THUNDERBOLT FROM NAVARONE

Alistair MacLean, who died on 2 February 1987, was the bestselling author of thirty books, including the world-famous adventure novels *The Guns of Navarone* and *Force 10 from Navarone*, both of which have been made into thrilling and internationally renowned films.

Sam Llewellyn is the author of several hugely successful nautical thrillers, including *Hell Bay* and *The Iron Hotel*, as well as *Storm Force from Navarone*, also inspired by Alistair MacLean's classic novels. An experienced sailor, he has sailed all over the world and now lives in Herefordshire.

SAM LLEWELLYN

THUNDERBOLT FROM NAVARONE

A sequel to Alistair MacLean's
Force 10 from Navarone

HarperCollins*Publishers*

HarperCollinsPublishers
77–85 Fulham Palace Road,
Hammersmith, London W6 8JB

www.**fire**and**water**.com

This paperback edition 1999
1 3 5 7 9 8 6 4 2

First published in Great Britain by
HarperCollinsPublishers 1998

ISBN 0 00 651104 X

Set in Meridien

Printed and bound in Great Britain by
Caledonian International Book Manufacturing Ltd, Glasgow

To Hex, Bert and Garlinda

PROLOGUE

Kapitän Helmholz looked at his watch. It was ten fifty-four and thirty-three seconds. Twenty-seven seconds until coffee time on the bridge of the armed merchantman *Kormoran*. At *Kapitän* Helmholz's insistence, coffee time was ten fifty-five precisely. A precise man, Helmholz, which was perhaps why he had been appointed to the command that had put him here in this steel room with big windows, below the red and black *Kriegsmarine* ensign with its iron cross and swastika board-stiff in the meltemi, the afternoon wind of the Aegean. Outside the windows were numbers one and two hatches, and under the hatches the cargo, and forward of the hatches the bow gun on the fo'c'sle and the bow itself, kicking through the short, steep chop. Beyond the rusty iron bow the sea sparkled, a dazzling sheet of sapphire all the way to the horizon. Beyond the horizon lay his destination, hanging like a cloud: a solid cloud – the mountains of Kynthos, blue with distance. It was all going well; neat, tidy, perfectly on schedule. Helmholz looked at his watch again.

With fifteen seconds to go until the time appointed, there it was: the faint jingle of the coffee tray. It always jingled when Spiro carried it. Spiro was Greek and suffered from bad nerves. *Kapitän* Helmholz raised his clean-cut jaw, directed his ice-blue eyes down his long straight nose, and watched the fat little Greek pour the coffee into the cups and hand them round. The man's body odour was pungent, his apron less than scrupulously clean. His face was filmed with sweat, or possibly grease. Still, thought Helmholz with unusual tolerance, degenerate Southerner he might be, but his coffee was good, and punctual. He picked up the cup, enjoying the

1

smell of the coffee and the tension on the bridge as his junior officers waited for the *Herr Kapitän* to drink so they could drink too. Helmholz pretended interest in the blue smudge of Kynthos, feeling the tension rise, enjoying the sensation that in small ways as well as in large, he was the man in control.

A mile away, in an iron tube jammed with men and machinery, a bearded man called Smith, with even worse body odour than Spiro, crammed his eyes against the rubber eyepieces of his attack periscope and said, 'Usual shambles up forward, Derek?'

'Probably,' said Derek, who was similarly bearded and smelt worse. 'Blue touchpaper lit and burning.'

'Jolly good. Fire one, then.'

From the spider's eyes of the torpedo tubes at the bow of His Majesty's submarine *Sea Leopard*, a drift of bubbles emerged, followed by the lean and purposeful Mark 8 torpedo. Tracking the deflection scale across the merchantman's rust-brown hull, Smith stifled a nervous yawn, and wished he could smoke. Three-island ship. Next fish under the bridge. That would do it. 'Fire two,' he said. It was not every day you bumped into a German armed merchantman swanning around on her own in the middle of nowhere. Sitting duck, really. 'We'll hang around a bit,' he said. 'Maybe they'll have some Schnapps.'

'Can but hope,' said the Number Two.

Helmholz's feeling of control did not survive even as long as it took to put his cup to his lips. It was one of the great ironies of his life that while at sea he was an automaton, as soon as he came in sight of land he was racked with an intellectually unjustifiable impatience. Suddenly his mind flooded with pictures of the *Kormoran* alongside the Kynthos jetty, unloading. The sweat of impatience slimed his palms. It was crazy to be out here with no escort; against reason. But there was such a shortage of aircraft for the direct defence of the Reich that the maintenance fitters had mostly been called back to Germany. So most of the air escort was out of action. The E-boats were not much better. Which left the *Kormoran* alone on the windy blue Aegean, with an important cargo and a pick-up crew . . .

He put his coffee cup to his lips.

Over the white china rim, he saw something terrible.

He saw a gout of orange flame leap up on the starboard side, level with number one hatch. He saw number one hatch itself bulge upward and burst in a huge bubble of fire that came roaring back at him and caved in the bridge windows. That was the last thing he saw, because that same blast drove the coffee cup right through his face and out of the back of his head. His junior officers suffered similar lethal trauma, but their good manners ensured that this was to the ribcage, not the skull. Perhaps Helmholz would have been consoled that things had been in order right until the moment of oblivion.

'Bullseye,' said Lieutenant Smith. 'Oh, bloody hell, she's burning.'

Burning was not good. Even if there was no escort waiting in the sun, the plume of black smoke crawling into the sky was as good as a distress flare. His thoughts locked into familiar patterns. The *Sea Leopard* had been submerged a long time. If there was to be a pursuit, now was the moment to prepare for it.

'Breath of fresh air, I think,' said Smith. 'Up she goes.'

And with a whine of pumps and electric engines, HMS *Sea Leopard* began to rise through the gin-clear sea.

They were not more than half a mile from the *Kormoran*. Great creakings came to them, the sound of collapsing bulkheads. Poor devils, thought Smith, in a vague sort of way; they were all poor devils in this war. They were all men stuck in little metal rooms into which water might at any minute start pouring.

'She's going,' said Braithwaite, the Number Two.

Sea Leopard broke surface, shrugging tons of Aegean from her decks. Smith was up the conning tower ladder and on deck with the speed of a human cannonball. The sea was steep and blue, the wavecrests blown ice-white by the meltemi. The black smoke of the burning ship leaped from the pale flame at its roots and tumbled away towards Kynthos. She was settling fast by the bow. One torpedo in her forward hold, one under her bridge. Nice shooting, thought Smith, wrinkling his nostrils against the sharp, volatile smell of the air. Not petrol. An altogether homelier smell; the aroma of stoves in the cabins of the little yachts Smith had sailed in the North Sea before the war. Alcohol. Not Schnapps: fuel alcohol.

The submarine began to move ahead, towards the wreck. In the

3

crust of floating debris that covered the water were shoals of long cylindrical objects. Smith's heart jumped. They looked like torpedoes. But they were too small. Gas bottles, they were; cylinders. He put his heavy rubber-armoured glasses on them. O2, said the stencilled letters. Oxygen. No bloody good to anyone.

There was a flash and an ear-splitting bang. When Smith could take notice again, he saw a great boil of bubbles. The ship was in half. Both halves sank quickly and without fuss.

The black cloud of smoke blew away. Except for the flotsam, the sea was empty, as far as you could see from a ten-foot conning tower among eight-foot waves. Petty Officer Jordan and a couple of ratings hooked a crate and hauled it aboard. 'Aircraft parts,' said Jordan.

Smith was disappointed. He really had been hoping for Schnapps. 'Better get going, what?' he said.

Jordan went below. *Sea Leopard* turned her nose west, for the friendlier waters of Sicily, away from the threatening smudge of German-held Kynthos. No survivors, thought Smith, raking the waves with his glasses. Pity. Couldn't be helped –

He paused. A couple of miles downwind, something rolled on the top of a wave, and what might have been an arm lifted. He opened his mouth to say, steer ninety degrees. A human? Wreckage? Worth a look.

But at that point his eye went up, climbing the vaults of the blue blue sky. And in that sky, he saw a little square of black dots. Aircraft.

He hit the klaxon and went down the conning tower and spun the hatch wheel. *Sea Leopard* sank into the deeps. *Kormoran* had been just another merchant ship in just another attack. Now it was time for *Sea Leopard* to take measures to ensure her own survival, to do more damage.

'Tea,' said Smith. They usually had a cup of tea sometime between eleven and half-past. Just now, he saw, looking at his watch before he wrote up the log, it was eleven minutes past.

ONE

Monday 1800-Tuesday 1000

It was raining in Plymouth, a warmish Atlantic rain that blanketed the Hoe and blurred the MTBs and MLs sliding in the Roads. In the early hours of their captivity the three men in the top-floor suite of the Hotel Majestic had spent time looking out of the window. They had long ago given up. Now they sprawled in armchairs round a low table on which were two empty brandy bottles and three overflowing ashtrays: men past their first youth and even their second, faces burned dark by the sun, eye-sockets hollow with the corrosive exhaustion of battle. They were in khaki battledress, without insignia. One was huge and black-haired. Another was tall and lean, with the hard jaw and steady eyes of a climber. The third was a rangy individual with a lugubrious face, glass of brandy in one hand, cigarette in mouth.

It was the third man who spoke. 'This is not,' he said, 'what I call a vacation.'

The third man's name was Miller. In so far as he had a rank, he was a corporal in the US Army Catering Corps. He was also the greatest demolition expert in the Allied armies.

The man who looked like a climber nodded, and lit a cigarette, and returned to his thoughts. This was a man you could imagine waiting for ever, if necessary; a man completely in control of himself. This was Captain Mallory, the New Zealander who before the war had been a world-famous mountaineer, and who had since done more damage to Hitler's armies than the entire Brigade of Guards. 'It's better than being machine-gunned,' he said.

Miller thought about that. 'I guess,' he said. He did not look sure.

'Soon,' said the big man, 'there will be work to do.' His accent was Greek, his voice soft but heavy, spreading a blanket of silence through the room. Andrea was a sleepy-eyed bear of a man, dark enough to look perpetually in need of a shave, his upper lip infested with a black stubble of regrowing moustache. He looked like the less respectable type of bandit, a mountain of sloth and debauchery. This impression had misled many of his enemies, most of them fatally. In fact, Andrea was a full colonel in the Greek army. Furthermore, he was as strong as a mobile crane, as fast and light on his feet as a cat, and as level-headed as an Edinburgh lawyer. When he spoke, which was not often, people gave him their full attention.

Miller and Mallory closed their minds to the soft rain on the window.

'They think we are spies,' said Andrea. 'They think we have made a deal with somebody and run away. It is not an unreasonable suspicion. Do you blame them?'

Miller took a swig out of his glass. 'They asked us to blow the guns on Navarone,' he said. 'We blew 'em. They asked us to destroy the Neretva Dam. Up goes the Neretva Dam. They sent us after the Werwolf subs. The Werwolf submarines get broken.' His long face was lugubrious. 'And now they tell us they have another job for us, and they pick us up in the Bay of Biscay and bring us all the way to Plymouth, and to demonstrate their everlasting admiration they lock us up in a fleabag hotel and put sentries on the door.' He coughed, long and loose and nasty. 'Sure, I blame them.'

'They've had ten-tenths cloud since the Werwolf raid,' said Mallory. 'They haven't been able to do a photographic recce, and there's no independent confirmation. And if you remember, it wasn't an easy job.'

'I remember,' said Miller, grimly.

'So look at it like this,' said Mallory. 'They locked us up here because they don't believe we could have achieved our objective. But we know we did. So we're right and they're wrong, and when they find out they are going to be very sorry. So it is all a very nice compliment, really.'

'I don't want compliments,' said Miller. 'I want a few drinks and some decent food and a little feminine society. For Chrissakes, Jensen knows what we can do. Why doesn't he tell them?'

Andrea put his hands together. 'Who can tell what Jensen knows?'

There was a small silence. Then Mallory said, 'I think we should go and talk to him.'

'Oh, yeah,' said Miller. 'Very amusing. There are thirty commandos on the landing.'

'I did not,' said Mallory, 'notice any commandos on the window-sill.'

Miller's face was suddenly a mask of horror. 'Oh, no,' he said.

Andrea smiled, a pure, innocent smile of great sweetness. 'Captain Jensen takes cocktails in the mess at ten minutes past six. The mess is in the basement of this hotel. It is now five past.'

'How did you know that?'

'I looked at my watch.'

'About the cocktail hour.'

'There is a chambermaid here from Roumeli,' purred Andrea. 'I talked to the poor girl. She was very pleased – are we ready?'

The room had filled with damp air. Mallory had raised the window. He was standing with his hands on the sill, looking down the sheer face of the hotel. 'Child could do it,' he said. 'We're off.'

The cocktail bar of the Hotel Majestic in Plymouth had been a fashionable West Country rendezvous in the 1930s, largely because it was the only cocktail bar in Plymouth, a town which otherwise found its entertainment in the more violent type of public house. It was eminently suited to wartime use. For one thing, it was mostly below ground, a comforting feature for those wishing their business to be undisturbed by the Nazi bombs that had all but obliterated large areas of the city. For another, its proximity to the naval dockyard gave the barman, an alert Devonian called Enrico, privileged access to the bottomless wells of gin which were as indispensable a fuel for His Majesty's warships as the more conventional bunker crude.

At six, the usual crowd were in: seven-eighths male, eight-eighths in uniform, talking in low voices from faces haggard with overwork and lack of exercise. At five past, Captain Jensen walked to his usual table: a small man in naval uniform with a captain's gold rings on the sleeve, a sardonic smile, and eyes of an astonishing mildness, except when no one was looking, at which point they

7

might have belonged to one of the hungrier species of shark. With him was a stout man with a florid face and the heavy braid of an admiral.

'Submarines,' the Admiral was saying. 'Damn cowardly, hugely overrated in my opinion.' He gulped his pink gin and called for another.

'Yes?' said Jensen, taking a microscopic sip of his own gin. 'Interesting point of view.'

'Not fashionable, I grant you,' said the Admiral, whose name was Dixon. 'But fashion is a fickle jade, what? Capital ships, I can tell you. The rest of it, well. . . Submarines, aircraft carriers, here today, gone tomorrow.'

Jensen raised a polite eyebrow. The Admiral's face was mottled with drink. He had recently arrived as OC Special Operations, Mediterranean, having been booted sideways from duties in the narrow seas before he could do any real damage. Jensen was interested in the Mediterranean himself – had, indeed, conceived and commanded some Special Operations of his own. It would have been reasonable to assume that he would have resented the arrival of a desk-bound blimp like Dixon as his superior officer. But if he did feel resentment, he showed no sign. Jensen was a subtle man, as his enemies had found out to their cost. Acting on Jensen's information, two Japanese infantry divisions had fought each other for three bloody days, each under the impression that the other was commanded by Orde Wingate. A German Panzer division had vanished without trace in the Pripet marshes, following a road on a map drawn from cartographic information supplied by Jensen's agents. Since early in the war, others of his agents had been the unfailing fountainhead of the cigars smoked by the most important man in Britain. Jensen had a finger in all pies. He had paid close attention to the development of his own career, but even closer attention to the question of winning the war. In the second as well as the first, he was known to be completely ruthless – a fact that might have given a more intelligent man than Dixon cause for worry.

But Dixon could not see over the mountain of his self-importance. Dixon had room in his mind for only one thing at a time. Just at the moment, that thing was gin.

'Lovely thing, drink after hard day at office,' said the Admiral, waving for his third pinkers.

'The Werwolf reconnaissance photographs,' said Jensen. 'I've seen them. Total success.'

'Yes,' said the Admiral. 'Where's that damn waitress?'

'Can I have your order to release my men?'

'Men?'

'The men you had confined to quarters.'

'Tomorrow, for God's sake. During office hours.'

'They might value a little liberty before the mission.'

'They'll do as they're damn well ordered. Waitress!'

Jensen's small, hard face did not lose its mildness, but he was conscious of a little twitch of anticipation. He knew Mallory, Miller and Andrea well; had indeed hand-picked them from a pool of the hardest of hard men. He knew them for excellent soldiers. But he also knew that they were not the kind of troops the Admiral was accustomed to. Locking them in a hotel room under heavy guard because you did not have the imagination to understand the stupendous success of their last mission was not a tactful move. Mallory, Miller and Andrea were not used to the close proximity of superior officers. They obeyed orders to the letter, of course. Still, Jensen had a distinct feeling that there would be trouble –

There was a small commotion by the entrance.

The Majestic was the kind of hotel whose frontage is criss-crossed with string-courses, cornices and swags of stone fruit. Mallory had sniffed the wet sea air, sighted on the fire-escape two windows along. Then he had lowered himself from the windowsill on to the bunch of limestone plums that decorated the lintel of the window below. Here he had paused, then hopped on to its neighbour. Miller, cursing inwardly, took a deep breath and followed him. Six storeys below, a cat the size of a flea prowled in a yard of trash cans. Miller got his feet on the fruit. He took another breath, and jumped for the next lintel. It was not more than six inches wide. Mallory had landed on it soft and quiet and confident as if it had been the flight deck of an aircraft carrier. To Miller, it looked about as accommodating as a child's eyebrow. His mouth dried out in midair. He felt his boot make contact, the toe bite, then slither. His stomach shrank, and as he teetered and began to fall his mind had room for one thought and one thought only. Navarone, Yugoslavia, the Pyrenees, and it ends here at the Hotel Majestic, Plymouth. How stupid –

Then a steely hand grabbed his wrist and Mallory's voice said, 'Hold up, there.' Then he was standing on the lintel, breathing deep to slow the thumping of his heart. Suddenly the fumes of the brandy and the cigarettes were blowing away and he had the sense that something had started again, like a machine that was winding up, moving on to the road for which it had been designed. The hesitancy was gone. Thought and action were the same thing.

He took the next two lintels in his stride. On the fire-escape landing he looked back. Andrea was drifting across the face of the hotel like a gigantic shadow. The Greek landed light as a feather next to them. They trotted down the iron stairs, spread out, automatically, with the discipline that had established itself these last weeks. Covering each other, covering themselves . . . Going out for a drink.

They flitted off the fire-escape, trotted through the alley to the front of the hotel, and up the grand stone steps into the lobby. The man behind the desk saw three men in khaki battledress without insignia. He had been a hall porter on civvy street, and he knew trouble when he saw it. Among the immaculate officers walking through the lobby, these men stuck out like wolves at a poodle show. Their boots were dirty, their eyes bloodshot, and they moved at a murderous lope that made him wish he could leave, fast, and become far away. Alarm bells started ringing in his head. Deserters, he thought, and dangerous ones. It did not occur to him that deserters were unlikely to be hanging around in smart hotels. These men made him too nervous to think. His hand went for the telephone. He knew the number of the Military Police by heart.

He told the operator what he wanted. But when he looked up, the men had gone. For good, he imagined, dabbing sweat from his pale brow with a clean handkerchief. There had been no time for them to cause any trouble, and they would not get past the sentries on the cocktail bar. He cancelled the call.

But the men had not gone; and they had indeed got past the sentries.

It had happened like this: three men in battledress without insignia had attempted to gain entrance to the mess bar. Challenged, one of them had barked the sentries to attention, an order the sentries had (for reasons they did not properly understand) found themselves obeying. Another, a very big man with black curly hair, had taken away their rifles with the confidence of a kind father removing a dangerous toy from a fractious child. The third, having passed remarks uncomplimentary to their personal turnout and the cleanliness of their weapons, which he had inspected, had followed his two companions into the hallowed portals.

As they gazed upon the shut door, the sentries became aware that they had failed in their duty. There had been no chance of their succeeding, of course; the situation had been out of their hands. But that was not going to make matters any easier to explain to the sergeant. They were on a fizzer, for sure. As one, both sentries went through the door.

Through the fog of smoke, they saw their quarry. All three of them were with a small naval captain. They were standing rigidly to attention. The small captain caught the sentries' eyes, and waved them away. 'Really,' he said, mildly, to the three men. 'You'll frighten the horses.'

'Thought we'd pop out for a drink,' said Mallory.

Jensen raised an eyebrow. Thirty commandos, said the eyebrow, and I hope you haven't bent any of them.

'We came down the fire-escape,' said Mallory. 'We were very thirsty.'

Into Admiral Dixon's brain there had sunk the idea that something untoward was happening. He did not expect his evenings to be interrupted by soldiers, particularly soldiers as scruffy and badgeless as this lot. He was further amazed when he heard Captain Jensen say, 'Oh, well. While you're here, I can tell you we've got the snapshots. Total success. Well done. Briefing scheduled for 2300 hours.'

Admiral Dixon said, in a voice like a glacier calving, 'Who are these men?'

'Sorry,' said Jensen. 'Captain Mallory. Corporal Miller. Colonel Andrea, Greek Army, 19th Motorized Division. Admiral Dixon, OC Special Operations, Mediterranean.'

The Admiral rested his gooseberry eyes on the three men. Miller watched the veins in his neck and wondered idly how much pressure a blood vessel could take before it burst. 'Why,' said the Admiral, 'are they improperly dressed?'

11

'Disgraceful,' said Jensen, with severity. 'But as you will remember, they have just completed a mission. They were confined to quarters on suspicion of collusion with the enemy, so they haven't had a chance to pop up to Savile Row. I think that in view of reconnaissance reports on the outcome of their mission, we can give them the benefit of the doubt. Unless you feel an Inquiry is necessary?'

'Hrmph,' said the Admiral, mauve-faced. 'Mission or no mission, can't have this sort of nonsense –'

'Walls have ears,' said Jensen smoothly. 'You have called a briefing for 2300 hours. That will be the moment to discuss this. Now, gentlemen. Refreshment?'

'I thought you'd never ask,' said Miller. There was a waitress. Jensen ordered. The three men raised their glasses to Jensen, then the Admiral. 'Mud in your eye,' said Miller.

'Here's how,' said Jensen.

The Admiral grunted ungraciously. He swallowed his gin and left.

'Well, gentlemen,' said Jensen. 'We're very pleased with you; most of us, anyway.' He smiled, that gleaming, carnivorous smile. 'You will be collected at 2245 hours. Till then, I bid you sweet dreams.'

'Dreams?' said Miller. It was not yet seven o'clock.

'I always think a little nap can be most refreshing before a lot of hard work.'

'Work?' said Mallory.

But Jensen was gone.

'Sleep?' said Mallory. 'Or drinks?'

Andrea pushed his glass forward. 'You can sleep on aeroplanes,' he said.

'Drinks it is,' said Mallory.

A car with a sub-lieutenant raced them through the blacked-out streets of Plymouth. The city was stirring like a huge, secret animal. The tyres kicked fans of water from deep puddles as they skirted piles of rubble and came to a set of high wire gates with naval sentries in greatcoats and bell-bottomed trousers. Beyond the gate was the dark bulk of a squat building with a sand-bagged entrance. The sentry led them through a heavy steel door into a disinfectant-smelling hall and down a flight of cement stairs, then another and another. Mallory felt the depth and silence pressing in on him. Suddenly he was tired, achingly tired, with the tiredness of two months of special operations, and the months before that . . .

But there was no time for being tired, because another steel door had sighed open, and they were in a windowless room painted green and cream. There were chairs, and a blackboard. Everything was anonymous. There was no clue as to where they were bound. There were three naval officers in the room, fresh-faced and wind-burned. Sitting apart was a willowy man in a Sam Browne over a tunic of excessively perfect cut. He was smoking a fat cigarette that smelt Turkish, gazing from under unnecessarily long eyelashes at the fire instructions behind the dais, and fingering a thin moustache. Mallory found himself thinking of Hollywood. It was an odd mixture of people to find a hundred or so feet under Plymouth.

Admiral Dixon and Captain Jensen walked into the room. With a scuffing of chair legs, the men stood to attention. 'Good evening,' said Jensen. 'Stand easy. You may smoke.' Dixon ignored them. He sat down heavily in a chair. His eyes were glassy and he was breathing hard, presumably from the effort of walking down all those stairs. Mallory reflected that if coming down had been that bad, someone would have to carry him up. Jensen, on the other hand, looked fresh as the morning dew. He stood on the balls of his feet, perky as a bantamweight boxer, while an orderly unrolled maps on the board.

Mallory knew that in the coastlines and contours of those maps their fates were written. There were the three fingers of the Peloponnese, blue sea, Crete, the island-splatter of the Dodecanese. And larger-scale maps: an island. Not an island he recognized, though when he glanced across at Andrea he saw him straight-backed and frowning.

'Very good,' said Jensen, when the orderly had finished. 'Now I said I had a job for you, a tiny little job, really. It's a bit of a rush, I suppose, but there it is, can't be helped.'

'Rush?' said Mallory.

'All in good time,' said Jensen. 'First things first. Admiral Dixon you already know. Gentlemen – ' here he turned to Mallory, Miller and Andrea ' – certain people are very pleased with what you achieved last week.' Admiral Dixon shook his head and sighed. 'So pleased, in fact,' said Jensen, 'that they want you to do something else. Probably much easier, actually.' He turned to the map at his back. Miller listened to the hum of the ventilation fans. It was all very well Jensen saying things were easy. He was not the one getting shot at. Miller doubted that he knew the meaning of the word.

The central map showed plenty of blue sea, and an island. It was the shape of a child's drawing of a beetle, this island: a fat body dark with close-set contours and a head attached to its north-eastern end by a narrower neck. 'Kynthos,' said Jensen. 'Lovely place. Delightful beaches. Very few Germans, but the ones there are particularly interesting, we think.'

Mallory and Miller slumped in their chairs. As far as they were concerned the only interesting German was a German they were a couple of hundred miles away from. But Andrea was still upright in his chair, his black eyes gleaming. Andrea was a Greek. The things the Germans had done to his country were bad, but they were much, much better than the things the Germans had done to his family. Andrea found Germans very interesting indeed.

'I'll start at the beginning,' said Jensen. 'Last year we bombed a place called Peenemunde, on the Baltic. Seems the Germans were building some sort of rocket bomb there; doodlebugs first, bloody awful things, but there was supposed to be something else. Germans called it the A3. Goes into outer space, if you can believe this, and comes back, wallop, faster than the speed of sound. Blows a hole in you before you've even heard it coming. Good weapon against civilians.' Mallory searched Jensen's face for signs of irony, and found none. 'We're expecting it any day now. And there's something else; bigger version, larger, longer range, more dangerous, good for use against troops. Questions so far?'

'Why bother with outer space?' said Miller.

'Think of a shell. Longer the range, higher the trajectory.'

'You'd need a hell of a bang to get it up there.'

Jensen smiled. 'Very good, Miller,' he said. 'Now what we believe is this. These A3 things are rockets. Thing about outer space, there's no air to burn your fuel. So your rocket needs to take its own air with it. These A3 things are supposed to burn a mixture of alcohol and liquid oxygen. One of our submarines sank a ship off Kynthos the other day, surfaced to look for, er, survivors. All they found was oxygen bottles. And a stink of alcohol.'

'Schnapps,' said Miller.

Jensen smiled, and this time even the artificial warmth was gone from the ice-white display of teeth. 'Thank you, Corporal,' he said. 'If that is all, I shall hand you over to Lieutenant, er, Robinson.'

Lieutenant Robinson was a tall, stooping man with round tortoiseshell spectacles and a donnish air. 'Thank you,' he said. 'Hmmyes. Kynthos. Typical Vesuvian post-volcanic structure, Santorini series, basalts, pumice, tufa, with an asymmetric central deposition zone –'

'Lieutenant Robinson used to teach geology at Cambridge,' said Jensen. 'Once more, this time in English, if you please, Lieutenant.'

Robinson blushed to the tops of his spectacles. 'Hmmyes,' he said. 'Kynthos is, er, mountainous. Very mountainous. There's a town at the south-western end, Parmatia, more a village really, on a small alluvial plain. The road from the town transits a raised beach –' he caught Jensen's eye – 'follows the coast, that is, mostly on a sort of shelf in the cliffs. There is no road across the interior suitable for motor transport. To the north-east of the mountain massif is another island, smaller, Antikynthos, connected to the main massif by a plain of eroded debris and alluvium –' here Jensen coughed '– a stretch of flat land and marshes. This smaller island is itself rocky, taking the form of a volcanic plug with associated basalt and tufa masses, and on this there stands an old Turkish fort and the remains of a village: the Acropolis, they call it, the High Town. There has always been a jetty on Antikynthos. Recently this has been greatly improved, and the aerodrome upgraded. In the view of, er, contacts on the island, some sort of factory is being established.' He took a photograph out of a file and laid it in an overhead projector. A man's face appeared on the screen: a round face, mild, heavy-lidded eyes behind wire-rimmed spectacles. 'Sigismund von Heydrich,' he said. 'Injured during the bombing of Peenemunde. Highly talented ballistician –' Jensen's eye again '– rocket scientist. He was spotted boarding a plane at Trieste, and we know the plane landed on Kynthos. They've built workshops in the caves under the Acropolis. But there's only a light military presence. Couple of platoons of *Wehrmacht*, nothing worse, as far as we know.'

Jensen stood up. 'Thank you, Lieutenant,' he said. The Lieutenant looked disappointed, as if he had planned to go on for some time. 'Well, there you are. Simple little operation, really. We want you to land on Kynthos and make a recce of this Acropolis. You'll be briefed on the development of the V4, which is what they're calling this one. Any sign of it, and we'd like it disposed of: air strikes will be available, but if they've got it a long way underground, well, Miller, we have the greatest confidence in your ability to wreck the happy home. Questions so far?'

'Yessir,' said Mallory. 'You say we've got someone on the island already?'

'In a manner of speaking,' said Jensen. 'There was a transmitter.'

'Was?'

'Transmissions ceased a week ago. It may be that the Germans found it. Or it may equally be that someone dropped it. Frightfully stony place, as you know.'

Mallory caught Miller's eye, and saw the wary resignation he felt himself. Jensen did not pick them for the easy ones.

'And of course there'll be Carstairs in case you need help. Now if you've got any questions, ask them now, and we'll get into the detail.'

Miller said, 'Who's Carstairs?'

'Good Lord,' said Jensen. 'Hasn't anybody introduced you? Very remiss. Perhaps Admiral Dixon will do the honours. Admiral?'

Dixon heaved himself to his feet. 'Captain Carstairs, make yourself known,' he said, and there was something in his face that much resembled smugness.

The man in the beautiful uniform stood up and saluted. His hair was brown and wavy, his moustache clipped into a perfect eyebrow. 'Gentlemen, how d'ye do?' he said.

'Captain Carstairs is a rocket expert,' said the Admiral. 'He is also experienced in special operations. Before the war he led expeditions up the Niger and in the Matto Grosso. He has overflown the North and South Poles, and climbed the north face of Nanga Parbat.'

Andrea caught Mallory's eye. Mallory's head moved almost imperceptibly from side to side. Never heard of him, he was saying.

'Wow,' said Miller. The Admiral looked at him sharply, but the American's eyes were shining with honest reverence.

'So I am very happy to say,' said the Admiral, 'that Captain Carstairs will make an ideal commanding officer for this expedition.'

There was a deep silence, full of the hum of the fans. Mallory looked at Jensen. Jensen was gazing at the place where the ceiling met the wall.

'Any questions?' said the Admiral.

'Yessir,' said Mallory. 'When do we start training, sir?'

The Admiral frowned. 'Training?'

'It'll take a month. Six weeks, maybe.'

Blood swelled the Admiral's neck. 'You're out of here on a Liberator at 0200 hours. You will transfer to an MTB near Benghazi. You'll be ashore and operating by 0300 tomorrow. There will be no training.'

'MTB?' said Mallory.

'Motor Torpedo Boat,' said Dixon.

'Bit indiscreet,' said Mallory, who knew what an MTB was. 'Noisy.'

'Can't be helped,' said Jensen. 'Sorry about the training, sorry about the MTB. But it's a matter of . . . well, put it like this. There's a bit of a flap on. These damned rockets are a menace to our rear and our flank in Italy. They can deliver three tons of HE with an accuracy of fifty yards. They need disposing of before they're operational, and we think that will be soon. We'd fly you in, but Staff say it's the wrong place for a parachute drop. So MTB it'll have to be. Time is of the essence.'

'Can't be done,' said Mallory. Suddenly he felt Jensen's eyes upon him like rods of ice.

The Admiral's neck veins swelled. 'Look here,' he said, in a sort of muted bellow. 'It is against my better judgement that I am using an insubordinate shower like you to perform a delicate operation. But Captain Jensen assures me that you know what you are doing, and takes responsibility for you. Well, let me make myself clear. If you do not obey my orders and the orders of Captain Carstairs in this matter, you will be charged with mutiny so fast your feet will not touch the ground – what are you doing?'

Mallory was on his feet, and so were Miller and Andrea. They were standing rigidly to attention. 'Permission to speak, sah,' said Mallory. 'You can get your court martial ready, sah.'

The Admiral stared, flabby-faced. 'By God,' he said. 'By God, I'll have you –'

Jensen cleared his throat. 'Excuse me, Admiral,' he said. 'Might I make a suggestion?' The Admiral seemed to be beyond speech. 'These men work as a unit. Their record is good. Might I suggest that rather than operating as a top-down command structure they be attached to Captain Carstairs as a force of observers, leaving Captain Carstairs in command of his own unit but without specific responsibility for these men, who would, as it were, be attached yet separate? This would obviate the need for special training, and establish the possibility of cross-unit liaison and cooperation rather than intra-unit response to *ad hoc* and *de facto* command structures.'

The Admiral's jaw had dropped. 'What?' he said.

'Mallory's the senior captain,' said Jensen. 'And of course there is a colonel in the force.'

'Who's a colonel?'

'I am,' said Andrea.

Now it was Carstairs' turn to stare. Andrea needed a haircut, and his second shave of the day. His uniform needed a laundry. Carstairs raised an eyebrow. 'Colonel?' he said, and Miller could hear his lip curl even if he could not see it.

The air in the briefing room was thick and ugly. 'Greek army,' said Andrea. 'Under Captain Mallory's command, for operational purposes.'

'Uh,' said the Admiral, looking like a man who had just trodden on a fair-sized mine.

Jensen said, 'Come out here, all of you,' and marched into the corridor. Out there, he said, 'You've got Carstairs whether you like him or not. I want you on this mission. I'm ordering you to take him along.'

'And wipe his nose.'

'Also his shoes, if necessary.' Jensen's eyes were bright chips of steel.

'Under my command,' said Mallory.

'I know about rockets,' said Miller. 'I know as much about rockets as anyone. We don't need this guy. He'll get in the way. We'll wind up carrying him, he'll –'

'We would be fascinated to hear your views,' said Jensen in a freezing voice. 'Some other time, though, I think.'

'So who needs this guy?'

'If you mean Captain Carstairs, the Admiral wants him. And that, gentlemen, is that. Now get back in there.'

They knew Jensen.

They got back in there.

The Admiral said, 'Captain Carstairs will be a separate unit, taking his orders directly from me.'

Carstairs smiled a smooth, inward-looking smile. Technically, Mallory was his superior officer. All the Admiral was doing was muddying waters already troubled. They stood wooden-faced, potential disasters playing like newsreels in their minds.

'Last but not least,' said Jensen. 'Local support. Lieutenant.'

Robinson stood up, spectacles gleaming. 'There is Resistance activity on the island,' he said. 'But we want your operation kept separate. Civilian reprisals, er, do not help anyone.' Andrea's face was dark as a thundercloud. He had found the bodies of his parents on a sandbank in the River Drava. They had been lashed together and thrown in to drown. He knew about reprisals: and so did the Germans who had done the deed, once he had finished with them. Robinson continued, 'We will be landing you in Parmatia. There is a gentleman called Achilles at three, Mavrocordato Street in Parmatia. He will provide you with motor transport up the island to the Acropolis. We'll have a submarine standing by at a position you will be given at midnight on Thursday, Friday and Saturday. If you're there, hang up a yellow fishing lantern as a signal. If not . . . well, he'll wait until 0030 on Saturday, then you're on your own. Got it?'

'Got it.'

'But avoid all other contact. We'd like you to be a surprise. A thunderbolt of a surprise. That's what this operation is called, by the way. Operation Thunderbolt.'

'After the weather forecast?' said Miller.

'How did you guess?' said Jensen.

'You did it last time,' said Miller.

Jensen did not seem to hear. 'Now,' he said. 'The detail.'

For the next two hours, in the company of the geologist and a man from SOE, they studied the detail.

'All right,' said Jensen, as they folded away their maps. 'Armoury next.'

The armoury was the usual harshly-lit room with racks of Lee Enfields. The Armourer was a Royal Marine with a bad limp and verbal diarrhoea. 'Schmeissers, 'e said you wanted,' said the Marine, pulling out boxes. 'Quite right, quite right, don't want those bloody Stens, blow up on you as soon as Jerry, go on, 'ave a look, yes, Corporal? Oh, I see you are the more discriminating type of customer, grenades, was it?' But even his flow of talk could not hold up over the grim silence that filled that little room. Mallory and Andrea sat down on the bench and disassembled a Schmeisser each, craftsmen assessing the tools of a deadly trade. The hush filled with small, metallic noises. Andrea rejected two of the machine-pistols before he found one to his liking, then another. Miller, meanwhile, was in a corner of the room, by a cupboard the size of a cigar humidor. He had a special pack, lined with wood and padded. Into this he was stowing, with a surgeon's delicacy of touch, buff-coloured bricks of plastic explosives, brightly-coloured time pencils, and a whole hardware store of other little packets and bottles.

Mallory reassembled his second Schmeisser. 'For you, Carstairs,' he said.

Carstairs looked languidly up from the sights of a Mauser. 'Never touch 'em, old boy.'

'You'll need one.'

'I'll be the judge of that,' said Carstairs, tapping a Turkish cigarette on a gold case. A silenced Browning automatic lay across his knees. 'Stand off is my motto. Works with impala. Works with Germans. Now look here, Sergeant, have you got a hard case for this?' He held up the Mauser carbine and a Zeiss 4X sniperscope. Several Mausers would be going to Kynthos – they were rugged carbines essential for long-range work. But the sniperscope was delicate as a prima ballerina's tutu – nothing to do with the kind of knockabout you could expect if you were storming a hollow mountain full of rockets.

As they left the armoury, Andrea fell in beside Mallory. 'What do you think?' he said.

'I think we should keep our eyes open.'

'Exactly, my Keith.' They walked on in silence. 'And what is this Nanga Parbat?'

'A mountain. In the Himalayas. There was an expedition to climb it in 1938.' Mallory paused. He hated what came next. 'A German expedition.'

'There was no war in 1938.'

'No.'

But all of a sudden Mallory's stomach was a tight ball. There was something wrong with this. It was the same feeling he had had on the south icefield of Mount Cook, watching his right boot go up and forward, watching the weight go on, but because of that feeling, not committing himself. Which had been just as well. Because when it felt the weight of that boot – brownish-black leather, new-greased, criss-cross laces in the lugs, that boot – the world crumbled and slid away, and what had been smooth ice had turned into a cornice over a ravine, a cornice that had crumbled under him and was swallowing him up.

Except that he had taken warning from that knot in the stomach, and kept his weight back, and walloped his ice axe behind him at the full reach of his arm, felt it bite, and hauled himself out of the jaws of death and back on to clean ice. And climbed the mountain.

The knot in the stomach was not fear, or at least not only fear. It was a warning. It needed listening to.

TWO

Tuesday 1000-Wednesday 0200

Al-Gubiya Bay is a small notch in the coast west of Benghazi. That morning, it contained a group of khaki tents, a concrete jetty, and one and a half billion flies. Alongside the jetty an MTB crouched like a grey shark. Her commander, Lieutenant Bob Wills, was sitting on the forward port-hand torpedo tube. The sun balanced on his head like a hot iron bar, and the flies were driving him crazy, but not as crazy as the orders he had received. He wondered what the hell they were dropping him in this time.

A three-ton lorry clattered on to the quay, stopped, and stood snorting in its cloud of Libyan dust. The canvas back of the lorry twitched and parted. Four men got down.

Three of them walked together, silent, closed-faced. Their faces were gaunt and sunburned. They looked at the same time exhausted and relaxed, and under their heavy equipment they walked with a steady, mile-devouring lope. Ahead of the three was a slenderer man. He was dressed like them in battledress without badges of rank. But his walk had more of a strut in it, as if he thought someone might be watching, and at the same time he moved uneasily in the straps of his pack. This and a certain finicky neatness in his uniform made the Lieutenant think that he was not completely at home.

The neat man had quick brown eyes that checked the MTB and the cuff-rings of the Lieutenant's tunic, hung from the barrel of the five-pounder. He said, 'Good morning. I'm Captain Carstairs.' The man smiled, a white, film-star sort of a smile. Wills was tired from months of night operations, and the smile was too dazzling.

He said, 'How d'ye do?' Carstairs' handshake was a bonecrusher. Wills' feeling of tiredness increased. 'Good fight?'

22

'Dreadful,' said Carstairs. 'Bloody Liberators. Can't hear a thing. Bring back Imperial. The Cairo run, what?'

'Yes,' said Wills. Himself, he had never been able to afford to fly in the Sunderlands of Imperial Airways. Lot of side, this Carstairs, he thought. He raised a hand to Chief Petty Officer Smith, who was loading stores down the quay. 'Chiefy. Help Captain Carstairs with his stuff, there's a good chap.'

During his brief chat with Carstairs, the other three men had climbed aboard the MTB and stowed their equipment. Without appearing to move very much they seemed to get a surprising amount done. The shortest of the three introduced himself as Mallory in a voice with a faint New Zealand twang.

'Morning,' said Wills.

Mallory saw a square youth with sun-bleached curly hair and a sunburned nose.

'Made yourself at home, I hope,' said Wills.

'Hope that's all right.'

Wills grinned. 'Top-hole,' he said. 'We don't stand on ceremony here.' He embraced with a sweep of his arm the blue bay, the parched dunes, the concrete jetty. 'You get out of the habit, in a tropical paradise.'

'Very attractive,' said Mallory, brushing away a couple of thousand flies.

'Wait till we get to sea,' said Wills. He was older than he looked, Mallory realized. From a distance, he might have been your standard British sixth-former. Close up, you could see the eyes. The eyes were a thousand years old.

'Been here long?' said Mallory.

'Long enough. Stooging around causing trouble on the island. Yachting with big bangs, really. Speak a bit of the lingo. Do what we can to make a nuisance of ourselves.'

'Quite,' said Mallory. He liked this youth. There was something in his eye that said he could really cause the Germans some trouble, if he put his mind to it, and putting his mind to it was what he was good at.

'We ready?' said Wills.

Mallory nodded.

'Top-hole,' said Wills. Carstairs was not his cup of tea, but these men were different. They spoke quietly, and looked at him steady-eyed, and when they shook his hand their grip was firm but economical, as if in this, as in anything else they did, they would use just enough force to get the job done properly, no more, no less. This fitted neatly with Wills' view of life, and he found himself favourably impressed. There was also another sensation lurking on the fringes of his conscious mind, and for a moment he did not know what it was. But ten minutes later, pouring the gin in the cupboard-sized wardroom, it came to him.

He was very glad they were on the same side as him.

'Excuse me,' he said. 'Couple of things to organize.'

The heavy throb of the MTB's engines came through the wardroom bulkheads, and the stink of high octane gasoline. The sleek grey boat scrawled a white question mark on the blue bay, roared out to sea and turned east.

It was a calm and beautiful day. Carstairs went on deck, thrusting his chiselled profile into the twenty-knot slipstream. Mallory, Miller and Andrea found plywood bunks, rolled on to them, and closed their eyes: except Mallory. Mallory lay and felt the bound of the MTB over the swell, and the tremor of the Merlin engines, and rested his eyes on the plywood deck above him. There were matters he needed to ponder before he slept.

As they had left the armoury, a runner had caught him by the arm. 'Telephone, sir,' he had said.

The voice on the telephone had been light but hard: Jensen.

'No names,' it had said. 'Something I wanted to say, between us two, really.'

'Yessir.'

'I wanted to say the best of luck, and all that.'

'Yessir.' Jensen would not have rung his mother to wish her luck. Mallory waited.

'Our new friend,' said Jensen. 'The expert. He's okay, but you might like to keep your eye on him.'

'Eye?'

'Just a thought,' said Jensen. 'I've got a feeling he might be on a sort of treasure hunt.'

'Treasure hunt? What sort of treasure hunt?'

'If I knew, I wouldn't be telling you to keep an eye on him, would I? Well, I expect you'll be wanting to get on your way.'

Mallory lay and watched the deckhead. There were undoubtedly problems on Kynthos. But Mallory strongly suspected there was also a problem on the MTB, a problem called Carstairs. Mallory did not trust the man. Nor, it seemed, did Jensen. So why did Jensen insist that Carstairs be part of the mission? Of course, it had not been Jensen who had insisted. It had been Admiral Dixon. Mallory found himself thinking that a spell on the bridge of a destroyer would do Dixon a lot of good: or on an MTB, a floating fuel-tank, a bladder of aviation fuel with two Merlin engines . . .

But Dixon was safe behind his desk, and that was a law of nature. Just like the fact that Carstairs was along for the duration.

Railing against the laws of nature was entirely pointless. Mallory was not given to doing pointless things.

A new vibration added itself to the bone-jarring roar of the twin Merlins. Mallory was snoring.

He awoke much later, prised a cup of coffee out of the galley, and climbed on to the bridge. The sun was sinking towards the western horizon, North Africa a low dun line to the south. As far as any German aircraft were concerned they were heading east, for somewhere in the Allied territory in the gathering shadows ahead.

A rating brought up a plate of corned beef sandwiches and more coffee. It was quieter on the bridge. Mallory wedged a deck chair in a corner. As he ate his mind kept coming back to Carstairs. Why would an experienced guerrilla fighter have chosen a sniper rifle with a notoriously delicate sight? If they were all on the same operation, why were they notionally two separate units? Why –

A shadow fell across him. It was Carstairs, slender fingers in the pocket of his battledress blouse: like Clark Gable, thought Mallory. His hand came out with the gold cigarette case. He opened it, offered it to Mallory. 'Turkish this side, Virginian that,' he said.

'Just put one out,' said Mallory. 'Tell me something. What are you doing on this trip?'

'Same as you,' said Carstairs.

'So what . . . qualifies you?'

Carstairs smiled. 'I've knocked about a bit.'

'And you're a rocket expert.'

'So I am.'

'Where did you pick that up?'

'Here and there,' said Carstairs, vaguely. 'Here and there.'

25

You got used to vagueness on Special Operations. It was a mistake to know more than you needed to know. So why did Mallory have the feeling that Carstairs was using this fact for his own purposes?

'Ever done armed insurgency work?' he said.

'Not exactly. But there have been ... parallel episodes in my life.'

'What's a parallel episode?' said a new voice: Miller's.

'A not dissimilar operation.'

'I had one of those, but the wheels dropped off.'

'I beg your pardon?' Carstairs' face was stiffening.

'All right,' said Mallory. Carstairs, it seemed, was too important to have a sense of humour. 'You're good in mountains. You can shoot.'

Carstairs yawned. 'So they told me on Nanga Parbat.'

'I thought that was a German expedition.'

'It was.' They stared at him. 'The Duke of Windsor asked me to go. Rather a chum of mine, actually, so one couldn't refuse. I speak pretty good German. I'm a climber. What's wrong with that?'

Mallory said nothing. The Nanga Parbat expedition had been supervised by Himmler in person. It had conquered the peak, but only by cementing in spikes and installing fixed ladders and ropes. They might as well have put scaffolding up the face. It was not what Mallory called climbing.

Carstairs said, 'The idea was to get to the top.'

Well, that was true.

'And the rockets,' said Miller, doggedly. 'Where did you find out all this stuff you know about rockets?'

Carstairs was not smiling any more. He said, 'We have all led complicated lives I am sure, and a lot of the things we have done we would not necessarily have told our mummies about. You can take it from me that I know what I know, and I am under orders from Admiral Dixon, Corporal. Now if you will excuse me I could do with forty winks.' And he went below.

'Temper,' said Miller, mildly.

Mallory lit a cigarette. He did not look at the American. 'I would remind you,' he said, 'that Captain Carstairs is a superior officer, and as such is entitled to respect. I would like you to give this thought your earnest attention.' His eyes came up and locked with Miller's. 'Your very close attention,' he said.

Miller smiled. 'My pleasure,' he said.

The MTB churned on down the coast. The sun sank below the horizon. Miller lay on the wing of the bridge, watching the last light of day leave the sky, and the sky fade to black, and upon it a huge field of silver stars come into being. Wills murmured an order to the man at the helm. Over Miller's head, the stars began to wheel until the Big Dipper lay across the horizon, the last two stars in its rhomboidal end pointing across an empty expanse to a single star riding over the MTB's bow.

They had turned north.

It was eight hours' hard steaming from Al-Gubiya to Kynthos. Rafts of cloud began to drift across the sky, blotting out patches of stars. The breeze was up, ruffling the sea into long ridges of swell. *M-109* made heavy weather, jolting and banging and shuddering as she jumped from bank of water to bank of water. Nobody slept, any more than they would have slept in an oil drum rolling down a flight of concrete steps.

Up on the bridge, Wills peered into the black and tried not to dwell upon the fact that *M-109* was the tip of a huge phosphorescent arrowhead of wake that shouted to anyone in an aeroplane 'Here we are, here we are'. This was not a subtle operation. 'Weave her,' he shouted into the helmsman's ear. The helmsman began to weave her port and starboard, panning the beam of the fixed radar scanner across the sea ahead.

'What you got?' said Wills to the man with his head in the radar's rubber eyepiece.

'Clutter,' said the man. 'Bloody waves –'

The MTB hit a wave, shot off into the air, and came down with a slam that blasted spray sixty feet in the air and buckled Wills' knees. His coffee cup shot across the bridge and exploded in a corner. Somewhere, probably in the galley, a lot of glass broke.

'Shite,' said the radar operator, and twiddled knobs. 'Dead,' he said.

'What do you mean, dead?' said Wills, though he knew perfectly well, because this always happened with radar. But they were deep in bandit country here, and the MTB was his first command, and this was his first Special Ops run, and he wanted things to go right, not cock up –

'Valve gone,' said the radar operator. 'Two, three valves.'

'How long?'

'Twenty minutes.'

Could be worse, thought Wills, lighting his sixty-third cigarette of the day. Could be better. Half an hour without radar, well, you can survive that.

So the MTB swept on blind under the stars: blind, but not unseen. Far down on the horizon, a dirty fishing caïque was hauling nets. In her wheelhouse, a man trained German-issue binoculars on the pale streak of water to the westward. Then he picked up the microphone of a military radio, and began to speak, giving first a call sign, then a course and speed that corresponded to the MTB's.

'Done, sir,' said the radar operator. 'No contacts.'

'Nice work,' said Wills, looking at his watch, then at the chart on the table under the red night-lights. 'Top-hole.' He rang for port engine shutdown, half-ahead starboard. *M-109*'s nose settled into her bow wave. One engine burbling heavily, she crept towards Kynthos, twenty miles away now. The breeze had dropped: the sea was like black glass.

'Still clear?' said Wills to the radar operator.

'Clear,' said the operator.

'Top-hole,' said Wills.

But of course the radar could not see astern.

As the engine note faded smoothly, Miller fell just as smoothly from a doze into a deep sleep. After what seemed like a couple of seconds he was awakened by somebody shaking him. 'Morning, sir,' said a voice, and an enamel mug was shoved into his hand, a mug hot enough to wake him up and make him curse and hear Mallory and Andrea and Carstairs stirring, too. When they had drunk the sweet, scalding tea, they went on deck.

There was no moon, but the Milky Way hung in a heavy swathe across the sky. By its light he could see a crumpled heap of rubberized canvas on the deck on the forward face of the wheelhouse. He groped for a foot pump, found one, plugged in the hose and started tramping away. The crumpled heap swelled and unfolded like a night-blooming flower, and became a rubber dinghy; an aircrew dinghy, actually, because unlike the naval dinghies it was boat-shaped instead of circular, and thus rowable; but unlike the dinghies used by the SAS, it was yellow instead of black, and would, if discovered by the enemy, be taken for the relic of a crashed aircraft instead of the transport of a raiding party. Andrea drifted up, silent as a wraith, and Mallory. Carstairs made more noise, his nailed boots squinching on the deck, grunting as he dumped his pack and his rifle.

'Three minutes to drop,' said a voice from the bridge.

Here we go again, thought Miller.

Then the night became day.

For a moment there was just stark blue-white light, the faces of the men on the bridge frozen, every pore mercilessly limned, the dinghy and the landing party in the slice of black shadow behind the superstructure. Then, very rapidly, things began to change.

The light blazed from a source as bright as the sun, behind them, low on the water. Someone was shouting on the bridge: Wills' voice. From behind the light came the heavy chug of a large-calibre machine gun. The bridge windows exploded. Glass splinters hissed around the dinghy, and someone somewhere let out a bubbling howl. Then more guns started firing, some from the MTB now.

'Stay where you are,' said Mallory, calm as if he were walking down the Strand. 'Two minutes to landing.'

'Shoot that bloody light out!' roared Wills, from the bridge.

They huddled in the shadow of the superstructure. Suddenly the blue-white glare vanished. The blackness that followed it was no longer black, but criss-crossed with ice-blue and hot-poker-red tracers. The MTB's deck jumped underfoot like the skin of a well-thrashed drum. Whatever was attacking was big, and heavily armed. They heard Wills' voice shout, 'Full ahead both!' The MTB started to surge forward.

But the tracers were homing in now. There was something like an Oerlikon or a Bofors out there. Into Miller's mind there popped the picture of the back end of the MTB: a huge tank of aviation gas, contained in a thin skin of aluminium and plywood. One Oerlikon round in there: well, two, one to puncture it, one to light it . . .

Miller found himself longing passionately for a row in a rubber dinghy on the night-black sea –

Crash, went something on the aft deck. Then there was a jack-hammer succession of further crashes. The MTB's machine guns fell silent. The engine note faltered and died, and she slowed, wallowing. An ominous red glow came from her after hatches.

Mallory's mind was clicking like an adding machine. Options: stay on board and get blown to hell; go over the side, with at least a chance that they would get ashore and on with the mission. No contest.

'Go,' he said.

The MTB had slewed port-side on to the tracers whipping out of the dark. They manhandled the rubber boat over the starboard rail and into the dark water. Miller climbed down, and stowed the packs and the oilcloth weapon bags as Mallory and Andrea lowered them. The orange glow was heavier now, beginning to jump and flicker, so Mallory could see Miller and Andrea working, and Carstairs, eyes flicking left and right, nervous for himself, not for anybody else. Not a team player, Carstairs. Hard to blame him, on top of a burning bladder of petrol in enemy waters –

Whump, said something the other side of the bridge, and the shock wave blew Mallory on to the deck. Then there was another explosion, bigger, and a blast of air, dreadfully hot, that carried with it a smell of burning eyebrows and more glass. Something crashed on to the deck alongside. By the light of the flames, Mallory saw it was Wills, blown, presumably, out of the glassless windows of the bridge. Unconscious at least, thought Mallory, ears ringing. If not dead –

Wills opened his eyes. His face was coppery with burns, his expression that of a sleepwalker. He started to crawl aft. Another explosion blew him backwards into Mallory's legs. The flames were very bright now, the air vibrating with heat. 'Into the dinghy,' said Mallory.

Carstairs went over the rail at a hard scramble, followed more sedately by Andrea. Aft of the bridge, the MTB was a sheet of flame. A man emerged, blazing, and fell back into the inferno. 'Come,' said Mallory to Wills. He half-saw other figures going over the rail, heard the splash of bodies.

Wills looked at him without seeing him, and started to walk into the wall of flame. Mallory grabbed his arm. Wills turned and took a swing at him. Mallory went under the punch, grabbed him by the shirt and trousers, and heaved him overboard. The deck was swelling underfoot like a balloon. Mallory went to the rail and jumped.

It was only when he hit the water that he realized how hot the air had been. He found himself holding the rope on the rubber flanks of the dinghy. 'Row,' he said. They already were rowing. There was another head beside him in the water: Wills, eyes wide and rolling. He scrambled into the dinghy and pulled Wills after him. Wills showed a tendency to struggle. He wanted to be with his ship –

The night split in two. There was a blinding flash. A shock wave like a brick wall hurtled across the water and walloped into the dinghy. Torpedoes, thought Mallory, against the ringing in his ears. Torpedoes gone up.

Then a thick chemical smoke rolled down on them. Under its black and reeking blanket they rowed and coughed and rowed again, squinting at the radium-lit north on Mallory's compass, for what felt like hours. 'Clearing,' said Miller at last. Overhead, the sky was lightening. They sat still as the fumes thinned around them, leaving them naked and exposed on the surface of the sea. But there was no one to see them. As the last of the smoke eddied away, it was plain that under its cover they had got clear. All around them was black night, with stars. The best part of a mile to the westward, the dark shape of some sort of coastal patrol boat lay half-wrapped in smoke, moving to and fro in the water, shining lights, looking for survivors.

And in that confusing patchwork of light and smoke, not finding any.

To the eastwards, the sky stopped well short of the horizon, cut out by the jagged tops of mountains: the mountains of Kynthos.

Mallory called the roll.

'Carstairs.'

'Here.'

'Andrea.'

'Here.'

'Miller.'

'Sure.'

31

'Anyone else?'

'Wills,' said Wills, in a strange, faraway voice.

'Nelson,' said another. 'And Dawkins. 'E's unconscious. I've 'urt me arm.'

'Okay,' said Mallory, level-voiced, though inwardly he was worried. There was work to do, and not the sort of work you could do if you were carrying maimed and unconscious sailors about with you. They had hardly started Operation Thunderbolt, and already it was in serious trouble.

Save it, he told himself. They were on the deep sea, with three extra people and a job to do. What was necessary now was to get ashore.

'Row,' he said.

They rowed.

After a while, a voice said, 'I'm getting wet.' A sailor's voice: Nelson.

It was true. The side of the rubber dinghy, which had been hard, was becoming flaccid. 'Probably the air inside cooling,' said Carstairs. 'The water's colder than the air, isn't it? So it'd shrink –'

'Got a leak,' said Miller. He found the pump and plugged it into the side. There was no chance of using his feet, so he squeezed the concertina bag between his hands. After two hundred, his arms felt as if they were on fire. But the tube was not deflating any more. 'Here,' he said to Carstairs.

'Sorry, Corporal?' said the drawling voice in the dark.

'Your go, sir,' said Miller.

Carstairs laughed, a light, dangerous laugh. 'I'm sorry, Corporal,' he said. 'I don't think I'm with you.'

Miller gave a couple more squeezes to the pump. The sweat was running into his eyes. 'Yessir,' he said. 'Yessir, Cap'n, sure thing.' Carstairs was only a dark shape against the stars, but Miller was sure he was smiling a small, superior smile –

'Give it to me,' said Andrea. Miller felt it plucked from his hands, heard the steady, monotonous pant.

'Carstairs,' said Mallory. 'You can row now.'

Carstairs' shadow froze. But Mallory's voice had an edge like a hacksaw. 'Delighted,' said Carstairs. 'Jolly boating weather, eh?'

For two endless hours, the oars dipped, and the pump panted, and the black mass of Kynthos crawled slowly up the stars. At

0155, Wills, who had been sitting slumped on the side, suddenly raised his head. 'Port twenty,' he said, in a weird, cracked voice.

'What?' said Miller, who was rowing.

'Left a bit.'

'Why?'

'There's a beach.'

'How do you know?' said Carstairs.

'Pilot book. Recognize the horizon.' Wills made a loose gesture of his hand at the saw-backed ridge plunging towards the sea ahead and to the right.

Carstairs said, 'You're in no condition to recognize anything.'

'So what do you suggest?' said Mallory, mildly.

'Straight for the shore,' said Carstairs. 'Up the cliffs.'

'Listen,' said Wills.

Miller stopped rowing, and Andrea stopped pumping. They listened.

There was the drip of the oars, and the tiny gurgle of the dinghy moving through the water, and something else: the long, low mutter of swell on stone. 'Cliffs,' said Wills. 'Doesn't feel like much out here, but there'll be a heave. Lava rock. Like a cross-cut saw. Two foot of swell, bang goes your gear, bang goes you.'

It was a lucid speech, and convincing. Carstairs could find no objection to it. He lapsed into a sulk.

Mallory had seen the beaches on the map, all that time ago in the briefing room under Plymouth. There were half-a-dozen of them at this end of the island, little crescents of sand among writhing contours and hatchings of precipitous cliffs. If it had been him in command of the Kynthos garrison, he would have watched them like a hawk.

The muttering grew.

"Scuse me,' said the voice of the sailor Nelson. 'It's Dawkins, sir. I think 'e's dead.'

'For Christ's sake,' said Carstairs, high and sharp. 'Save it for later. We'll –'

But Mallory had moved past him, and had his fingers on Dawkins' neck. The skin was warm, but not as warm as it should have been. There was no pulse. 'I'm afraid you're right,' he said.

'Throw him overboard,' said Carstairs. 'He's just dead weight.'

'No,' said Mallory, pumping.

'You –'

'I'm taking operational responsibility for Able Seaman Dawkins,' said Mallory.

There were cliffs on either side and ahead, now, not more than fifty yards away. The dinghy lifted spongily in the swell. They were in a sort of cove.

Andrea said, 'Wait here.'

'What are you doing?' said Carstairs.

Andrea did not answer. He seemed to be taking off his battledress. A pair of huge, furry shoulders gleamed for a moment under the stars. Then he was gone, quiet as a seal in a small roil of water.

'Reconnaissance,' said Mallory. 'Hold her here, Miller.'

Cradled in the bosom of the sea, protected on three sides by a small, jagged alcove of the cliffs, they waited.

THREE

Wednesday 0200–0600

Private Gottfried Schenck was not in favour of Greek islands. The beer was terrible, the food oily and the women hostile, particularly in the last couple of days. Still, it was better than the Russian Front, he supposed. He had thought it a place completely without danger, until the unpleasantness on Saturday. Tonight he had seen the flick of tracer and the flash of a big explosion out at sea. It looked as if things were getting worse. He had commandeered a bottle of wine from a peasant he had met with a flock of goats; vile stuff, tasted like disinfectant, but at least it stopped the jitters. He looked at his watch. Two o'clock. Four hours till his relief at dawn. Time to have a look in the next cove, perhaps have a crafty fag with his mate Willi.

He turned and walked along the edge of the sea, his boots making only the faintest of crunches on the sand.

From his vantage point by a rock thirty yards to seaward, Andrea watched him go, waited, counting; saw the sudden flare of a match beyond the headland . . .

Not that anybody normal would have seen this. But Andrea's eyes were used to weighing matters of life and death in thick darkness. He waited in the milk-warm water, counting, watched the sentry come back on to the beach, throw away the glowing butt. Then, with no fuss or turbulence, he sank below the surface.

The cigarette had not done Private Schenck any good. He felt sleepy, and there was a filthy taste in his mouth. What he really needed was a swim, but if anyone caught him swimming on duty there would be hell to pay –

He had arrived at the end of the beach. He turned round and started back, moving smartly to wake himself up, shoulders square, eyes on the tip of his nose, trying as he often did to feel the way he had felt all those years ago at Nuremberg in the temple of searchlights, when he had believed in all this damned Nazi nonsense –

Behind him, something rose from the water beyond the small waves that broke on the shore: something impossibly huge that gleamed with water in the starlight and took two loping steps towards him, clapped a vast hard hand over his mouth and hauled him through the breakers and bent him creaking towards the water, as he tried to shout, but managed no sound at all, like a child in the hands of this terrible thing from the sea. Schenck had given up even before his face hit the water, gently, oh so gently, and stayed there, under those huge, remorseless hands, until his mouth opened and the bad taste of cigarettes and old wine became the taste of salt, and he breathed.

Andrea waited until the bubbles ceased to rise. Then he swam back to the dinghy, and talked low and short to Mallory. A minute later, the dinghy was heading for the beach.

Things now began to move very fast for the still-dazed Wills. As soon as the dinghy's nose touched the sand, they were out, dragging the packs on to their backs, hustling him and Nelson up the beach and into the low scrub of thorn and oleander at its back. 'Watch them,' said Mallory to Carstairs. Carstairs looked as if he was going to protest, but suddenly Mallory and Miller were gone, and there was nowhere else to go, so Carstairs had no option.

Dimly in the starlight they saw Andrea drag Dawkins' body from the dinghy, and tow him out through the little breakers and into deep water. Nelson started forward, but Wills put a hand on his arm. They heard the hiss as Miller enlarged the hole in the dinghy and left it in the surf, watched Mallory and Miller brush out the footprints on the beach, reversing up into the bushes.

Wills' head was buzzing like a hive full of bees. He was streaming sweat, and he felt sick, or rather he felt as if someone else a lot like him felt sick, because he was somewhere else. Nearby, Andrea was climbing back into his fatigues. Wills heard himself say, 'All right, Nelson?'

'Shouldn't have done that to poor Dawks,' said Nelson.

'He's dead,' said Wills. 'He doesn't know. He's being useful.'

'It ain't right,' said Nelson. He sounded aggrieved: bit of a barrack-room lawyer, Nelson. ''E needs burying. There's no call to chuck 'im in the sea.'

'There was a guard,' said Andrea. 'I killed him. Now the Germans will think he found poor Dawkins, and they fought, and both drowned.'

'You 'ope,' said Nelson, who did not hold with foreigners.

'Yes,' said the foreigner, in that lion-like purr of his. 'And so should you, if you do not want to die.'

Hearing the voice, Nelson realized that he desperately and passionately wanted to live.

'Miller,' said Andrea. 'Have a look at Nelson's arm.'

Miller pulled out a pencil light, lodged it between his teeth, and unwrapped the strip of rag from the seaman's right forearm. The cut gaped long and red against the white skin. 'You'll live,' said Miller. 'Sew you up later.'

'Jesus,' said Nelson weakly. 'It's really bad. Oh Jesus. It feels bloody terrible.'

'You won't die,' said Miller. 'Not of a cut arm, anyway. No bleeding, and all nice and clean and tidy with seawater.' He sprinkled sulfa into the wound, bound it swiftly and expertly with a bandage from the first-aid kit, and made a sling out of the rag. 'Good as new,' he said.

But as he tied the sling, he could feel that despite the warmth of the night, Nelson was shivering.

Mallory said, very quiet, 'Put out that light and let's go.'

They crossed a stony track along the back of the beach. Inland, the ground rose steeply. Mallory halted them in a grove of oleanders. 'Wait here,' he said. Nelson sat down with a heavy thump.

'Shut up,' said Carstairs, too loud.

Silence fell: a silence full of the rustle of the breeze in the oleanders, and the trill of the cicadas, and the small crunch of the surf on the shore.

And German voices, talking, from the next beach.

It was just the chatting of sentries bored by a long night duty. But it ran a bristle of small hairs up Nelson's spine. And suddenly the silence of the group was not just six people keeping quiet, but a sort of frozen hole in the middle of the night noises. He felt sick, with burning petrol, and his shipmates gone, and a nauseating pain in his arm, and poor old Dawks chucked in the sea. And now he was mixed up in God knew what with a bunch of bandits, in enemy territory. He had signed up for the Navy, not the bleeding Commandos. What he wanted now was a nice POW camp, not to get shot out of hand for raiding enemy territory with the skipper and these four hard nuts . . .

These two hard nuts.

As Nelson counted the heads against the sky, he saw that in the middle of the silence – quieter than the silence itself, in fact – the big one and the thin one had vanished.

Mallory and Andrea went quickly down the track, one either side. They moved quiet as shadows, stooping to avoid the tell-tale flick of a silhouette against the sky. Their packs were with Miller in the oleanders. They carried knives and Schmeissers, and the knowledge that if they used either they were dead, and the mission was finished.

As he trotted on, part of Mallory's mind was chewing at the problems of the mission. There were several ways of adding up a fire at sea, a cut-up rubber dinghy, a dead British matlow and a drowned German sentry. Some of them were innocent – a survivor of the wreck, a fight in the shallows. Others were not. The rubber boat was a type used in aircraft, not MTBs. Why would a guard drown, having fractured a British seaman's skull? Anyone with any brains was going to bump into these questions, particularly on an island as sleepy as Kynthos. Perhaps in a couple of *Wehrmacht* platoons, there would not be too many brains.

But from Mallory's experience, there would be brains in plenty: thorough, inquisitive, fine-slicing brains . . .

Speed was what was needed.

They had rounded a headland. There was a low, regular lump that might have been an observation post. They skirted it to the rear, and found the road improving, running round the back of a half-mile beach of pale sand washed with the drowsy roar of the small surf. Behind the beach, an untidy huddle of rectilinear blocks gleamed white in the starlight. Houses. Parmatia.

They moved inland, through a belt of scrub and onto a valley floor tiled with little gardens and lemon groves. A couple of dogs barked lazily as they passed. The air was warm and still.

Mavrocordato Street was a long jumble of small farms and sheds. Number three was shuttered up tight against the sickly influences of the night air. Round the back, a shutter stood open. Andrea and Mallory took a last look over the dark plain. Then Andrea went in through the window.

If Miller had not been Miller, he would have been getting bored. Instead, once he had closed the cut in Nelson's forearm with a neat line of stitches he had propped his head on his pack, felt a large regret that in their present circumstances it was not possible to light a cigarette, and closed his eyes. Not that he was asleep. It was merely that Miller was a man who hated unnecessary effort. In the darkness of the rocks, the only thing you got from a visual inspection of your surroundings was eye-ache. Also, by closing your eyes you gave your ears the best possible chance. He lay there, and sorted the sounds of the night: breeze in the leaves, the rustle of the sea, cicadas, the small click of a beetle rolling a pebble, the breathing of Wills and Nelson and Carstairs –

No breathing from Carstairs.

Carstairs had gone.

Carstairs had gone God knew where.

Miller was a gambler. Before the war, he had spent much of his life in the weighing of odds. Since he had been mixed up with Mallory and Andrea, not much had changed, except that the consequences of losing a bet had become more deadly. And even in the old days, the kind of people Miller had played poker with were not the kind of people you welshed on and lived.

So Miller weighed up the odds. Carstairs was reputed to know what he was doing. Miller was a corporal, Carstairs was a captain, running his own show under the Admiral.

Carstairs was on his own.

Mallory waited outside the window in a horrible silence, the dreary silence of the hours before the dawn, when nature is at its lowest ebb and sleep most closely approximates to death. His finger rested on the trigger of his Schmeisser. He tested the night sounds, found nothing amiss. He was a soldier, Mallory, and a mountaineer, a man not given to fantasy or speculation. But once again he felt the tightness in his stomach he had felt on the way out of the armoury in Plymouth. This warm world that smelt of farms lay under the shadow of death –

The shutter creaked faintly. Andrea's voice said, 'Come.'

Mallory found himself in a cool room that smelt of scrubbed floors and old wine. The shutter closed, and there were fumbling sounds, as if someone was draping the window with a cloth. A match scraped, and a mantle flared and began to glow. The person who had lit it was small, with a hood over his head and a long, Bedouin sort of robe. 'Achilles?' said Mallory.

'Achilles is dead,' said Andrea. 'The partisans have blown up the road. The Germans took reprisals. One hundred and thirty-one people were killed in the square on Saturday. Achilles was one of them.'

Mallory said nothing. If there was no road, it would be hard to get the Thunderbolt force across the mountains even if there were no wounded. With wounded, it would be next to impossible –

'I will take you,' said their host, and swept back the hood of the robe. Swept it back from a tangled mass of black hair, and a smooth face with a straight nose and big, black eyes that glowed with tears and fury.

'This,' said Andrea, 'is Clytemnestra. She was the sister of Achilles.'

'For twenty-three years,' said the woman. 'Twenty-three years, and two months, and three days, and four hours, before those pigs . . . those worse than pigs' – here she plunged into a machine-gun rattle of abuse in a dialect that Mallory recognized from his months in the White Mountains in Crete – 'saw fit to take him away and murder him.' She pulled a wine bottle and some glasses out of a worm-eaten cupboard. 'But we are together,' she said. 'We will be together again. Together, we will take you across the mountains.' She sloshed wine into the glasses.

'You know the paths,' said Andrea.

'Of course I know,' she said. 'And if I do not know, then my brother Achilles will walk at my side, and show me.'

They drank in silence. Mallory heard the glass rattle against her teeth. Too wild, thought Mallory. He made his voice calm and

40

level, the voice of a policeman at the scene of an accident. 'Could you bear to tell me what's been going on, this past week?'

She did not look up. 'The more people who know, the better,' she said. 'It should be carved in letters four feet high on the cliff of the Acropolis, so people can see –' She caught Andrea's eye. Then her head bowed again, and she took his mighty hand, and for some time could not speak.

After a little while, she dried her eyes on her rusty black shirt and took a deep breath. 'Forgive me,' she said.

'There is nothing to forgive,' said Andrea, and the slow fire in his eyes kindled hers, and she nodded. 'Tell us, and we will avenge your brother.'

'Achilles was a farmer,' she said. 'A farmer and a policeman. There were half-a-dozen men in the mountains, klephts, thieves, what have you. We all on this island hate the Germans, we do what we can to make their lives awkward, in small ways, you understand. But these klephts in the mountains, they were always causing trouble. For their own pleasure, not Greece's freedom. They stole Iannis's wine, and Spiro's sheep, and they raped poor Athene, and every man's hand was against them, because they were bandits, not fighters. Then last Monday they tried to steal a German patrol truck, and they were drunk, so they made a mess of it and one of them got killed.' Her head dropped.

'Steady,' said Andrea, squeezing her hand.

She nodded, pushing the hair out of her eyes. 'So on Tuesday there arrived many aeroplanes at the aerodrome, with many soldiers. And the word went round the island that from now on it was a new world, with no mercy. But these klephts either did not hear or did not want to hear. So in revenge for the killing of their man they planted a big charge of explosive at a place where the cliff overhangs the road to Antikynthos and the Acropolis, the only road, you understand.' Mallory nodded. He understood all too well. 'And they blew the cliff down on to the road. Nobody was passing, of course.' Here she looked disappointed. 'But these new soldiers came, and they climbed over the rubble. They had a new kind of uniform, mottled-looking, like the sun in an olive grove. There was one man, with a crooked face and very pale eyes, the officer. He took one person for every metre of road destroyed, he said.' The tears were running again. 'One hundred and thirty-one people, men, women, children, it didn't matter. The women and children he machine-gunned. The men he hanged.' She fell silent.

Mallory left her in peace for a couple of minutes. Then he said, 'And the partisans?'

'They left the island the night before the hangings. Saturday. They stole Kallikratides' boat, and went away, who knows where, who cares? They left a note saying it was a tactical withdrawal. But we know that they were frightened that someone would catch them, us or that man Wolf, it didn't matter –'

'Wolf?' said Mallory.

'That's this officer's name. Dieter Wolf, they call him, may he rot in hell. He hanged Kallikratides, too. With his own hands.'

'The same Dieter Wolf?' said Andrea.

'Sounds like it.'

Andrea nodded, heavily. In his mind he could see a village in the white mountains of Crete, dry mountains, full of the song of grasshoppers and the smell of the herbs the peasants plucked from the wild plants to eat with their lamb. But today there was another smell wafting across the ravine. The smell of smoke, the black plume that rose from the caved-in roof of the village church. The church into which a *Sonderkommando* had driven the women and children of the village; the church to which they had then set fire. All this because one of the patriarchs of the village had shot with his old shotgun one of the *Sonderkommando* he had found in the act of raping his daughter . . .

Andrea and Mallory had lain in cover across the unbridged ravine that separated them from the village. They had arrived too late. In the shaking disc of his field glasses an officer stood: a man in scuffed jackboots, with a white, crooked face and no hair, cleaning a knife. Later, they discovered why the knife had needed cleaning, when they found a grandfather disembowelled by the roadside. Even at this range, the officer's eyes caught the sun pale and opaque, like slits of brushed aluminium. Then he and his troops had boarded their armoured personnel carriers and roared away down the road to Iraklion.

Andrea had found out that this man was Dieter Wolf, and promised himself and the dead of that village that he would have his revenge.

'Sometimes,' he said, 'God is very good.' He looked at his watch. 'It will be getting light,' he said.

42

'I will get dressed,' said Clytemnestra. 'Then I will show you across the mountains.'

She went. Doors slammed. Mallory poured Andrea a glass of wine, drank one himself, lit a cigarette.

According to Lieutenant Robinson in the bunker at Plymouth, Kynthos was a soft target. But if Dieter Wolf was here taking reprisals, that meant only one thing. Cambridge don or not, Robinson had been wrong.

He ground out his cigarette and tossed the butt into the stove. The door opened. Clytemnestra was wearing baggy black breeches, soft leather boots, a fringed shawl at her waist, a worn embroidered waistcoat lined with sheepskin over her black shirt. Her hair was bound into a black silk scarf. She looked dull, crow-black, a thing of the shadows. Only her eyes were alive, burning –

There was a thunderous knocking at the door. She shooed Andrea and Mallory on to the stairs. 'Coming, coming,' she said, and opened up.

Andrea's world was keyhole-shaped. He could see very little, and his breathing was deafening in his ears. The kitchen seemed to have filled with people. There was silence, except for the shuffle of boots on tiles: not jackboots, though; boots with unnailed soles. The talk broke like a wave; a Greek wave. Despite all the noise, there were only two visitors.

'Be quiet, be quiet!' cried Clytemnestra. 'Please!' She seemed to be a woman people listened to. Silence fell. 'Now. Ladas, what is it?'

'There was this man,' said Ladas. 'Iannis the Nose saw him. He was snooping in the square, looking into cars, windows, you name it. Dressed in a soldier's uniform. Not a German uniform: British, maybe, Greek, who knows? Straight away we thought, the partisans are back. And you may call us cowards, but you know yourself they were no better than thieves, and my poor Olympia that they shot . . . for a victory perhaps it might be worth losing a sister, but for those damned thieves of partisans, those *Kommunisti* bastards, never, God's curse on –'

'You are right,' said Clytemnestra, soothingly, without impatience. 'Tell me more about this man, in whom I must tell you I do not believe.'

'He has curly hair and a thin moustache, so thin, like a worm on his lip. He carries a rifle, many grenades. When he saw me I thought he would shoot. But he vanished only, into the dark, like a ghost.'

'Perhaps he is a ghost.'

Ladas scowled so that his mighty eyebrows nearly met his mighty moustache. He did not look like a man who believed in ghosts. 'You know this town,' he said. 'It is full of spies. If a spy says to this German pig, "I have seen a ghost", this German pig will kill people until the ghost comes to life. What can we do?'

'Watch and pray until the ghost goes away.'

'How can you know?'

'This can only be a ghost. This is the way you deal with ghosts.'

There was a silence. The man with Ladas had a heavy, stupid face with small, suspicious eyes. He looked like a man who might believe in ghosts. He said, 'She is wearing her clothes.'

'Yes,' said Ladas. 'You are wearing your clothes.'

Clytemnestra looked drawn and weary. 'When you have no man in the house,' she said, 'you must take the sheep to the mountain yourself. And it will soon be dawn. Now back to your beds. Some of us have work to do, even if you want to run around in the dark squeaking of ghosts.'

They left.

Clytemnestra opened the stairs door. 'What is this?' she said. 'Who is in the village?'

'Hard to say,' said Mallory. But he knew. It was Carstairs, of course. There were things he needed to say to Carstairs. 'It will soon be light,' he said.

Outside, the air smelt sharp and fresh. The sky over the mountains was still deep blue and thick with stars, but low down, towards the peaks, the blue was paling.

'This man,' said Andrea to Clytemnestra. 'He is one of our people.'

She walked fast through a maze of paths that wound among the gardens. 'Then you should control him,' she said. 'Why is he wandering in the village like a madman? He will get people killed.' They walked on in silence.

Something was worrying Mallory. 'And you,' he said. 'You shouldn't be with us. We are soldiers, in uniform. We have no

44

connection with you. There will be no reprisals. But if they find you with us –'

'If I don't come with you, how will you find your way across the mountains?'

'We have maps.'

She laughed, a large, scornful laugh that sent a couple of doves flapping from their roost. 'Use them to roll cigarettes,' she said. 'If you use the tracks you will see on them, the Germans will find you. They have the same maps –'

'Hush,' said Mallory.

They were on the road through the dunes, approaching the southern end of the beach.

'Down!' said Andrea. A figure stood suddenly outlined against the paling sky. Its head was blocky with a coal-scuttle helmet, its shoulders tense over its rifle. '*Wer da?*' it said.

Mallory's breath was loud in his ears as he lay face down in the dunes. Andrea was at his side. Mallory knew what he would be thinking, because he was thinking it himself. The pre-dawn was quiet. The cocking lever of the Schmeisser would sound like a train crash. One shot, and it would all be over . . .

Clytemnestra walked forward, hips swaying insolently. 'Who wants to know?' she said, in Greek. 'What murdering son of a whore comes to my home and gets between me and my work?'

'*Vas?*' said the soldier.

'I looking for my sheeps,' said Clytemnestra, in terrible German.

The soldier stood undecided. Mallory could not work out whether he had seen them. Beside him, Andrea sighted on the place under the man's left shoulder blade where he would drive the knife. He put one mighty palm on the gritty soil, tensed his legs to spring –

'Go on, then,' said the soldier.

'I evacuate my bowels on your mother's grave,' said Clytemnestra, in Greek. 'I dig up her remains and feed them to my pigs, who vomit.'

'Nice meeting you,' said the German, in German, and stamped back down the beach.

Mallory took his hand away from the cocking lever. The palm was wet with sweat. He and Andrea rose from cover. After that, they marched in silence.

As they turned up the track behind the beach, Andrea said, 'Wait.'

They waited.

Ahead, over the noise of the cicadas, there came the sound of a stone rolling under a boot.

'Three minutes,' said Andrea's huge, purring whisper by Mallory's ear. Then, silent as a shadow, he was gone.

The path unreeled under Andrea's boots as he ran. He could feel the blood taking the power around his body, the thing that made him not a man in the grey pre-dawn, but a hunting animal closing with its prey. He saw the figure ahead, clambering up the path. He was alone, moving probably quite fast, but to Andrea slow and clumsy.

Andrea looked around him with that special radar of his. He sensed the town, Mallory and Clytemnestra behind him, the German soldiers on the beach, the two corpses in the surf, the little party ahead.

He sprang.

A great hard hand went over the mouth. The other hand went to the nape of the neck. He began the pull sideways to dislocate the vertebrae.

It was the smell that stopped him.

It was the smell of hair oil; a hair oil that Andrea had smelt before, on the MTB, in the dinghy, tonight. A powerful smell, sickly even by Greek standards. Expensive.

The smell of Captain Carstairs.

Andrea decided not to break the neck, after all. Instead he kept a hand over the mouth, and said, 'No noise, or you die.' Then he waited for Mallory.

So Miller lay with his eyes closed, devoting himself to analysis of the night sounds.

He heard Carstairs coming up the path, and rolled to his feet, Schmeisser in hand. Then he heard Andrea's attack. After the brief scuffle came the brief bleep of a Scops owl. Mallory's signal. Miller let out a long breath as three dark figures arrived in the camp.

'All right,' said Mallory's voice. 'Moving out.'

'Where to?' said Miller.

'Germans on the beach,' said Mallory. 'Silence.'

Wills was already upright. Nelson's cut had stiffened, and he needed some persuading. 'Hurts,' he said, whining.

'Up,' said Wills. 'Show a leg.'

Grumbling, Nelson got up. Then they were slinging packs and weapons, starting up a steep, stony path among the bushes. And very soon the path was so steep that there was no spare energy even for wondering, or indeed doing anything except keeping the feet moving and the breath rasping and the heart beating. All the time, the sky in the east grew lighter.

FOUR

Wednesday 0600–1800

Just after six o'clock, the sun hauled itself over the mountain. 'Stop now,' said Clytemnestra. 'We eat.'

They slumped to the hot, stony ground and started fumbling for cigarettes and chocolate. They were on a ledge, a bare shelf of rock made by a crack that ran across a great cliff that seemed to rise sheer from the sea. Nelson said, 'Water.' Miller passed him his canteen. The seaman drank avidly, water spilling down his face and on to his shirt. Miller twitched the water bottle out of his hand.

'Sod that,' said Nelson. 'I've got a mouf like a bleeding lime kiln.'

'We all have,' said Miller. He pulled a cigarette from his packet and lit it with a Zippo. He had been a Long Range Desert Group man, doing damage behind enemy lines in the Western Desert. Water was more important than petrol, which was more important than motherhood, religion and the gold standard. 'You drink in the morning and at night. Drink in the day, you just sweat it right out again. Now let's have a look at your arm.'

Nelson would not let him. His face was bluish and hostile under his sweat-matted red hair. ''S all right,' he said, and fell back into a sullen silence.

Wills said, in his odd, marble-mouthed voice, 'Pull yourself together, man.' But Nelson would not meet his eye.

In daylight, Wills was a mess. He had no eyebrows, and no hair on the front part of his head. His skin shone with tannic acid jelly, and there was a great bruise on his right temple. As he looked out over the blue void of the sea, his eyes were glassy and his hand trembled. Mallory guessed that he was thinking about his ship. He offered him a slab of chocolate and a wedge of the bread they had brought from Mavrocordato Street. Wills shook his head.

'Sorry about your ship,' said Mallory.

Wills made a face that made him look ridiculously young. 'Poor chaps,' he said.

'First command?' said Mallory.

Wills nodded. There were tears in his eyes.

'Can you go on?'

'Of course.'

'Good man.'

'Don't worry about Nelson,' said Wills. 'Top-hole chap.'

Mallory nodded. Loyalty to your men was a good thing. He just hoped that it was a two-way process.

Carstairs was sitting off to one side, by himself. There was dust in his greasy curls, and his eyebrow moustache was distorted by a wet red graze. 'How are you doing?' said Mallory.

'Fine,' he said, very curt.

'I want you to stay close,' said Mallory. 'You could get hurt.'

'Now you look here,' said Carstairs, as if he was talking to a taxi driver who had taken him to the wrong street in Mayfair. 'This is not the first time I've been behind enemy lines. Believe it or not, I am capable of looking after myself. And if you have any worries on that score, I suggest you cast your mind back to Admiral Dixon and the briefing. It is none of your damn business whether I get hurt or not.'

Mallory smiled, a peaceful white smile. 'How's your neck?' he said.

Carstairs' face filled with sullen blood.

'Listen,' said Mallory, 'it's my job to look after my men, and avoid reprisals against the islanders. So any time you want to do a little freelance snooping around the civilian population, I should be grateful if you would talk to me first.'

'Ask your permission?' he said. 'Go to hell.'

'Liaise,' said Mallory.

'Go to hell.'

Mallory was not smiling any more. He said, 'Admiral Dixon is a long way away. You nearly had a nasty accident with Colonel Andrea. You are lucky to be alive. Think about it.'

Carstairs thought about it. 'Where is Andrea?' he said.

'Sentry duty,' said Mallory.

'A colonel's work is never done,' said Carstairs, and smiled a superior smile.

'So what were you doing in the village?'

'I was looking for transport,' said Carstairs. 'Not that it's any affair of yours.'

'Transport where?'

'To the Acropolis.'

Mallory pointed to his boots. 'You're looking at it.'

'Sorry?'

'The partisans blew up the road.'

'Fine,' said Carstairs. He grinned, suddenly. 'I should have asked. Saved myself a stiff neck.'

Mallory nodded. It was nearly an apology. 'All comes out in the wash,' he said, getting to his feet. 'Five more minutes, gentlemen. Make the most of them.'

The ledge where they had paused was in dead ground. But from Andrea's vantage point above and to the side, he could see the beach where they had landed, and the bay of Parmatia, and the white town spread out like a map below.

Things were happening down there.

As he watched, three field-grey lorries moved out of the town and along the road behind the bay. For a moment they were hidden from view. When they came out, there were only two lorries. They halted at the landing beach. Ant-like figures spilled out, clotted into groups at the waterside.

It looked very much as if someone had found the bodies of Dawkins and the sentry. And the third lorryload of soldiers might have stopped to look for seashells.

Then again, they might have decided to start up the track into the mountains.

That might or might not be dangerous. As an army the *Wehrmacht* were fine soldiers. As individuals, a lot of them were conscripts, and a lot of them were going through the motions, waiting till it was time to go home, win or lose.

The *Sonderkommando* were different. The *Wehrmacht* felt a sort of horrified scorn for Dieter Wolf and his men. They were volunteers, hand-picked for fitness, ruthlessness and cunning – soldiers who loved killing for killing's sake, particularly when it was seasoned with plenty of rape, loot and torture. Dieter Wolf was the nearest thing the Nazis had to a special forces leader. He was a known intimate of the legendary Otto Skorzeny. The presence of his *Sonderkommando* on the island meant two things.

One, the Germans had no desire to be interrupted in whatever they were doing in the Acropolis.

And two, these mountains would soon be swarming with soldiers.

When Andrea went back to the ledge, the rest of the party was already upright. Wills put out a hand to steady himself, missed the rock, and sprawled in the dust. Carstairs raised an eyebrow. Miller helped him back on to his feet. His eyes seemed to be looking in different directions. 'Sorry,' he said, in that voice that sounded as if there were marbles in his mouth. Concussion, thought Miller. How would you understand an Englishman with concussion?

'Up,' said Clytemnestra. She kicked her boot-toe on to a small ledge, hoisted herself upwards and disappeared. The party followed; all except Nelson.

Nelson stayed at the bottom, shaking his head, shoulders bowed. He had a mop of red hair, white skin, a face flushed and sulky. Andrea, the rearguard, said, 'You want help?'

'My arm hurts,' said Nelson.

'Everybody hurts,' said Andrea. 'If we don't walk, we get hurt worse.'

'I'm not a commando,' said Nelson. 'I'm a bleeding matlow. What am I doing running around on cliffs like a poxy goat?'

'Your duty,' said Andrea. Gentle as a mother with a child he picked him up, and put him on the first step of the path. Nelson looked white-faced over his shoulder and downwards. Then he started climbing, using both feet and both hands. It struck Andrea that a man who could climb with such vigour might not have very much wrong with his arm at all.

All morning they climbed, at first on steep sea-cliffs, and then in a tangle of ridges and small valleys grown with scrub. By eleven o'clock they were five thousand feet above sea level, in a little valley of juniper and holm oak. Goats wandered among the boulders, their bells clonking mournfully. The men walked heavily, mouths parched, tormented by the small gurgle of the stream in the valley's bed. 'Too hot,' said Clytemnestra, wiping sweat from her forehead. 'We'll rest here three hours.' She led them on to a ledge overlooking the valley, and pushed aside a huge old rosemary bush. Behind the bush was the dark entrance of a cave.

Mallory was impatient to be pushing on. But he could see that Wills was just about done up. All of them could do with a rest: eight hours, never mind three.

Patience.

Carstairs had the map out. The mountains here formed ridges that spread from the central plateau like the fingers of a right hand. They had climbed from the beach between the first and second fingers, and crossed the ridge to the valley between the second and the ring fingers. Beyond the next ridge, between the ring finger and the little finger, the road ran. It was here (Clytemnestra said, pointing) that the partisans had blown the cliff down on to the road and blocked it solid.

Carstairs offered to stand sentry. Mallory settled down in the corner of the cave next to Miller and lit a cigarette to drive off the stink of goat dung.

'Nice place,' said Miller. 'Reminds me of a boarding house I used to use in San Francisco.'

'The carpet, you mean?' said Mallory.

'That and the fleas.' Mallory's eyes were closing. 'I'll do it,' said Miller.

'Yes.' Mallory was asleep.

They both knew that what Miller had been talking about was keeping an eye on Carstairs.

So Miller sat and smoked. Andrea and Mallory snored, Wills fell into a sort of twitching stupor, and Nelson curled into a ball. As for Clytemnestra, she had gone into another compartment of the cave, and it was impossible to tell whether she was asleep or awake, though now he came to think of it, Miller could not imagine her asleep.

After about half an hour, Miller got quietly to his feet and crept to the mouth of the cave.

Carstairs had taken up position in the ruined walls of a hut further up the ledge, commanding a view of the entrance to the valley and the ridge opposite. It was a good place to see without being seen. Miller walked up to it quietly. The valley shimmered in the heat, and a lizard scuttled away over a stone. Inside the shadows of the ruin, Carstairs made no sound. Miller went to the door, and looked in.

Carstairs was gone.

Miller stood quite still, thinking. There could be reasons. Went behind a rock, Miller told himself; call of nature. But even as he had those thoughts his binoculars were out, and he was scanning the valley, rocks, trees, a goat dragging at a branch with its teeth –

There.

High on the ridge opposite, a small, khaki figure was toiling towards the crest, rifle over its shoulder. Miller lowered the glasses. For a moment he considered giving chase. But the ridge was steep, and God knew what lay beyond, and Miller was no mountaineer.

He went back to the cave and pressed Mallory's hand. The New Zealander's eyes snapped open.

'Sorry, sir,' said Miller. 'Carstairs gone.'

Mallory said, 'Take guard.' Then he slung over his shoulder his Schmeisser and a coil of silk rope, and went out at a fast lope.

Miller watched the rangy khaki figure jog into the bottom of the valley, step from boulder to rickety boulder with the casual stride of a man taking a morning stroll. A speck in the air caught Miller's eye; an eagle soaring on a column of hot air. He watched it idly for a minute or so. When his eye returned to Mallory, he was surprised to see him already at the far side of the valley. Miller put the glasses on him, saw him come to the bottom of a cliff that anyone short of a fly would have walked around. But Mallory put his hands on it and went up it without fuss or difficulty, as if lighter than air. Miller propped himself against a rock, checked his weapon and lit a cigarette. As befits one who understands demolition, beneath his leathery exterior he was a sensitive man. He felt a sort of distant pity for anyone on the wrong end of that pursuit.

Even Carstairs.

Out of the shadow of the cave, it was hot; hot enough to swell Mallory's tongue in his head and bring the sweat rolling down the creases at the corners of his eyes and down his hollow cheeks. The air in the valley hung still and heavy, full of the smell of thyme and baking stone, and the cigarettes Mallory had smoked all these days and nights and weeks of bad food and snatched sleep.

At first his head felt sore and out of step with the world. But after a couple of minutes he got his mind fixed on Carstairs. Carstairs taking off on his own, with a long-range weapon. Carstairs was a dirty little mystery who needed solving before he blew the mission.

So Mallory hitched up his Schmeisser and trotted across the bottom of the valley, and went straight up the cliff on the far side, feeling the life return to his fingers and back and legs as he shifted from hold to hold on the firm, warm rock. Within half an hour he was standing on the crest of the ridge: not on top, where someone could see him, but below the skyline, in the little puddle of shade at the foot of a boulder. Here he pulled out his binoculars.

It took ten patient minutes of searching that wilderness of rock and scrub before he saw the little flicker of movement: a man, moving at a steady, plodding walk towards a range of low ridges in the distance. Khaki battledress, slung rifle. Carstairs.

Mallory started after him.

The Englishman was not more than twenty minutes ahead. Not even a mile, in this terrain. Steadily, Mallory wore down his lead.

They crossed a couple of low spurs of hill. Mallory checked his compass, and pulled the map out of his blouse pocket. After an hour and a quarter, the ground dipped sharply. Ahead, Carstairs flicked into shadow, and became invisible. Mallory was not worried. He knew where his man was heading.

What he did not know was why. He brushed through a fringe of scrub, and stopped dead.

In front of him there was no more ground. Beyond the lip of the cliff was a deep gulf of air, in which swallows hawked and swooped, and beyond that, the vast blue void of the sea. He lay down, and peered over the edge. He was looking down a three-thousand-foot precipice. Somewhere far below, hidden by overhangs, the sea muttered at the island's rocky skirts. A thousand feet below, the swoop of the cliff was interrupted by a flat platform of rock that ran along it like a step. It was fifty yards wide, this step, its outside edge scattered with wind-blasted shrubs, its inside blurred with the rock falls of centuries.

Vertically below Mallory's eyes, a green fur of trees grew on a glacis of rubble. To his right, the glacis was huge, extending most of the way up the thousand-odd feet of the cliff, new and raw, blocking the shelf completely.

Along the shelf there snaked the white ribbon of the road, vanishing into the great cone of rubble. This must be what was left of the overhang the partisans had blasted down to cut the island in half.

It was not going to stay cut long. The sound of diesel engines clattered up to Mallory's ears. Round the bulge of the landslide, there ran a pale band of levelled and compacted rock. As Mallory watched, a mechanical digger trundled round and deposited a load of rubble into what might have been a hole. It looked very much as if the road was nearly open again.

And Mallory was not the only one who thought that way. At the foot of the slide stood a little queue of vehicles: a horse and cart, three German army trucks, and a field ambulance, the red cross on its roof shimmering in the heat. A small knot of men sat in the shade of a little stand of pines.

And a couple of hundred feet down the cliff, masked from the vehicles by a buttress the size of a cathedral tower, a little khaki figure dangling like a spider on a thread.

Carstairs, descending.

Mallory watched him for a moment, weighing the odds. Let him go, catch him. Shoot him. Shooting him was the option he would have preferred, just now. But the Admiral was Jensen's superior officer. Shooting involved noise, which would attract attention, and besides, he was well out of Schmeisser range. Shooting was just a beautiful dream.

Mallory moved in dead ground to the top of the buttress. Carstairs had doubled his rope around a natural fin of rock. Mallory pinched the ropes together and tied a constrictor knot around the pair. If Carstairs wanted to pull the rope down so he could descend further, he was in for a disappointment.

Mallory looked down. The rope was a white line ruled down the cliff, disappearing at an overhang. Mallory measured out enough of his own rope to reach the overhang. Then he belayed it on a knob of rock, turned his back to the void, and leaped out and down. The pyramid nails of his boots bit once, twice. Then he was by the overhang, holding, looking down.

There was a ledge below, thirty feet wide, running diagonally downwards to the slide area. It was broad enough to have trees on it, and an undergrowth of juniper and caper bushes. The doubled rope terminated in a small area of broken stone. Carstairs was nowhere to be seen.

Mallory went down Carstairs' rope, braking just before he reached the bottom to avoid the tell-tale crunch of boots. Carstairs had left a flattened trail in the scorched grass by the bushes. Very quietly, Mallory pulled out his knife and followed it.

The ledge followed the curve of the cliff face for fifty yards, wide as a road, sloping towards the ravine floor at an angle of forty-five degrees. Through the head-high scrub Mallory could see grey vehicles, men moving, the red cross on the field ambulance's roof. He moved on, very stealthy –

'Don't move,' said a voice in his left ear. Something pushed into his left kidney. He knew without looking that it was the barrel of a silenced Browning.

'What the hell do you think you're doing?' he said.

'Minding my own business,' said Carstairs. His immaculate hair was disarranged, and sweat was rolling into his silly moustache. His eyes had a wild, dangerous look.

Mallory said, 'If you shoot me, you'll have fifty Germans after us.'

The gun in his kidney did not waver. 'Why are you following me about?' he said.

'Because you were standing sentry and deserted your post.'

'Don't be damn silly –'

'You listen here,' said Mallory. 'I don't care how many admirals you are taking your orders from, I am your superior officer by seniority and I would remind you that you are subject to my orders even if you are not directly under my command.'

There was a very faint lessening of pressure. Seventy-five feet below, the red cross on the ambulance roof glowed in the sun.

'You won't get through this alone,' said Mallory. 'It's team work, or nothing.'

The pressure of the Browning faded. Mallory watched as Carstairs holstered it and half-turned, performing some operation that made a small, metallic sound, putting something in his pocket. Carstairs nodded, smoothed his hair, gave a rueful film-star smile slightly marred by the scabbing graze on his upper lip. 'Just thought I'd pop and have a look,' he said. 'When I was in the town they said the road would be opening soon. So I thought, well, it'd shorten the journey, know what I mean?'

Mallory had a very good idea of what he meant. But what Carstairs meant had nothing to do with what Carstairs said. 'We'll carry on over the mountains,' he said.

Carstairs shrugged. He bent and picked up his sniper rifle, and started back up the path towards the rope. A dove, disturbed by his passing, clattered out of a holm oak tree. Three more, disturbed by the first, zigzagged away over the road in a kerfuffle of wings. Carstairs and Mallory stood still, holding their breath. For a moment, a thick, pregnant silence hung over the gorge. Then there broke into that silence a voice, giving orders, steady and professional, in German. 'Schmidt,' it said. 'Take two men and get on to that ledge and see what's going on.'

Mallory and Carstairs turned and ran. 'Go,' said Mallory, when they reached the bottom of the rope.

Carstairs grabbed hold and went up, kicking his feet into the rock, making a lot of noise about it, Mallory thought as he unslung his Schmeisser, but travelling at commendable speed. When Carstairs got to the overhang, Mallory shouted, 'Cover me!' turned and gripped the rope, and started to walk the wall.

The rock was coarse and pitted, so it took no more than a couple of minutes to reach the base of the overhang. German shouts came from below. Mallory decided that this was one of those occasions when speed was more important than technique. He went over the overhang hands only, expecting to find Carstairs waiting, covering the cliff base, ready to open fire. But Carstairs had not bothered to wait: look after number one was Carstairs' motto. He was a pair of bootsoles half-way up the cliff. Even as Mallory glanced up, a rifle banged down below, and a bullet kicked chips from the wall by Carstairs' shoulder. The fixed rope was taut over the overhang. A German was coming up. Mallory pulled the pin from a grenade, let the lever spring back and counted to three, listening to the fizz of the internal fuse. On four, he tossed the grenade over the edge.

The sound of the airburst rolled around the hard faces of the cliff. The rope slackened suddenly. There were screams. Mallory tossed another grenade, five seconds this time, and started up his own rope. By the time he heard the flat bang from the ledge, he was half-way up. Someone was firing down there. He could hear the bullets strike, wild and far away. He found a perch, pulled another grenade out of his pouch, hauled the pin out with his teeth, and let it rattle down behind him. There was traffic manoeuvring in front of the landslip. They would be trying to get some vehicle-mounted weapons to bear. *Bang,* said the grenade. No sound from above. He was at the top.

Carstairs was hauling in his rope, coiling it. He glanced at Mallory, completed his coil, and started away uphill. Mallory caught him.

'I said cover me,' he said.

Carstairs cocked an eyebrow. 'Didn't hear,' he said.

'We've got to show ourselves.'

'Don't be silly.'

Mallory found that his Schmeisser was in his hands, pointed at the ground between him and Carstairs. 'We need to show them it's an Allied operation. Not partisans. In case of reprisals.'

'Oh for God's sake –'

'If you disobey a direct order I shall regard it as a mutinous act.'

Carstairs saw in Mallory's face what that meant. He flinched as if he had received a smack in the teeth. He laughed, a weak laugh. 'Christ,' he said. 'I . . . oh, if you say so.'

Mallory took him along the clifftop in dead ground. Above the slide, he went to the edge of the cliff. The vehicles were still below. The men had gone: taking cover. Mallory stood up, dragging Carstairs with him. 'Allied regular troops!' he roared, in English and German. Then he threw his last grenade into the void and stepped back. A storm of machine-gun fire tore the air where they had been standing.

'Now move,' said Mallory, and started back the way they had come.

They were in trouble. The element of surprise was gone. If that had been *Wehrmacht* down there, it was big trouble. If it was Dieter Wolf's *Sonderkommando*, it was big, big trouble.

Whatever shape the trouble came in, there was no doubt who lay at the root of it.

Carstairs.

They got over the top of the first ridge without being shot at, trotted into the valley beyond and scaled the far side. As Mallory went up the last low cliff to the summit, a bullet cracked by his ear. A rock by his right hand exploded into stinging chips. The ridge was there, knife-sharp against the blue sky. He jumped for it and hauled himself over. As he lay in cover to calm his breath, a burst of machine-gun fire pulverized the top six inches of the rock plates behind which he lay. Carstairs was beside him, spitting out powdered stone.

'Give me the rifle,' said Mallory. 'Go and tell the rest of them.'

Carstairs said, 'Oh, really.' Then perhaps he remembered the conversation in the dead ground above the cliff, or perhaps he saw the look in Mallory's eye. Whichever the case, he handed over the rifle and ran.

Mallory moved fifty yards below the skyline, resurfacing in a notch between two boulders, and rested the fore end of the Mauser on the ground in front of him. He snapped the guards off the telescopic sight, took a couple of deep breaths, and cuddled the butt to his shoulder. Into the disc of the sight floated rocks, low, dark-green bushes. The disc settled. And across it jogged a figure in field-grey uniform, coal-scuttle helmet, Schmeisser held across the body.

Mallory put the cross hairs on the centre of the chest and squeezed the trigger. The Mauser bucked. The grey figure flung its arms out and slammed backwards into the rocks. Behind it, Mallory saw the quick, dancing flicker of a machine-gun's muzzle flash, heard the crash and whine of the rounds smacking rock. He paid no attention. His eye was back on the sight, and he was searching among the rocks, finding the grey cobblestones of the Spandau crew's helmets. The machine gun opened up again. Mallory could just see the dark upright of the loader's jackboot as he knelt by the weapon. He raised the sight a couple of clicks. Then he shot the man just below the knee. The gunner turned his face. Mallory shot him in the side of the head, and transferred his attention to the men advancing across the notched and rock-strewn plain –

There were no men. On the grey, ridged valley floor nothing moved but the bushes, fretted by the small wind from the sea.

Mallory began to crawl backwards, knees and elbows, behind the cover of the ridge. Once in cover, he doubled under the lee of the rocks. A *Wehrmacht* garrison would have been ragged and dull-edged. The men in cover looked sharp and well-disciplined.

Behind the smell of thyme and rosemary and his own sweat, he seemed to detect the keen, ugly whiff of Dieter Wolf.

He went back to the ridge. A figure moved over to the right, out of the ground, over a rock, back into cover, fast as a rabbit. He sent a Mauser round after it, heard the whine of the ricochet. Missed. He slung the rifle and ran down the ridge, from stone to stone across the valley floor, hurdled the stream, went up the other side and into the cave.

Carstairs was back. He and the others were waiting, loaded up, ready to go. Mallory glanced in his direction. 'You're under arrest,' he said.

Carstairs' face turned blank, fish-white. 'You can't –'

'Disarm him,' said Mallory to Miller. Mallory's Schmeisser just happened to be pointing at Carstairs' stomach.

Stiff-faced, Miller removed Carstairs' Browning and knife.

Carstairs said, 'I didn't mean –'

'You have jeopardized the operation,' said Mallory. 'You will be dealt with later.' He pulled out a map, beckoned Clytemnestra. 'We've got thirty men after us,' he said. 'Where do we go?' He gave her a pencil.

She drew a line: a tenuous line that zigzagged on to a tight bunch of contours until the contours ceased, giving way to the hatchings of rock faces. 'We'll mark the path with piled stones,' she said.

He put his finger on a narrow white stripe among the contours and hatchings. 'What's this?' he asked.

She told him. Then they made a rendezvous, and she led the party out and along the ridge: Wills and Nelson, Wills still dazed-looking and rubber-legged, Nelson scared, sunburned under his carroty thatch, hugging his arm, grey-faced with pain or fear or both, and Miller with his big pack, and Carstairs somewhere between hangdog and arrogant.

'Get up in those hills,' said Mallory, handing Miller a copy of the map reference. 'See you later.'

Miller tilted his head back, looking at the hills. If they were hills, so were the God damned Himalayas, he thought. And soon he was going to be up there, making like the abominable snowman or an eagle or something. Miller was a creature of the American Midwest. His idea of the ideal landscape was a billiard table, flattened out a little.

'Take it easy,' he said to Mallory.

'We'll do our best.' Mallory's face was set, his eyes remote. He was loading rounds into a Schmeisser magazine, already working on the problem of thirty Germans against two Allied troops who had first to fight a rearguard action and then to complete an operation.

'We'll be with you in two hours, maximum,' he said. 'If we're not, you go on.'

Miller turned away, grim-faced. He shouldered his big pack, and set off in the wake of Carstairs, Clytemnestra and the two sailors.

The path led upwards: over the ridge, down the other side, along a little ribbon of flat ground that wove through a great field of boulders, and on to the face of a mountain – hill, Miller told himself, remember it's only a hill – that if it had been by the seaside you would have called it a cliff.

The sweat ran into Miller's eyes. The pack straps dug into his shoulders. From below came the hammer and crack of small-arms fire. Mallory and Andrea were busy.

Ahead, Wills stumbled and crashed into a rock. 'All right,' he mumbled. 'All right.'

'Help him,' said Miller.

Clytemnestra pulled at his arm. She said, 'He is too big for me, poor man.'

'Cap'n Carstairs?' said Miller.

Carstairs scowled at him. Then, grudgingly, he hauled the sailor's arm around his neck. 'Move it,' he said.

Haltingly, the procession climbed on.

Back by the cave, things were getting complicated.

The *Sonderkommando* had sneaked up behind the ridge, making maximum use of cover. It had done them very little good. There was always a moment when they were going to be silhouetted against the skyline. They were superior in numbers. But they had no artillery and no mortars, and it did not look as if they ran to air support. While it was small arms against small arms, there was not a lot of progress that could be made against two determined defenders.

So Andrea and Mallory moved from the cave towards the ruined hut, keeping in cover, stopping to snipe at the matchhead-sized helmets that popped over the skyline, but never stopping in the same place twice. The sun was moving across the sky, but it was still hot.

At four thirty-one, there was a pause in the firing on the ridge opposite the cave. Mallory and Andrea were only ten yards apart. They looked at each other, then at the ridge opposite. Nothing moved. For a moment, birds sang, and the breeze blew, and there might have been no war at all. Then something a long way away made a small, flat explosion, and Mallory and Andrea grovelled on the ground, because they knew what that meant.

High in the air, a fleeting black dot came into being, hung for a moment, and fell to the ground thirty yards in front of them. There was a sharp, ear-damaging *crump*, and shattered stone flew past their ears. Mortar. When Mallory ran between two rocks, a gun opened up with a low, heavy clatter. They had brought up a mortar and re-manned the Spandau, and they were both on the other side of the ridge.

Mallory wiped away the blood that the stinging chips of stone had brought to his forehead. The idea of fighting a pitched battle against a numerically superior enemy with mortars and heavy machine guns was not appealing. But fight they must, to give the rest of the party time to get clear. He crawled to the other end of his line of rocks and fired. The machine gun opened up again. Under cover of its sheet of lead, five field-grey figures bounced out of cover, scuttled across five yards of open ground, and dived out of sight. Another mortar round pitched into the rocks, closer this time.

Andrea shouted. 'Going, my Keith!' he roared. It could have been a cry of pain: but Mallory knew it was precisely the opposite. Andrea was out to even the odds.

Andrea went up and over the ridge behind Mallory's position, ran along it in dead ground for two hundred yards, recrossed the spine, and began to worm his way across the valley floor like a giant lizard. He heard firing and explosions up to his right; Schmeisser fire from Mallory now, the sound of battle, several defenders working hard; or of one man, moving around, making noise and fuss. They were a team, Andrea and Keith Mallory. So far, it was all satisfactory.

The ground had begun to slope uphill. There would be men posted to protect the flanks. Andrea lay still as a stone, moving his head up inch by inch.

Twenty feet to his right, a German soldier was sitting behind a stone, scanning the rocks down the valley.

Andrea allowed his head to sink away. He moved over the ground like a giant shadow, seeking the strips of darkness along the sides of bushes, the lee of small stones. He moved not like a man moving over ground, but like a huge ripple of the ground itself. In four steady minutes, he completed a semicircle. He was looking at the back of a helmet, a tunic with a leather harness, corrugated canisters at the waist, tense shoulders . . .

Andrea moved forward, silent as a shadow, knife in front of him. There was a brief struggle, without sound. The German made a sharp exhalation. No inhalation followed. Andrea laid the body in the dust, wiped his knife on its tunic, and went with great caution forward over the ridge.

Here he crouched behind a boulder and waited. He heard the *whap* of the mortar, the explosion on the other side of the valley. He saw the heads of the men around the mortar, the gleam of the sun on the tube of the weapon. And further up, in a nest of rocks on the reverse slope of the ridge, the machine-gunners. He noticed that the arc of fire from the Spandau pit was ahead only, and that apart from the man he had killed, there was nobody protecting the flanks. This must be a hastily-assembled squad, sent up the cliffs in hot pursuit, undermanned and under-equipped . . .

All this went through his mind in the blink of an eye. During this blink he had wormed through the rocks to the machine-gun pit. The gunner fired a burst at the hill opposite. In Andrea's mind, the field-grey figures facing Mallory got up, ran forward, flopped down again: advancing.

From cover, Andrea threw three grenades into the mortar pit. Then he unslung his Schmeisser and stood up.

Mallory knew he was in trouble. The *Sonderkommando* were in Schmeisser range now. The mortar fire had ceased, presumably for fear of scoring own goals. He had laid aside the rifle, and was trying to look three ways at once. Under cover of the last burst of machine-gun fire, the enemy had come within a hundred and twenty feet. He had seen one scuttling away to the right, and up to the left he thought he had seen movement, though he could not swear to it. He was going to find out, though. He settled himself grimly behind the rock, and waited for the Spandau to open up: short burst, to get his head down and signal to the men. Then the longer bursts, the blizzard of metal that would keep his head down while the *Sonderkommando* swarmed aboard –

The Spandau burped; the short burp. Then there was a huge explosion: bigger than a grenade. It sounded like a lot of mortar bombs going off at once. Hot on the heels of the explosion was a long burst of Schmeisser fire, with screams.

In the silence that followed, he sighted through the crack in the stone wall. He saw the grey helmets rise, squeezed a short burst over the rock. Then the machine gun opened up again, and through the crack he saw the men rise from cover. He waited for the metal rain to start pelting around his ears. The machine gun started its deadly hammer. But the rain did not come.

He put his eye to the sighting cranny.

Down below him, the field-grey figures were up and advancing, but not under a curtain of friendly fire. They had risen into the open at the first burst of the machine gun. And the second burst had whipped not over their heads, but into the thick of them. The rocks below Mallory were strewn with field-grey corpses. To the right, a man was groaning. To the left, movement caught Mallory's eye. He turned. A camouflage uniform, much stained with new blood, was lurching at him through the rocks. He put a short Schmeisser burst into the helmet. The man went over with a crash.

On the far side of the valley, a figure stood up. Acting on reflex, Mallory went for the rifle. Then he stopped.

It was Andrea.

Andrea walked quickly across the valley and up to the cave. By the time he got there, Mallory had his feet up on a rock and was smoking a cigarette. 'That was useful,' he said.

Andrea nodded. He was a superlative craftsman in the art of war, and he had done his job. Mallory gave him a cigarette. He lit it, shouldered his pack, and loped off up the hill. Mallory went after him.

At the top, he looked back at the valley where thirty men had died or run away. The shadows were lengthening towards evening.

Evening of the first day. There was nothing to feel good about. The Germans knew there was a British force in the mountains. They did not know it contained two wounded sailors and a man who did not know how to obey orders. They would come looking, and soon.

What had happened in the valley had been a victory. But it had been only one battle in what looked like a very long campaign.

FIVE

Wednesday 1800-Thursday 0300

After the field of stones, the path led on and up. It was not much of a path: more a strip of bare mountainside, marked with stones placed one on another like the little men children put up on beaches to knock down with more stones. As they passed the markers, Mallory kicked them down. It was six o'clock, and the sun was heading for the rock-masses of the western horizon when they reached the top of the slope and found themselves at the base of a cliff.

'What are we,' said Andrea. 'Flies?'

Mallory shook his head. He took a mouthful from his water bottle, and cast left into deep shadow, to a place where the cliff seemed less than vertical. At the base of the slope was one of Clytemnestra's little stone men.

The slope was not a hill. It was more like the leading edge of the dorsal fin of a fish – a dorsal fin a thousand feet high and three feet wide, made of rotten rock, tapering away into the far distance. Mallory pointed at the map.

'It's a ramp,' he said. 'A stepladder. Up there, it gets wider.'

'And then,' said Andrea, sighing, 'it gets narrower again.'

He had a point. But the sun was sinking, and this was no time for debates.

They went up.

It was easy climbing. Andrea plodded away, keeping his eyes in front of him, not thinking about the void on either side of the blade of rock – keeping his mind on the far side of the mountains; on the marshes, the Acropolis, how to cross the one and get into the other . . .

The path was broadening. It became a sort of plateau. Mallory came up behind him, and went ahead to reconnoitre.

From somewhere far away there came a small, remote buzzing.

Andrea found himself a ledge with a bush growing off it, squeezed himself in, and watched, cursing, as evening fell over his beloved country.

To the west, the island fell ridge on ridge to the mottled blue sheet of the sea. The valleys below were blurred with veils of haze, veils tinged faintly with flame-colour and blood-colour, prophesying the sunset. And above it all, flying out from the high blind cliffs ahead, gleaming silver in that low sun, was an aeroplane.

Mallory watched that plane, too. Ahead of him the ridge threaded across to a maze of cliffs and canyons, cliffs piled on cliffs, and above them the summit of Mount Skaphos. And above the summit cliffs a sky of purest blue, and in that blue the aeroplane. A Fiesler Storch; a slow-flying aeroplane, with an observer. Looking for them.

The Storch banked gently, and began to spiral downwards. It came lower and lower, until from his position in the rocks Mallory could see the pilot's head, catch the glint of binoculars in the observer's seat . . .

He turned his face to the ground, and hoped the bloody thing would go away.

On the mountain shoulder at the far end of the ridge, Miller heard the engines, too. The rendezvous map reference was a cave – no more than an overhang of the cliff, really. Clytemnestra was dozing, Wills muttering in a half-sleep, Nelson sitting with his back against the cliff, hugging his slashed arm, staring bug-eyed at a boulder, as if it was showing him a film about things he did not find pleasing. As for Carstairs, he was in a clump of bushes in front of the cave, unarmed still, watching the ridge and the valley below.

'What's that?' said Nelson.

'Plane.'

'What do they want?'

'If I was a bird, I'd ask them.'

Nelson shook his head, an odd, feverish shake. Miller reckoned he was a nasty mixture of ill and frightened. Miller was a demolition man, not a nursemaid. But his good nature made him say, reassuring, 'We'll keep still, and not show our faces, and we'll be fine.' And then what? he thought. All the way over the mountains to storm some huge God damned bunker, and we say, listen, you wounded and you crazy, hang loose in the mountains till you hear a great big bang, and then Poppa will make sure you get home . . .

Sure.

He took out a cigarette and stuck it in his mouth. He did not light it: on an evening like this, a spotter plane could see the flash of a buckle, the white of an eye, a puff of cigarette smoke.

In the back of the cave, Wills said in a loud, definite voice, 'Henry!'

There were no Henries. 'Back to sleep,' said Miller. 'There's a good lootenant.'

'Damned plane's late,' said Wills. 'Got to be in Paris for lunch. Camilla's waiting.' He got to his feet, stood swaying. 'For God's sake,' he said.

'Sit down,' said Miller, alarmed now.

'You,' said Wills. 'You, that man. Siddown and shaddup.' He came to the front of the cave. Miller stood up, to stop him going out on to the ledge. 'Honestly,' said Wills.

'Please,' said Miller. 'Sir.' The Storch was at the outer edge of its spiral, turning back towards them.

Wills said, 'Stand away. She's my fiancée y'know. We're lunching in Paris. Top-hole. Special treat.' His eyes were glassy, looking at things in a different world; customs at Croydon aerodrome, perhaps. He rummaged in the pocket of his filthy, sweat-stained jacket. 'Here y'are.' He might have thought he was pulling out his passport.

What he actually pulled out was his cigarette case. His silver cigarette case, highly polished. He waved it in Miller's face.

'Put it away,' said Miller.

But Wills kept waving it. A flash of westering sun bounced off it and into Miller's eyes. Horrified, Miller grabbed it out of his hand.

Behind them, the Storch's engine-note changed from a drone to an angry buzz. The pilot opened the throttle wide, banked steeply, and flew straight as an arrow over Mount Skaphos, heading east.

It looked very much as if the pilot had seen it too.

Mallory watched the change of course, heard a second later the new roar of the engine. He knew what it meant, and so, judging by the way he came loping across the rocks, did Andrea.

They hit the ridge at a dead run, pebbles scattering under their feet and looping out and into the void below. Ten minutes later they were climbing a steep, near-invisible path among genista bushes, and Miller was materializing out of the rock face ahead.

'Moving out,' said Mallory. 'Where's Carstairs?'

Carstairs stood up in his bush. 'Cigarette?' he said, producing his case. 'Turkish this side, Virginian that.'

'Put it away,' said Andrea. 'Captain Carstairs, I have something to say to you. Atten-shun!'

Carstairs dropped his cigarette and came to attention. His face was like the face of a man who, walking down the street in the dark, has just realized that what he has trodden on is not a paving stone but an open manhole.

'Captain Carstairs,' said Mallory. 'I am changing our operational basis.' His voice quiet and level, as always. But there was a cold power to it that made the hair rise on Carstairs' scalp. 'For the remainder of this operation you will consider yourself under my command and the command of Colonel Andrea. When the occasion presents, you will face court martial for desertion in the face of the enemy. Is that clear?'

Carstairs said, white-lipped, 'That is not –'

'Any complaints should be set out in writing and submitted after the conclusion of the operation,' said Mallory. 'Meanwhile continue to consider yourself under arrest. Your conduct under arrest will be taken into your account at your court martial.'

There was a silence. Carstairs stood pale and numb. The penalty for desertion in the face of the enemy was death. The message was clear and simple: behave or die.

Andrea said, 'Corporal, return this man's weapons.'

'Pleasure,' said Miller.

Carstairs found himself sweating. For a moment, this loose array of bandits had turned into a sharp, formal military unit. Carstairs realized that he had underestimated them; underestimated them badly.

From now on, he would have to use new tactics.

Mallory said, 'Clytemnestra. We'll need to go on into the mountains. Hide till dawn.'

'Of course.'

Mallory drank water, shouldered his pack. 'We'll move out,' he said. Clytemnestra took the lead. He walked beside her. 'What are the chances of the Germans getting ahead of us?' he said. 'Cutting us off?'

'Not tonight,' she said. 'The other sides of the island are very steep. It is bad country up there.'

Miller was trudging behind them, cigarette hanging out of his mouth. 'You wanna know what I'd do?' he said. 'I'd put some guys in a plane, maybe two lots, one ahead of us, one behind. And I'd fly them up here and I'd make them jump out, and they could chase us the hell and gone and their legs wouldn't even ache.'

They toiled on up the thread of a path that zigzagged towards the summit of the steep slope above the cave. The breath rasped loud in Mallory's ears. He was tired, but not yet tired enough for Benzedrine. There was a strange buzzing in his head . . .

There was a strange buzzing in the air. It grew, became a drone, then a roar.

He looked up.

Three aeroplanes rumbled across the sky: Tante Jus, Junkers Trimotors, lit gold by the sun like squat, ungainly millionaires' toys. The doors in their sides were open.

Not toys.

Mallory's head felt dry and empty, filled with the sound of his breathing. He made himself walk more quickly.

The rest of the group knew death when they heard the beating of its wings. They began to walk more quickly too.

Under Wills' nose, the Gieves sheepskin-lined seaboots went trudge, trudge in the shale. It seemed to Wills that he had been walking for ever; up and up and up, with his feet boiling and his brain banging around in his skull like a turnip in a dixie. It hurt like hell, he would grant it that. It hurt like hell and tasted blue

70

and smelt like aluminium and it felt sad as velvet. But he could remember his own name, now, so he supposed he was getting better. He also remembered that at some point in some world or other he had had a ship, and there had been a bang, and now he had no ship any more.

There was a slope up, and after the slope some rocks. And now there was a wall on his port-hand shoulder and to starboard a great deep swoop of nothing, and in his head the roaring, whining, zinging hum of blood, or aeroplanes, or something. He looked to the right, out over the void, even though the sun hurt his eyes. It was red, the sun, blood-colour. It shone on sea and land and jellyfish.

Jellyfish?

Jellyfish in the sky, floating down in to the deep shadows of the ground.

Something wrong with the above statement. Check details.

Details of what?

Under Wills' nose, the Gieves sheepskin-lined seaboots went trudge, trudge in the shale.

Down below, the white silk parachutes of the *Sonderkommando* drifted earthward, each one pink as a baby's fingernail in the warm glow of the sunset, on to the flat patch at the foot of the steep ridge Andrea and Mallory had climbed after their defence of the cave.

'How long till dark?' said Mallory.

Clytemnestra shrugged. 'Forty minutes,' she said.

Mallory looked at the slow laborious trudge of Wills, the agonized hobble of Nelson. The men on the parachutes were fresh. The people on this cliff path had climbed five thousand feet, and had not slept for twenty-four hours.

The path they were on was a narrow ledge running across the face of a sheer cliff. Ten minutes later, the ledge joined another ledge. The main path went off to the left. Another, scarcely visible, snaked away to the right. Andrea spoke at length with Clytemnestra, in Greek, then to Mallory. They bent their heads over the map. Then Mallory said, 'Carstairs. You go with Clytemnestra and the wounded. Andrea, Miller, come with me.'

'Smashing,' said Carstairs, with a frank Boy Scout grin.

Mallory did not smile back. He said, 'The Germans will be here in twenty minutes. Get a move on.'

Carstairs got a move on. The small, shuffling file disappeared up the thready path to the right.

Miller sat on a boulder. Twelve hundred feet below his boots, stunted olives rocked in the small evening wind. Beyond them, a file of tiny grey figures trotted towards the base of the slope. Miller lit a cigarette.

'Okay,' said Mallory. 'Now listen.'

Miller listened. When Mallory had finished, he said, 'Are you serious?'

Mallory looked him in the eye, hard and steely. He said, 'What do you think, Corporal?'

Miller sighed. He reached above his head and stubbed his cigarette on the left-hand fork of the track, wide, obvious, well-used by men and goats. He said, 'I guess you're serious.'

'Thank you,' said Mallory. 'Now, shall we get on with it?'

Averting his eyes from the frightful emptiness below, Miller began to scramble along the left-hand path.

It did not take long to find what he was looking for: a place where the ledge bulged out from the cliff face on a cornice of rock, with a little pile of debris at its inner edge. Miller dropped to his knees and began scuffling in the dirt on the inside of the ledge. He found what he was looking for: a letter-box-sized crack in the rock. Reverently, he opened his pack, took out four sticks of gelignite, and taped to them a time pencil. He snapped the glass ampoule in the time pencil, tamped the bomb into the letter box, wedged rocks over the top, and replanted the rosemary and spurge he had disturbed with his digging.

'Done,' he said.

Andrea nodded. The lower limb of the sun was kissing the horizon, drawing a road of fire across the sea. He was watching the place where he and Mallory had been hiding when they first heard the Storch. It lay empty under the sky, pink in the sunset.

Then it was not empty any more.

Suddenly, the empty area was striped with the shadows of men; one shadow, then two, shadows that dispersed quickly into the rough ground, taking cover. Andrea had counted sixty parachutes. He waited until he had lost count of the men on the outcrop. Then

72

he took his Mauser, settled the sight on one of the helmets down below, and took up the first pressure on the trigger.

'Ready?' he said to Miller.

Miller was never ready for this kind of thing. But he nodded anyway. Andrea fired.

A quarter of a mile up the path, Mallory had found a narrow chimney; a seam between two plates of rock, polished smooth by the action of winter rains. He settled the two coils of silk climbing rope around his shoulders. Then he put in a boot, turned his foot to wedge the sole, stepped up, and raised his hand. He heard the crash of Andrea's rifle, and the clatter of a Schmeisser. He kept climbing. The crack got narrower up here. He jammed in his right forefinger, and bent it to enlarge the knuckle. With his free boot, he groped the wall until he found a hold, no more than a pimple of rock. The pyramid nail of his boot bit home. He moved the first foot, got a new hold in the crack with the knuckle of his other hand. If he had looked down, he would have seen that he was already a man's height above the ledge with the path, that the precipice was opening out below him. He did not look down. Instead, he concentrated on the rock-sheets in front of him, climbing from the hips, body out from the wall. Before the war, they had called it the Mallory Float; a perfectly balanced stance on the face that took him drifting up, defying gravity. One of the great rock climbers, they called him: and one of the great mountaineers. A man who could walk for thirty-six hours, and climb five thousand vertical feet at the end of it.

As long as nobody shot him.

After a couple of hundred feet the crack petered out. Mallory paused, drove in a spike with the leather-bound lead hammer in his belt, belayed to it the first of the two silk climbing ropes around his shoulders, and paid out the coil. The rope fell away into the shadows below. Then he went on up, climbing on hammered-in spikes until he came to a zone of rougher rock; rock about as rough as an old brick wall. To any climber except Mallory, it would have looked smooth and impossible. To Mallory, it might as well have been a stepladder. He went on up, slow and steady, not bothering with spikes. At three hundred and thirty feet, he came upon an area of rotten rock that gave way to soil. He had arrived at the top.

He belayed the second rope to a boulder, and dropped the free end down the face of the cliff. Then he lit a cigarette and told the weary ache in his limbs to be still, and settled down to wait.

Andrea and Miller were sitting down too; but not for reasons of repose. The inside of the path represented dead ground, so on the inside of the path they were sitting, backs to the wall, while a steady covering fire from the German troops below whanged up into the cliff face above their heads. Every now and then, Andrea stuck the barrel of his Schmeisser over the edge and squeezed off a short burst.

'Go,' said Andrea, after ten minutes.

They went.

As they belly-crawled along the ledge, the sun was a small red glow on the western horizon, and the stars were coming out. Andrea leaned over the path edge, blasted half-a-dozen rounds into the void, ducked quickly back, and carried on up the path. The space below suddenly crackled with blue-red muzzle flashes, the bullets splashing against the rocks safely to the rear. On the hook, thought Miller, with a solemn cheerfulness. Bless your innocent hearts.

On they crawled, the full quarter-mile, until Miller's hand brushed the rope. He took a deep breath, and swallowed whatever it is that you swallow when your mouth is as dry as a Saharan cave floor. Then he grasped the rope and started to climb.

Down on the ledge, Andrea took the clip from his Schmeisser and groped for one he had reserved in a special pocket of his pack. His fingers found the two tapes he had wrapped around the magazine to identify it as tracer. He slapped it into the machine pistol, and fired: fired along the line of the ledge this time, back the way he and Miller had come, five rounds, tracer. The bullets smacked rock, tumbled in a firework display that said: up here; we went this-a-way. Then he fired another burst off to the right. From below, on the plain where the parachutists had landed, and where a radio operator might be sitting, it would look as if a battle was starting on the path.

Andrea slung his Schmeisser, gripped the rope and started to climb. When he reached the spike, he coiled the first rope and worked the spring-steel piton out of the rock. Then, light as a feather, he went up the second rope and over the cliff edge.

Mallory and Miller were sitting with their backs against boulders, dim, looming figures against the stars. From three hundred feet below, there came the clink of metal and the crunch of jackboots on shale: men, running in silence, chasing an enemy.

An enemy who was no longer there.

When the sound of pursuit had died away, Mallory, Miller and Andrea turned their faces east, for the precipices of Mount Skaphos and the plains beyond.

Private Emmanuel Gruber was a proud man and a good soldier. He was proud to be in the *Sonderkommando*: proud that *Hauptmann* Wolf had singled him out, proud that he had achieved the objectives of the training course, proud to have received a hint that he was in line for promotion to *Feldwebel*. And proud that tonight he had been ordered to bring up the rear of the pursuit squad; forty men, another twenty waiting at base as reinforcements. It was safe back here, too; though of course (Gruber told himself hastily) if *Hauptmann* Wolf ordered him into the jaws of death he would leap in without hesitation.

So on went Gruber at the double, supremely fit, right shoulder to the cliff, left shoulder to the void. He could have run all night.

Except that on the inside of the widening in the path he had passed a second previously, the time pencil of Miller's blasting charge had come to the end of its sixty-minute career.

A gout of flame blasted straight out of the cliff face, and a clap of thunder drove Gruber's eardrums together in the middle of his head. He staggered, head ringing. A flying chunk of stone caught him in the small of the back, and he would have staggered again, except that the foot meant to take his weight found not ground but space. He fell with a long, depressed cry, bounced twice, and had time to regain terminal velocity before he went into the olive trees below.

So he was not in a position to see what his comrades in the pursuit squad of the Wolf commando saw: that in the area of the blast the path they had been following no longer existed, and in its place was a cliff face as clear and lacking in footholds as a billiard table stood on its end.

Not that there was any point worrying about it. As the *Leutnant* lost no time in explaining, nobody was going back anyway. The order of the night was hot pursuit. The enemy had attempted to mine the path. Poor Gruber had taken what had been meant for all of them. Meanwhile, there was no time for hanging around.

The *Sonderkommando* turned and resumed the chase.

They trotted up the path, along the cliff, into a steep-sided valley. It was dark, and the radio did not work in this place of cliffs and ravines. After three hours' running, they found themselves on a bare mountainside, in a steep-canted field of boulders that stood silent and ominous on the starlit rock. Here the *Leutnant* rejected with fury a suggestion that they should bivouac, the better to continue the search at dawn. *'Vorwärts!'* he cried. 'Onward!'

At that precise moment, seven miles, three gorges and two thousand five hundred vertical feet away, Able Seaman Nelson was reaching the end of his tether.

They were still walking. Nelson had difficulty remembering a time when he had not been walking. His feet were sliding in his boots, whether in blood or the fluid of burst blisters he did not dare look. The cut in his arm had always been painful. Now it had set up a deep, deadly throb that travelled up the inside of his bicep and into his armpit. It would have been at the centre of his world, that throbbing, had there been room for it.

But all there was room for at the centre of Nelson's world was terror.

Not that he was a coward. You could not be an AB on an MTB, and fight your way through nights full of tracer bullets and high-octane petrol, and be a coward. Ashore in Portsmouth, after an air raid, he had come close to a George Cross, burrowing into the teetering pile of rubble that had once been a house, ARP and fire brigade shouting at him, don't be a bloody fool, come back, she'll collapse; but Nelson had kept going, found the middle-aged woman in the flowery housecoat, dragged her back out into the rain and the searchlights and the metallic clink of falling shrapnel.

But the MTB and Portsmouth had been with his mates. Now, Nelson had a hole in his arm the size of a slit trench, and he was blundering around some mountains with the Old Man, who had gone barmy, four bandits in uniforms without insignia, and a Greek bint with rolling eyes and grinding teeth who gave him the willies. It was the people and the mountains that were getting to Nelson. At sea, you fought your gun and took your chance with your mates, and while you did not like it unless you were bloody cracked, you could put up with it, like. The dry land was too bloody dry, and the people were too bloody violent, and you could see the look in their eye while they tried to kill you, and that was just not bloody on. A couple of hours ago there had been all that shooting down the hill, and a hell of a bang, God knew what that had been about. And now they were on this terrible path, black as the inside of a cow, and any minute now some Jerry might pop out from behind a rock and say, boo, you're dead –

For the seventy-third time since sunset, Nelson caught his boot on a rock, stumbled, jolted his arm, and bit his lip to stop himself whimpering. Because this was not going to end. You had to face it. Things were going to get worse, not better. It gave him the willies, and that was bleeding that.

Ahead, Clytemnestra's voice said something in Greek. Nelson followed the dim hulk of the person in front up a steep slope towards a small light that had somehow started to shine. Another bloody cave.

But it was not a cave. The walls were too smooth, the angles too perfect. In the middle of the floor was a sort of raised stone plinth. On the plinth, the big Greek man – he must have joined the file in the dark, though Nelson could not remember seeing it happen – was spreading the little tins of compo rations, a bottle of brandy, a radio.

Nelson slumped to the ground, propped his back against the wall, and let his head loll on his breast. The lanky American spoke, in Greek. Clytemnestra replied. Nelson did not like not understanding. 'What does she say?' he said, querulous.

Miller looked at him, saw a blue-white face, black circles under haunted eyes. 'I said what is this place. She said it's a tomb.' He gestured at the plinth. 'The dining table there is where they laid the stiff. Eat something.' He waved a hand at the compo and the brandy.

But Nelson's stomach was a small, clenched fist. He could not eat. He could only sit there and strain his ears at the night, at the thousand miniature nights contained in the shadows of this house of the dead. This house of the soon-to-be-dead . . .

He tried to get up. The muscles of his legs were too stiff. He toppled sideways. Someone was shouting, frantic, in his voice. Hands grabbed him, laid him out, tipped brandy down his throat.

He fell into a sort of coma. He was dimly aware of someone doing something to his bad arm, of a pinprick. Then there was a deep, buzzing silence.

They sat around the stove. The little blue flames cast fluttering shadows on the tomb's ceiling. Nelson and Wills sprawled along a wall, Nelson's arm new-dressed, half a syrette of morphine running in his blood; Wills snoring in a heavy, exhausted drone. Clytemnestra had folded her hands over her stomach and put her head on her pack, and was sleeping quietly as the tomb's original tenant.

The remaining four men did not sleep; not yet. Their cigarettes pulsed and glowed. They were resting, but it was the rest of a hunting animal, or a latched spring, ready to leap from repose into violence with no intervening period of acceleration. Carstairs sat a little apart from the others, cleaning his machine pistol.

Mallory said, 'Captain Carstairs, the court martial is in session.'

Carstairs raised an eyebrow, not lifting his eyes from the breech mechanism.

Mallory said, 'By your actions this afternoon you have endangered the lives of your comrades and the success of the operation.'

'Operational necessity,' said Carstairs. He yawned, and lay back on the musty floor.

Andrea spoke. His voice had a note in it that Mallory had never heard before, and in the flicker of the stove-flames his bear-like shoulders seemed to fill the vault of the tomb. 'Captain Carstairs,' he said. 'The charge is that today, having been posted sentry, you did desert your post in the face of the enemy. The penalty is death. You may speak in your defence.'

Under the cold lash of that voice, Carstairs seemed for a moment to freeze. Then he laughed, a thin, nervous laugh. 'I don't think Admiral Dixon will agree,' he said.

'I am not interested in Admiral Dixon.' Andrea's hands moved. There was the metallic sound of a Schmeisser cocking lever.

Carstairs looked at his own weapon, in pieces on the groundsheet. He looked at Mallory and Miller, and found no comfort. His face was impassive, faintly quizzical, but there was a little sheen of sweat on the upper lip. He said, 'If you put it like that.' He took out the gold case, and selected a cigarette with deliberation.

'There is an explanation,' he said, eventually. 'I have orders of my own, from Admiral Dixon. Who incidentally will not be very pleased to hear that you see fit to override his authority and haul me in front of a kangaroo court –'

The Schmeisser in Andrea's hand moved upwards an inch, so Carstairs could see all the way down the barrel. Carstairs did his best to look bored. 'But since you want an explanation, you can have one. There was a survivor.'

'A survivor?'

'After the *Kormoran* was torpedoed. Before she went down. Apparently someone hopped on to a life raft, bit of driftwood, God knows, and paddled off downwind and landed on Kynthos. This person was picked up by the Germans, in a very bad way, in a coma, actually, just before the partisans blocked the road.'

'How do we know this?' said Andrea.

'Agent in Parmatia radioed in,' said Carstairs. 'That's who I was looking for in town last night.' He made it sound as if he had been doing the rounds of the night spots. 'But apparently they got themselves killed shortly after they sent the signal.' Andrea's face was like stone. 'Anyway, they told me in the village that this survivor was in the ambulance, in the convoy heading over the road as soon as it opened. Like today. He's still unconscious, apparently. Important fellow in ways I am not at liberty to disclose. I have orders to debrief him. If you don't like that, you can always check with Admiral Dixon, or your Captain, what d'ye call him, Jensen.'

Andrea said, 'That's it?'

Carstairs shrugged, nonchalant as his voice. His eyes were not nonchalant, though. They shifted between Mallory and Miller. 'Just about,' he said. He put his hands on his knees, and composed his features into something like manly frankness. 'Look here. I can't say I liked sliding off into the blue. But I thought, well, an hour and a half, make a recce, and it would be just my neck, not everyone else's. How was I to know that Captain Mallory would come bumbling in and queer my pitch, what?'

Miller was watching Mallory. The New Zealander's face was still and mild, but he was watching Carstairs closely. 'You wanted to talk to this . . . survivor,' said Mallory.

'That's it.'

'And how were you planning to do that?'

'I told you,' said Carstairs, with the exasperation of a teacher repeating a lesson to a small child. 'It was a recce. I wanted to see if the road was open. How am I meant to talk to an unconscious man in a military ambulance?'

Mallory said, 'Why do you need to debrief this man?'

Carstairs smiled, all teeth and superiority. 'Sorry, old boy,' he said. 'Love to help. But, well, Admiral's orders. No can do.'

Silence fell, except for Wills' snores and the bluster of the wind in the tomb's entrance.

Finally, Mallory said, 'He's got a point.'

Miller said, 'Has he hell.'

Andrea's black eyes snapped at him. 'Thank you, Corporal,' he said. 'That will be enough.' The Schmeisser moved away from Carstairs' eye. 'Captain Carstairs, you are a member of this force, and will in future communicate your operational intentions to its field commander. The record will show that you have been reprimanded without loss of pay.'

Carstairs nodded, as if at a waiter who had brought him his change. He said, 'I knew you'd see sense. Now if you'll excuse me, I'll get forty winks.'

Mallory took first watch, sitting outside the tomb under the thick mat of the stars. The night was quiet, except for the sigh and bluster of the breeze in the rocks.

There was a faint movement at his side. When he looked round, he saw Andrea, blotting out a sizeable patch of sky.

'What do you think?' said Andrea.

'Jensen says he's okay.'

'Jensen's in England.'

'Quite.'

There was a silence. Andrea and Mallory had worked together for a year; the kind of year that contains more than most lifetimes. They knew each other well. 'So,' said Andrea. 'There is a problem, my Keith?'

Mallory lit a cigarette. 'He says he was on a recce,' he said. 'So when I caught up with him, he was standing on the cliff directly above the ambulance, with a grenade in his hand and the pin out. And I thought, strange kind of recce. That's the problem.'

'I see,' said Andrea. 'Truly, I see.' There was another pause. 'But we must keep this man, because these are the orders of Jensen. Mouth shut and eyes open, I think.'

'Of course,' said Mallory. Andrea was right. But it was the last thing you needed, on an operation like this.

'I'll do the dawn patrol,' said Mallory. Andrea nodded, and went in to sleep.

SIX

Thursday 0300–1200

Miller woke Mallory three hours after midnight. He tumbled out thumping-headed, dry-mouthed, to stand his guard. It came hard to some soldiers, this wakefulness in the dead time before dawn, when the metabolism was at its slowest. But Mallory was used to early mornings. He had spent his life in mountains where you could not climb after eleven a.m. because of the deadly rain of rock let go by melting ice fields. So he lay a second, his eyes wide open. Then he put his hand to where he knew his weapon would be, swung on his pack and went out into the air.

The stars still hung in the sky. He went up a slope of rocks and stationed himself above the tomb entrance, in a niche of the boulders. There was nothing but the rock, and the stars, and the clean night air. His mind flew back to other mornings on the shoulders of Mount Cook, the white peaks of the Southern Alps all around, waiting in frozen stillness for the first pink touch of the sun.

He pulled out a slab of chocolate and a round of flat Greek bread, ate until he did not want to eat any more, then kept on eating. It was going to be the sort of day when a body needed all the fuel that could be crammed into it:

He analysed the possibilities. The two sailors would have to be parked somewhere; here, perhaps. Must ask Clytemnestra. There was Clytemnestra herself. Clytemnestra needed to be kept out of sight, or there would be reprisals.

And Carstairs. Carstairs was a climber. Carstairs could fight. But Carstairs was the most dangerous of the lot. Mallory had never seen the Greek as angry as he had been last night. The Schmeisser-point court martial might have looked theatrical, but Carstairs had been within seconds of having his brains on the tomb roof –

Mallory stiffened.

The sky was lightening now, turning a darker-than-battleship-grey that cast the jagged peaks around him into sharp relief. But that was not what had made Mallory sit up and very quietly work the cocking lever of his machine pistol.

Down among the ravines and gulches they had travelled the night before, he had heard the short, sharp yip of a hunting dog.

He got up, and slid down the slope and into the tomb. It smelt of sleep. He passed among the supine forms like a cold wind, Miller and Andrea first, then Carstairs and Clytemnestra. 'They've got bloodhounds,' he said. 'We must leave.'

'We go on,' said Clytemnestra. 'It is downhill. Not so difficult.'

Mallory left her to wake the others, and tumbled outside again. He, Miller and Andrea faded into the rocks. The dog yipped again, very close. Five men in S S camouflage smocks came round the corner. The one in the middle had a lead in his hand. On the end of the lead, straining, was a black-and-tan dog. A Doberman, actually, thought Mallory, with the inconsequence that comes of extreme stress. Not a bloodhound.

The dog started a continuous strangled baying, and turned up the hill towards the tomb mouth. Mallory put his Schmeisser to his shoulder and opened fire.

Nelson had slept badly. It was more like a coma than a sleep, a sort of delirium in which the dreams writhed below the surface like maggots in a wound. Everything was burning: the terraced house in Coventry where he had been brought up, the B S A motor bike he rode to work, the house where he had gone to rescue the woman in the housecoat, the MTB's bow gun crew: all solid and living one minute, the next stripped by the flames to rafter and bone, brick and tile and flesh melting away like wax. And the noise: the throbbing of his arm like an engine in the armpit, across to the heart, and with every heartbeat the engine accelerating in the horror of the dream, until the noise was continuous and Nelson knew he could not stand any more of this –

Then the real noise started, and Nelson slammed awake.

The roof was flickering with a hard blue-white light, and it was difficult to breathe because the tomb was full of fumes; the fumes of gunsmoke. In the blue-white flicker bodies were moving, made jerky by the flashes. There was the American running towards the door, and the big Greek in the entrance itself, rolling over and over, rising on one knee to squirt bullets into the dark, then rolling on and out beyond the light. Even Wills was up, dazed-looking, fumbling with the bolt of a big rifle.

Nelson hugged his arm, thirsty, head bloated with fever. He understood that there was nothing he could do. He could not shoot. He could not run. All that remained was to sit here and wait for the Germans to come barrelling in through the entrance – there would be a lot of them, he was sure of that, and the skipper and the Greek and the rest of them would be flattened by sheer weight of numbers. And when the Germans came in they would first look him in the eye and then blow him into little bits.

Nelson cringed at the thought.

Then he had an idea.

He was no good for fighting, not in this state. He was no bloody good to anyone. He would get himself out of the way, nice and safe.

Suddenly everything seemed radiantly simple.

But Nelson was leaving one thing out of account. In his veins there ran not only blood, and the throb of his wound, but also a considerable amount of morphine.

Andrea and Miller had had the same idea as Mallory. The rocks chattered with gunfire. The five Germans rolled over and were still. The dog, his handler dead, slunk whining into the boulders. Mallory lowered his gun.

Twenty-five more Germans came round the corner.

Mallory slammed a new clip into his Schmeisser and cursed. The new men were not in formation, like their late comrades in the dog squad. They had heard the gunfire. They were spread out among the boulders, bad targets for the Mauser, too distant for the Schmeissers. Normally, Andrea and Mallory and Miller would have faded into the landscape. But Clytemnestra and Carstairs and the sailors were still inside the cave.

Mallory began to sweat. This was the guerrilla's nightmare: an assault by superior enemy forces on a fixed position. Either you faded, or the operation was finished. It was an evil decision to have to make.

Then all thoughts of the decision went out of his mind, and he was frozen by a strange and terrible sight.

A figure had walked out of the tomb; a strange figure, dressed in rags, with a blue-white face and red hair in a halo round his head. Nelson. Nelson with his good hand in the air, and his bad hand in its sling, and his eyes spinning in his head with terror and morphine. 'Oi!' he yelled in a high, cracked voice. 'Me sailor. Me not soldier. Me non-combatant, prisoner of war, you savvy, cock? You no shoot, got that?' He stumbled down the little path towards the rocks where the Germans lay hidden. The silence was so intense that Mallory could hear the squinch of a pebble under his foot.

There is a German behind that rock, thought Mallory, as Nelson approached a tall, pyramid-shaped slab. And I can't cover Nelson because he won't know what to do if I open fire . . .

Nelson was nearly at the pyramid rock, still waving his good arm and yelling. As he passed the rock, a camouflaged arm shot out and grabbed his collar, and a black boot kicked him behind the knees so they collapsed and he was suddenly kneeling on the path, sideways-on to the observers above the tomb. As Mallory watched, a hand with a Luger came out and dug into the nape of Nelson's neck. The dull *whap* of the shot floated up the hill.

Nelson smashed forward on to his face and lay twitching.

Mallory had seen a lot of life, and a lot of death, too. But this cold assassination of an unarmed man in the process of surrender froze him to the spot. And that split second he stood frozen he heard a soft, metallic sound, and a voice behind him said in heavily-accented English, 'Drop your gun.'

He dropped it. There was no chance of doing anything else. The order had only been an order, but the sound had been a rifle bolt. He waited for the bullet in the back of the neck, his mind clear of thoughts, his eyes on the mountains, rank on serried rank under the pink dawn sky.

The shot did not come.

The voice behind him said, '*Marsch*.'

Mallory marched.

He saw Miller walking towards him, a rifle at his nape. He saw the tomb mouth full of camouflage smocks, heard shouting, saw

Carstairs come out, hands in the air, Wills, stumbling, eyes screwed up against the painful light of dawn.

A German strutted up to Miller, a *Leutnant*, sharp-faced under a grey peaked cap. 'Is this all?' he said, in English.

'All what?' said Miller.

'All your people,' said the German.

'Nope,' said Miller.

Mallory's eyes rested on him with some curiosity. He trusted Miller. But he trusted Andrea too. And Andrea had disappeared, and so had Clytemnestra. He and his fellow-prisoners might be in considerable danger. But with Andrea on the loose, so were the Germans. What was Miller playing at?

'Where are they?' said the German.

'As a citizen of the United States of America,' said Miller, 'I see all people as my people. Like it says, "Bring me your poor, your huddled millions" –'

'Masses,' said Mallory.

'I thought it was millions,' said Miller.

'Silence!' yelled the *Leutnant*. 'Kneel!'

Miller looked at him, then at Mallory. They knelt.

'What is your mission on Kynthos?' snapped the *Leutnant*.

'Name, rank and number,' said Mallory. 'I will give them to your superior officer.'

The Germans behind the rocks were coming out of cover, drifting towards them, curious now they had caught up with their quarry. Bunch up, said Mallory in his head. That's good.

'Together,' said Wills, who sounded stronger and more definite, 'with an official protest. How dare you.' He was angry to the point of incoherence. 'How dare you in contravention of the Geneva Convention summarily execute one of my –'

The *Leutnant*'s jackboot sent him sprawling among the rocks.

'Now,' said the *Leutnant*. 'Tell me now, or I will shoot you, this man first.' Mallory could hear the shuffle of boots on rock as the men gathered round. *Sonderkommando* behaviour, he thought. Not *Wehrmacht*. *Wehrmacht* were soldiers. This lot were murderers.

'Noo!' cried Miller. 'Please!' He cast himself on the ground. Mallory cast himself down too, abasing himself.

And incidentally taking cover.

A sleet of lead blasted out of the rocks and the tomb mouth. The

Leutnant screamed and fell across Mallory. Mallory grabbed the man's Schmeisser. A German saw him move and brought his machine pistol round. Mallory saw the muzzle flash, felt the officer's body shake as the rounds meant for him thumped into the *Leutnant*'s torso. Then his own Schmeisser was hammering, and the German's machine pistol was firing in a great arc in the sky as his dead finger tightened on the trigger.

After that everything was quiet, except for a voice, shouting. At first it shouted in German. 'Hands up!' it said. 'You are covered!'

The three Germans left standing raised their hands. 'Keep hidden!' roared the voice, in Greek. Talking to Clytemnestra. Mallory climbed to his feet. Miller was already up.

Somewhere, a radio said, in German, 'A Force, A Force, come in.'

Mallory found the set under a body, rolled it aside, lifted the mike to his mouth. 'A Force,' he said. 'Mission complete.'

'Please give me a code word with that,' said the voice.

Mallory took his thumb off the transmit switch. 'What is the code word?' he said to the nearest living German.

'Schultz, *Feldwebel*, 175609 –'

Something moved at the corner of Mallory's eye. It was Carstairs, with a Luger. He knocked the German to the ground with the barrel and jammed it into the man's mouth. Mallory heard the pop as a tooth broke. 'The man said, code word,' said Carstairs. He pulled the gun out of the man's mouth. 'One. Two –'

The German had no way of telling whether Carstairs was going to count to three or fifty, but with a gun muzzle half an inch from his eye socket he was not going to hang around to find out. 'Wild Hunt,' he said.

Mallory thumbed the transmit switch. 'Wild Hunt,' he said, and released it.

The set hissed an empty wash of static. There was no reply.

The German with no front teeth laughed. 'You are out of time. They are looking for you already.'

'Bastard,' said Carstairs, and cocked the Luger. The German turned grey. Sweat stood on his forehead as he stared at death.

'Leave him,' said Mallory.

Carstairs raised an eyebrow.

Mallory said, 'Take their clothes.'

'Clothes?' said Carstairs, looking down at his own immaculately-tailored tunic. 'They won't fit.'

'Best-dressed corpse in the mountains, right?' said Miller, who was already taking off his trousers. 'Change everything but your boots.'

'Why?'

'So your feet don't get sore,' said Miller, struggling into the camouflage smock and hanging the radio on his belt. 'Move it.' He grinned at Carstairs, a grin not at all sincere. 'Pardon me. Move it, Captain.'

Carstairs moved it.

They rolled the bodies over a cliff. They took away weapons and ammunition, and the survivors' boots and socks. Then they bound and blindfolded them, and left them barefoot and helpless in a field of razor-edged lava rock. Nelson they buried as best they could. Then they resumed the march, Mallory first, Wills after him, then Carstairs and Clytemnestra, with Andrea bringing up the rear.

They were on a sort of plateau now, a high, windswept place without cover, still cold with the morning chill, but brilliantly lit by the low sun. They marched on, towing long shadows from their boot heels, squinting against the sun in their eyes. Mallory hoped nobody would put any aeroplanes up. It was a forlorn hope, he was pretty sure. German uniforms or no German uniforms, German radio procedures were cast in stone. A dud procedure meant trouble. And these were not the kind of people who closed their eyes to trouble –

Someone stumbled into Mallory's back. He looked round in time to see Wills plough off to the right, trip over a stone and fall flat on his face.

'Leave him,' said Carstairs.

Mallory ignored him. He went and crouched beside Wills. For the first time, he saw the damage the *Leutnant*'s boot had done. The man's face was a mask of blood, the bruise on his temple the colour of blue-black ink.

'Leave me,' mumbled Wills.

Miller came up, squatted and took out the first-aid kit. He said, 'Hold up,' and trickled drinking water between his cracked lips. 'Think you can walk?'

'Course,' croaked Wills. 'Dizzy spell.' He got half-way to his feet, then toppled sideways in the dust.

Andrea said, 'Come.' He lifted Wills like a child, and hauled him on to his back. 'We'll find some shade.'

'Quickly.' Clytemnestra was chewing her lower lip. 'We must cross this part. Then the ground is broken. Safer –'

Mallory held up his hand.

The breeze sighed in the rocks. Above the breeze, another sound: the small, faint drone of an aeroplane's engine.

It was the Storch again; the same Storch. It saw them straight away, circled lazily in the deep blue morning.

'Wave,' said Mallory.

They all waved, even Wills, on Andrea's back, raised a lethargic hand: a patrol of *Waffen-SS* saluting their comrades in the wilderness.

But Mallory was thinking radio. The observer would have been talking. Either the ground patrols had a listening schedule, to which they should have responded. Or he was talking to his base station, reporting five men and a Greek heading east, and the base station would be checking where the Greek fitted in . . .

After another half-hour's march they were in broken ground, sloping away to the eastward. Clytemnestra walked out ahead now, moving fast and light among the hillocks and boulders like a hound making a cast. After ten minutes, she stopped and beckoned. They walked over to her.

She was standing at the head of a seam of the ground, deepened by running water into a groove no more than three feet wide. She led them down the groove. After a hundred yards it was already a ravine, plunging steeply downwards, disappearing from view round a colossal buttress of rotten stone. There was a path along the right-hand side of the ravine; a narrow ribbon of flat ground. This path Clytemnestra took. Another God damned goat path, thought Miller gloomily, trudging along. The German who had originally owned the smock he was wearing had been an eater of raw onions, by the smell of it –

'Here,' said Clytemnestra.

They had arrived at the end of the gorge, on a ledge balanced like an epaulette on a vast shoulder of rock. The ledge was perhaps thirty feet wide. On it were a couple of walls that might once have been part of dwellings. On its inside edge the cliff was patched with the stone fronts of cave-houses. 'Very hard place to find,' said Clytemnestra. 'Once, klephts live here, bandits. Now, nobody.' She walked across to a patch of green moss and ferns between two of the walled caves. A trickle of water fell from a projecting rock into a bowl roughly carved from the stone. 'Everything you need,' she said.

Mallory was looking east.

Beyond the ledge, the ground dropped away three thousand feet in a series of precipices over a vast and hazy gulf. The bottom of the gulf was flat and green, marked into rectangular fields. At the southern end of the fields, a dark line, presumably a fence, separated out what looked like a group of huts and a brown-and-yellow expanse of baked earth and dry grass that must be an aerodrome, its eastern and northern sides formed by the sea.

Mallory raised his glasses to his eyes.

Beyond the fields was a stretch of reeds and whitish flats in which water glittered under the sun. It must have been the best part of a mile wide. On the far side the ground rose again, steep and black; the remains of a plug of magma, Lieutenant Robinson's volcano, remnants of a cone of pumice and ash washed away by time. There were buildings up there, some white and gleaming, others ruined; and some, as Mallory focused his glasses, trailing a faint plume of dust.

'Aerial,' said Carstairs.

Mallory panned his glasses up an apparently endless face of bare black cliff. At the cliff's summit, he saw the spider-like tracery of wires and pylons. An aerial array, all right.

'They are building something,' said Clytemnestra. 'They take stone across, from the place down there.'

Three thousand feet below, a ruler-straight line ran from the base of the cliff, across the marshes, to a group of huts at the base of the Acropolis. 'What is it?' said Carstairs.

'Railway line,' said Clytemnestra. 'For stone and gravel.'

'Where's the quarry?' said Mallory.

She pointed straight down.

'I'm a guy, not a fly,' said Miller.

Mallory was not listening. He said, 'Ropes. Weapons. Anything not vital, leave it up here. Clytemnestra, can you stay here for twenty-four hours? We'll be back.'

She pointed down the ledge, to a place where the path narrowed, and there were the hard outlines of more ruined buildings. 'There is the Swallow's Nest,' she said.

'Password,' said Mallory. 'You'll need one.'

'Jolly boating weather,' said Wills.

'Shoot anyone who doesn't use it.'

'Jolly what?' said Clytemnestra.

'Never mind –'

'Quiet,' said Andrea. Over the dim rumour of humanity from the vale below there came once again the sound of an aeroplane engine.

They were standing on a wide part of the ledge, smooth as a parade ground, without cover. Standing up or lying down, they would stick out like a poached egg on a black table.

'Wave,' said Mallory.

The Storch came round the escarpment at eighty knots, not more than a hundred feet out. The people in S S uniform waved, the way they had waved last time. Mallory could see the faces of the pilot and the observer, curious, blank behind their goggles, not waving back. It went past once. 'That's it,' said Carstairs.

The Storch dropped a wing and turned, so slow and low it almost seemed to hover. Mallory could see the observer's lips moving as he spoke into his microphone. They were being checked up on. The carnage by the tomb would have been discovered by now.

'Wave,' said Mallory. Bluff, and bluff again, and hope like hell it worked, though hope grew harder to sustain –

But Carstairs had his Schmeisser at his shoulder, and its clatter was ringing in the cliffs, and the Storch was banking away, and a long line of pock marks appeared in the Storch's unarmoured belly. The plane's bank became a roll, a staggering roll that turned into a sideslip that would have been a spin except that half-way through the first turn the face of the escarpment came out to meet the aircraft. A wing touched delicately, crumpled like the foil from a cigarette packet. The propeller churned into the rock, the nose telescoped, a tiny spark of flame flicked back on the cowling, and among the noise of buckled and cracking metal came the big, solid whoomp of the fuel tank blowing. The Storch came momentarily to rest, perched nose-up on a sixty-degree slope, blazing from propeller boss to tailskid. Mallory could see the observer beating at the cockpit cover, jammed because of the heat. Then the plane began to slide tail-first into the abyss, gathering speed, leaving a long plume of black smoke, bouncing out from the cliff, over and over, breaking up as it fell.

Then it was gone, and all that remained was the smoke, tangled in the crags and bushes in the morning calm.

If you wanted a pointer to this place, thought Miller, you could not have done much better unless you had picked up a dirty great paintbrush and made an arrow on the cliff and marked it SHOOT HERE.

'Good show,' said Carstairs, stroking his silly moustache.

'Excellent,' said Miller, wearily.

Mallory felt tired to the marrow of his bones. And it had not yet begun. There would be men up here. A lot of men.

'All right,' he said. 'As I was saying before we were so rudely interrupted. We'll get down there. Clytemnestra. Situation's changed. You'd better come too.'

Clytemnestra said, 'No.'

'Oh?'

'Wills cannot move, not just now. The hiding places up here are very good. There will be no trouble. If we came, we would be in the way.' She smiled, a ferocious flash of teeth in her face. 'I think you are good fighters, you three.' She turned to Carstairs. 'But you will get yourself killed.' She said in Greek, 'And these other people, too. You are like a barnyard cock. A lot of noise and fuss, but that is all. No patience. A child, not a man.'

'What does she say?' said Carstairs.

'She admires you intensely,' said Miller, who had learned good Greek in the process of blowing up targets in Crete and the Peloponnese.

'Objectives,' said Mallory, hurriedly. 'Listen.'

'Permission to, er, speak,' said Carstairs.

Mallory grinned at him, a grin without humour. 'No,' he said. 'You will for the purposes of the next phase of this operation consider yourself under my orders, and keep quiet. Do I make myself clear?'

Behind its mask of sweat and grime Carstairs' face was smooth, his eyes remote and distant. 'Perfectly,' he said.

'Our objective is to destroy the rocket factory,' said Mallory. 'Yours is different. I authorize you to disclose it, to avoid confusion.'

'It would be a great pity if we . . . interfered with one another,' said Andrea. His big hands were resting on the Schmeisser, light and casual. The ledge was full of a studied politeness; but under the politeness lay a wire-taut thread of violence.

Carstairs was not stupid. He knew that for the third time, he had made life complicated and dangerous for the rest of the Thunderbolt Force. He knew that these men were used to achieving their objectives, and did not let anyone or anything stand in their way. The time had come for a dose of frankness – carefully measured, but a dose none the less. 'I'll go after the aerials,' he said.

Mallory had been sitting apart, binoculars on the plain and the Acropolis. 'It's a bad climb to solo,' he said.

'I'll manage,' said Carstairs. He had his own glasses out. Things were moving on the airfield. A Trimotor was taxiing, and a group of vehicles was parked at the root of the causeway that took the road across the marsh to the Acropolis. There was an ambulance among them. 'I'm off,' he said.

'Your objectives,' said Andrea. This time, the hands on the Schmeisser looked firmer. 'The aerials. Then this person you have to . . . debrief?'

'For Christ's sake,' said Carstairs. 'This is need-to-know information.'

'We need to know,' said Andrea flatly.

Far below, the Trimotor was taxiing to the downwind end of the runway.

'Very well,' said Carstairs. 'If you insist. The *Kormoran* was boarded before she sank. She was carrying new German code books. Maybe this . . . survivor saw the boarding party. Highly likely, actually. In Parmatia they said he was unconscious. I'm hoping he still is. If he has woken up and told the Germans what he saw and they transmit the news back to Berlin, or Italy, or anywhere else, then bang goes a very useful intelligence source. A vital intelligence source, you might say. So I don't care what you men are doing, I'm going after those aerials to shut them up. And then I'm going to find the man who was in the ambulance, awake or asleep.'

'And then?' said Mallory.

Carstairs' face was hard as stone. 'Use your imagination, Captain,' he said.

So now they were assassins, thought Mallory. Not soldiers. There was a difference.

'Over there,' said Mallory, pointing at the dark massif opposite. 'Northern end. There's a village.'

'Once a village,' said Clytemnestra. 'Now a prison. For slaves.'

'Slaves?'

'The men of the island. The Germans make them work in their factory.'

'Well, well,' said Mallory. 'We rendezvous there at midnight.'

'Where?'

'There is a little street by the church,' said Clytemnestra. 'Athenai Street. It is dark. There are no guards.'

'How do you know?'

'We go there.'

'I thought it was a prison.'

'It is. But we are Greeks. We will wait from midnight here.' She pointed to a spot on the map in her hand. 'Then if you have not found us we will come to find you at dawn.'

Far below, the Trimotor was up and off the runway, a minute grey cross chasing its shadow over the dim marshes. Soon, the plateau above would be full of paratroops.

'Moving out,' said Mallory.

How come I always say never again, thought Miller, and every time I say it I am doing it again within twenty minutes?

'Go,' said Mallory.

Miller did not look down. He knew what was underneath him: three hundred feet of cliff, with a slope of sharp scree to bounce on, then another precipice –

He braced the doubled rope over his shoulder and up between his legs, and started to walk backwards down the cliff. His packful of explosives wanted to unbalance him. His knees wanted to shake him loose. His breakfast wanted to fling itself into the glad light of day –

'Hold up,' said Carstairs' voice. Miller found himself teetering on something that Mallory would probably have called a ledge, but as far as Miller was concerned was no bigger than a bookshelf, and a shelf for small books at that.

'Between the legs,' said Carstairs, with his oily smile. 'Up the back. Round the –'

But Miller had gone, bounding out into space, half a hundredweight of explosives on his back. He did not like heights, but he liked Carstairs even less.

When Miller hit the scree slope, Andrea was already there. Carstairs and Mallory followed, pulled the ropes down and belayed again. Andrea and Carstairs, then Miller and Mallory went down again, and again, until they were standing on a scrubby shoulder of rock, a stratum that had stood up to rain and wind and sun better than the rest of the cliff. Mallory and Carstairs were coiling the ropes, making the coils fast, slinging them on their small packs.

Once Miller's knees had stopped shaking, he had time to recognize a change in Carstairs. Miller on a cliff was a fish out of water. But as he watched Carstairs coil the rope and run his eye over the next pitch, he recognized that this was a man in his element.

The hard stratum made a broad, rubbly road along the cliff face, inaccessible from above and below. They had already lost two thousand feet in height. The valley floor was closer now, and from somewhere ahead and downhill came the pant and clank of heavy machinery.

The Tante Ju had gone overhead twenty minutes previously. If the Germans had dogs, they would be on the ledge by now. Miller wondered how Wills would be doing. Okay, as long as he had Clytemnestra there.

Miller frowned.

Clytemnestra reminded him of someone, for a moment he could not think who. As he scrambled through the dense and thorny underbrush, he remembered. Those eyes, that jaw, that figure; Darling Miss Daisy.

Darling Miss Daisy had been a good friend of his in Chicago during the Dirty Thirties. Darling Miss Daisy's speciality had been removing all her clothes except a garter in front of the patrons of the El Cairo Tearooms, a rendezvous whose definition of tea was loose at best. As a token of their appreciation, the tea drinkers would stuff high-denomination banknotes into Miss Daisy's garter. Miss Daisy had been a good friend of Miller's, and had one night asked him along to witness the performance. This he had done with much appreciation. By the close of her act Darling Miss Daisy, nude except the garter and a pair of high-heeled pumps, had collected some eight hundred dollars, in those days a most considerable sum.

At this point, a citizen called Moose Michael had jumped out of the crowd, grabbed Miss Daisy from behind, and pushed a gun into her swan-like neck. Miss Daisy was no stranger to this sort of carry-on, and relaxed. Guys with what this guy had on his mind on their minds always made a bad move sometime, and that was when you set the dogs on them.

But Moose Michael's hand was not groping for Darling Miss Daisy's outstanding assets. It was groping for the money in the garter. This was not in the rules. Miss Daisy clenched her perfectly-formed fist, rolled her flashing black eyes, and gun in her neck or not, broke Moose Michael's jaw in four places.

Miller could see a lot of Darling Miss Daisy in Clytemnestra. Trudging on through the scrub, he crossed her and Wills off the worry-list.

Ahead, the clank of machinery was getting louder.

SEVEN

Thursday 1200–2000

Leutnant Priem had been in North Africa, and at the invasion of Crete, and most recently in Yugoslavia. As he skirted the shoulder of the ravine (they could have done with a dog; but the dogs had disappeared) he thought: this could be a great posting, this island, if the commanding officer used his brains. One stupid Storch crashes, observer's been drinking Metaxa, screaming down the radio, and Wolf panics, and here we are pretending to be mountain goats, heading for his bloody map reference as if we were doing a security sweep for a Führer visit . . .

The path came out on the ledge. Cicadas trilled in the noonday sun, and the air was heavy with the whiff of thyme and rue. Priem cast a scornful eye over the ruined buildings. How could you believe in the glories of Greek culture when the people lived in such hovels? Degenerate scum. No better than animals. Of course, nobody had been here for years . . .

'Search the place!' he barked. He lit a cigarette and sat in the shade. A lizard lay on a slab of rock, bringing itself up to temperature for the next hunting trip. Lucky damned lizard. Nothing to do but sit around in the sun all day. While Priem had to make a pretence of searching these places where nobody had been, ever. That was Wolf for you. Savage, but *gründlich*. Thorough –

'*Herr Leutnant*!' yelled a voice.

Priem stamped out his cigarette and went to interview the sergeant.

'Buildings empty,' said the sergeant. 'Found this here, sir.' He pointed with the tip of his jackboot at a little pile of golden cylinders. Cartridge cases.

Priem was suddenly not relaxed any more. 'Good,' he said. They were Schmeisser cases. 'And the aeroplane?' he said.

'Over here,' said the sergeant. 'One hundred and three metres down.'

'Rope,' said Priem.

'Rope in place,' said the NCO.

The wreckage of the Storch was draped over a crag. Priem climbed round it, scrutinized the burned remains of the pilot and the observer, frowning slightly. He paused to examine the line of bullet-holes starting at the wing-root and vanishing under the belly.

He climbed back to the ledge in silence. 'Sergeant,' he said. 'We will establish a field HQ here. Search again, particularly down the cliffs. And give me that radio.'

Higher on the mountain, in what would once have been the uppermost street of the bandit village, Clytemnestra and Wills lay in darkness. It was a cool darkness, smelling slightly of mould, but that was not surprising, since their hiding place was situated under the ruins of the washing-copper in the corner of four walls that had once served as a laundry.

This village of bandits was a village for which searches and razzias were no novelty. The crusaders had rummaged it, then the Turks, then the Greeks. The Germans were merely the latest in line.

Just as long (Clytemnestra reflected, listening to the concussed muttering of Wills) as they did not bring their dogs.

It was a tidy enough quarry, as quarries went; a big horseshoe cut in the cliff, fans of fallen stone at the base, a couple of diggers moving across a white floor trailing clouds of dust. There was a crusher, a big machine with a hopper and a black funnel that belched smoke, panting and grinding, discharging crushed stone into another, larger hopper. Under the larger hopper ran a railway track. As the men on the quarry lip watched, a train reversed into the quarry and positioned the first of its four trucks under the hopper. The hopper-release opened. A dose of crushed stone roared into the truck. The locomotive moved on. Another dose roared into the second truck. Move. Roar. Move. Roar. The locomotive hissed steam and began to pull out, gathering speed.

'Well?' said Carstairs.

'Wait,' said Mallory, eyes down on his watch.

The train bustled off across the plain, shrinking on its converging lines, speeding on to a causeway across the marsh, shrinking still. At the far end a cloud of white dust rose, then whipped away on the breeze. The breeze was up, now. A long edge of grey was travelling down the sky from the north. 'Twelve minutes,' said Mallory. 'Down we go.'

'Why?' said Carstairs.

The other men were slinging their packs. Miller pointed behind them, up the cliff, where little figures were descending on ropes, rummaging every ledge and hollow. 'They're still looking,' said Mallory. 'If we don't keep moving, they'll spot us.' Carstairs' mouth went dry. He scrambled to his feet, and down the flank of the quarry.

Far away, a long steam-whistle blew. The stone train had emptied its trucks. Now it was on its way back.

The four men went down the big fan of rubble on the quarry's northern side. The sun beat hot on the white stone as they ran, jumping from stone to stone, slithering in the small gravel, dust trailing from their heels. Men below looked up; labourers, mostly, in dusty overalls, trailing shovels, smoking cigarettes. They saw four men in camouflage smocks and *Wehrmacht* caps sliding down a pile of rubble. They were used to seeing soldiers; too many soldiers.

A sentry walked over, *Wehrmacht*, a *Feldwebel*, bored and dusty. The *Sonderkommando* had only been on the island three days. Mallory was betting that between the *Wehrmacht* guards and the *Sonderkommando* there would be no love lost. 'What do you want?' said the *Feldwebel*.

Mallory said, 'Mind your own damned business.'

The *Feldwebel* blinked. 'It is my business.'

'Perhaps you would like to explain that to *Hauptmann* Wolf.'

It did not work. 'I have my own officers,' said the *Feldwebel*. 'I do not need to talk to your nasty little *Hauptmann*.'

Mallory said, 'Very wise,' and started to walk past him towards the rock crusher.

'One moment,' said the sentry. 'Papers.'

'Don't be bloody stupid,' said Mallory. They were all walking now, towards the shade of the crusher, the sentry nearly running alongside them. The cloud had covered the sun. The air felt thick and moist.

The sentry got in front of them and unslung his rifle. 'Papers,' he said, and in his eye there was a meticulous glint, the legendary obstinacy of the German NCO. Mallory's heart sank.

'All right,' said Mallory. 'Shall we go and see your commanding officer?' Andrea was standing close behind him. Above them, the stilts of the rock crusher towered like the legs of an enormous insect. Mallory could feel Andrea moving. The guard's life was hanging by a thread. He looked Mallory up and down . . .

And saw his boots.

They were caked with dust, scuffed and battered. They were variations on a theme of British paratrooper's boots, manufactured for Mallory by Lobb of St James' Street, London, in collaboration and discussion with Black's of Holborn, expedition outfitters, fitted on his personal last, studded with pyramid nails hand-sharpened with the file Mallory carried in his pocket.

They should have been regulation German army jackboots.

There was no way of knowing what was in the *Feldwebel*'s mind, but Mallory could guess. The *Feldwebel* was a high priest of order and regulation, and the boots were heresy and sacrilege. The rifle came up. The eyes went round. The mouth opened to shout.

Mallory caught hold of the rifle barrel and pushed it sharply aside, stepping aside himself as he did so. Something very big and very fast came past him. The *Feldwebel* made a loud whooshing sigh, and crumpled forward over Andrea's fist. Andrea heaved him upright. He whipped out the knife he had driven up and under the man's ribs and into his heart, and in the same movement pushed the body back into the shadows under the crusher. The air was thick and still. A couple of big raindrops made dark blots in the dust.

Mallory lit a cigarette. Nobody said anything. Mallory blew smoke and said, 'Listen.'

They listened. Thunder rumbled. The rails were humming. Three minutes later, the train came in.

In the cab, the driver yawned. He was German, and so was his fireman. Give a Greek this job, and nothing would get done. The soldiers were as bad. They were meant to sign each load in and out as the train went through the gate in the fence by the guard-house. But they were *Wehrmacht*, not railwaymen. They had made him do all the signing at the beginning of his shift, so he could come and go as he liked –

The hopper roared. He pulled forward to the second red post, applied the brakes, turned to tell the fireman to chuck a bit more coal on. The fireman was blond, with blue eyes in a sooty face. The engine driver's mouth fell open.

This was not him. This was a man with a lean brown face and the coldest grey eyes the driver had ever seen.

The engine driver was about to shout when he felt something press against his leather jerkin. Something sharp. He felt the sting of cold steel in the fat on his belly. He closed his mouth. 'Fill up,' said the man. 'Then drive.'

The engine driver did not ask what had happened to his fireman. He said, 'The pressure is down.'

There were two men in the cab with him now: the lean-faced man and another with an eyebrow moustache. The man with the eyebrow moustache opened the firebox, and shovelled in coal. 'All right,' he said. 'Off we go, what?'

The driver blew out his oil-stained moustache. 'No,' he said. The thing in his belly moved a couple of inches. Skin broke. Blood rolled. It was raining now, hot, steamy rain, but the driver was suddenly bathed in cold sweat. 'Sorry,' he said. 'Yes. Of course. Very well.' His hand went to the regulator.

The leg of the hopper started to move. The train gathered speed. The quarry face faded into a grey curtain of rain. The gate loomed, guard post beside it. Mallory crouched on the footplate, and Carstairs bent, shovelling. The driver stared straight ahead, not acknowledging the wave of the crop-headed sentry drinking coffee in the wooden hut. And the train was travelling on an embankment over green fields. To the right was young corn and rain-grey sea. To the left was more young corn, terminated abruptly by a tall fence of mesh and barbed wire, with sheds and what looked like a fuel dump. Tailplanes stood like blunt sharks' fins beyond the sheds. Ahead, down the cylinder of the ancient locomotive, the fields fell away. The train rattled through a belt of reeds. Then there were rain-pocked pools of water on either side, dead-looking, dotted with clumps of sickly vegetation. The margins of the pools were crusted with white deposits. The place had a flat, washing-soda stink. When Mallory licked his lips, his tongue was dry with lime.

Over to the left was another causeway, carrying a road. At its landward side it passed between high fences, with red-and-white-striped barriers, huts for a platoon of soldiers, and a machine-gun post on either side, one to cover the approach, the other to cover the causeway itself. Mallory was glad he had decided to come by train.

The far shore was upon them: first a glacis of new stone, then a flat area that looked as if it had been reclaimed from the marsh. Beyond the flat area, the basalt colossus of the Acropolis rose like a wall. On the far side of the reclaimed area, behind a chainlink fence, was a vehicle park. As Mallory watched, an ambulance rolled in. The doors opened. A pair of orderlies lifted out a stretcher and ran with it through the rain and into a steel door set in the face of the cliff.

Mallory glanced at Carstairs. Carstairs was watching the ambulance too.

The tracks ran across the reclaimed area on a trestled viaduct ending in a set of buffers. Below the viaduct was a pile of crushed stone. Two huge concrete mixers churned alongside the rock piles.

The train slowed to a crawl. The driver raised his hand to another lever and pulled it. The train shuddered. Looking back over the tender, Mallory saw the hopper of the first wagon tilt sideways, and dump its cargo over the side of the trestle with a roar. An explosion of dust mingled with the rain and spread over the cab.

'Out,' said Mallory into the fog.

When the dust settled, Carstairs was gone.

The driver reversed the engine and opened the throttle. The train shuttled back across the marshes and the fields, past the bored sentry and into the quarry. Men were still moving on the escarpment, searching. They were lower down, now.

It was only a matter of time, thought Mallory. The clock had been ticking. And now it was about to strike.

The train slowed. The locomotive came to a halt by the first red post. The driver pointed. On the steel staging beside the cab was a lever. Mallory stepped off the footplate and hauled. The hopper opened with a roar. The truck filled. Miller and Andrea appeared out of the shadows. 'In,' said Mallory.

Up ahead in the sentry box, there was turbulent movement. The sweaty guard came out of the door into the rain, cramming a steel helmet on to his cropped head with one hand, waving a rifle in the other. He was shouting, his words drowned by the roar of the diggers and the huge metallic pant and grind of the crusher.

It was time to leave.

The sentry had slung his rifle and was dragging the gates shut across the railway line, boots slipping in the big puddles. The train picked up speed. Mallory saw his face, red-eyed. Then the locomotive hit the gates with a crash, and there was a squeal of tortured metal, and the train was through. When Mallory looked back, he saw a wisp of smoke coming from the guardhouse window. His eyes fell on Miller. 'I guess he sat in his ashtray,' said Miller, returning his gaze with great innocence.

The wisp of smoke became billows, turning orange at the roots as the Thermite bomb Miller had tossed through the window burned its way through the desk and into the floor, consuming paper and timber and the sentry's lunch, and most importantly the Bakelite of the telephone system.

'Now listen to me,' said Mallory.

They all listened. Even the train driver listened. He did not understand, but he trained his ears with maximum concentration on the string of incomprehensible syllables that came from the New Zealander's lips. All of them knew that what was about to happen in the next five minutes was a matter of life and death. The train driver thought it would probably be death.

As it turned out, the train driver did not need to understand. The train thundered through dense curtains of rain into the marshes. As he stood trembling with terror, he felt himself seized by strong arms and flung like a human cannonball at the swamp. He landed in a pool of foul-smelling water that stung his eyes like caustic. When he could breathe again, he struggled on to a mud bank and lay there coughing. After a while, he heard a terrible noise.

The engine driver was a railwayman, not a soldier. He decided that discretion was the better part of valour. He still was not seeing too well. But he could locate the noise, all right. He began to crawl, swim and flounder as fast as he could in the opposite direction.

*   *   *

103

Andrea threw the engine driver out of the right-hand side of the cab, away from the greatest number of prying eyes. Then Mallory hit the throttle and jammed it right forward. Even with a full quota of trucks, the locomotive was over powered for the job. Now it was only half-loaded. As steam blasted into its cylinders it leaped forward, belching smoke, and shot across the last of the embankment. By the time it hit the trestled dumping section, it was travelling at forty miles an hour, all thirty-five tons of it.

'Go,' said Mallory.

As Miller jumped, he could see a steam-shovel working, hazy and grey in the rain, but he was not thinking about witnesses, because he had fifty pounds of high explosive in his pack, and besides, Mallory and Andrea were beside him in mid-air. Then they were hitting the side of a pile of crushed stone a terrible whack, rolling over and over in a soup of falling water and wet stone dust.

The train thundered through the buffers, corkscrewed into mid-air, drive-wheels spinning. It lost momentum, crashed on to the rubble bed of the reclaimed ground, and tobogganed forward into the cliff. The basalt face crumpled its nose like a cardboard mailing tube and drove its boiler back into its firebox. There was a mighty roar and a thunderclap detonation. The reclaimed ground was suddenly obliterated by a scalding fog of escaping steam and rain and stone dust.

In that fog, a voice close to Miller's ear said, 'Go now.' Mallory's voice. In the background was shouting, and the churn of the concrete mixers, and a klaxon.

Miller got up, and ran behind Andrea in what he assumed was the right direction. Somewhere, the klaxon was still screaming.

Andrea was bleeding. Miller imagined he was probably bleeding himself. There was an entrance ahead, a hole in the cliff. The klaxon noise was coming out of the horn above the hole. Andrea said, in German, '*Herein*.' In. Somewhere a sergeant was shouting, a *Feldwebel*, telling people to take cover. Wait a minute, thought the rational part of Miller, that is a German secret weapon factory, you can't go in there. Besides, where's Mallory?

But by that time he was inside the mountain, and with a steady hum of hydraulics the steel door was easing to . . .

Was shut.

*   *   *

In the cellar of the ruined house above the ledge, Clytemnestra woke suddenly from a fitful sleep. Next to her she could hear the breathing of Wills: regular breathing, shallow. He was improving, she thought. Men do improve after a few days, unless they die ... Her thoughts strayed towards Achilles: her own dear brother Achilles, tall and strong and quick to laugh, his falcon's beak of a nose above the moustache, his eyes glittering with kindness and amusement. The whacking of rifle-butts on the door. The dragging away of Achilles, and her next – her last – sight of him, on the cart in the square, the Nazi swine yanking the noose taut over his head; the look in his poor eyes, that said this is really happening, to me ...

Clytemnestra dragged her thoughts back from that thing too dreadful to contemplate. It had filled her mind with a turbulence that broke against the edge of her consciousness in waves of rage. She reached out her hand for her gun. She closed her fingers on the cool metal. It had a grounding effect, drew her back to the here and now.

To what it was that had woken her up.

When she remembered what that had been, she drew in her breath and did not let it out. And in the silence, that thing came again: half-way between a howl and a yelp, the distant sound of a dog. Not the sheepdogs they used in the mountains: a more purposeful sound. The sound of a dog hunting. One of the black-and-tan dogs the *Sonderkommando* used for hunting people.

She reached out and squeezed Wills' hand. The feel of his warm flesh gave her encouragement. 'What is it?' he said.

She told him.

'Well,' he said. 'We'd better do something about it, eh?' As he said it, he felt a sense of wonder: his head was clear, his thoughts sharp. He remembered very little about the past twenty-four hours, except a blurred procession of images, feet walking over rock, Nelson, terrible dreams ...

But that was all over now. He groped for his Schmeisser and snapped in a new magazine. Clytemnestra had her eye to the spy-hole in the wall. 'How many?' he said.

'Four. And the dog.'

'One feels they may be in for a bit of a shock.'

Clytemnestra said, 'A very big shock.' She did not go in for his English understatement. After all, there was no shock like dying.

'Good dog, Mutzi,' said Tietmeyer, the handler.

Marsdorff did not agree. This damned animal had dragged him and Schmidt and Kohl up a cliff in the noonday sun. It had relieved itself on a handhold, which he had then put his hand on, and of course everyone had found that very amusing. Marsdorff was a pudgy, maggot-coloured man, who owed his place in the *Sonderkommando* more to a lack of scruple than to any positive military talent. Basically, Marsdorff was very good at hanging people, an accomplished hand with a red-hot iron and a pair of pliers, and no beginner when it came to the process of gang rape – a business that in Marsdorff's view was often approached crudely and without thought. A really well-handled woman could keep a squad amused for some days –

'Good dog,' said the handler. The Doberman on the choke lead growled and slavered, claws scritching on the bare rock as it hauled Tietmeyer up the path towards the ruined house. It had needed some persuasion to come out of the rocks by the tomb, into which it had fled after the death of its previous handler. Now it was back at work, though, it seemed enthusiastic to make amends. 'There's been someone in there, all right. Gone now.'

'Oh, good,' said Marsdorff, with sarcasm. 'Eagles, are they? Or mountain goats?'

'Let's hope they're goats,' said Kohl, who disliked Marsdorff. 'I don't mind shagging a goat, but eagles are right out.'

'You have to draw the line somewhere,' said Marsdorff, sagely. He was not joking. 'On a bit.'

Negligently, the four men approached the next group of ruins. They did not believe anyone was on this island who was not supposed to be. Apparently there had been shooting. Well, they would believe it when they saw it.

The path had come to a narrow place, a defile dug out between a blade of rock and the cliff. The defile ended in a sort of groove, shoulder-deep in bare rock, leading to another group of ruined houses, the first of them a massive stone building, with loopholes staring blankly at the defile and the groove. They entered the groove, Tietmeyer in the lead. In one of the loopholes, something moved; a short, slender pipe. The barrel of a machine pistol. Tietmeyer said, nervously, 'I don't –' There was a large and dreadful noise, and the groove filled up with bullets. All of them jumped. None of them hit the ground alive.

Wills walked up to the bodies. He was pale again. 'Christ,' he said.

Clytemnestra squatted by Tietmeyer's body and liberated his Schmeisser, half-a-dozen magazines and a bunch of stick grenades. Then she spat in the dead face, and moved on to the next corpse. Wills watched the place where the path came round the bend in the rocks. 'They'll be back,' he said. 'Unless they're deaf.'

Clytemnestra raised a scornful eyebrow. 'So let them come,' she said. She pointed upwards, to where the cliff bulged out in an overhang like the brow of a stone genius. 'If they come there, we swat them like spiders.' She pointed over the lip of the path. 'There, they will not come unless they are birds. From this way' – she pointed to where the path ended among the houses – 'also, you will need to be a bird. And up the path, all must pass between the narrow rocks. It is like the path at Thermopylae. But you have never heard of Thermopylae, I expect.'

'Battle in ancient Greece,' said Wills. 'Played in a mountain pass. Three hundred Spartans v. a hundred thousand Persians. Home team triumphant. Leonidas played centre forward.'

'So now help me with these bodies, and we should get back to the houses.'

'Quite,' said Wills. It would have been bad taste to point out that the heroes of Thermopylae had died while achieving their victory. He helped Clytemnestra topple the bodies over the cliff. Then he gathered up an armful of guns and bombs and scrambled after Clytemnestra back to the Swallow's Nest.

They were not the first people to have had the idea of defending this eyrie. The Swallow's Nest was the fortress-like building commanding the defile, a tower that overhung the abyss like a swallow's nest in the eaves of a roof. Wills' boots rang in the thick-walled rooms. He put his head into something that might have been a waterspout, or a nozzle for boiling oil. The valley was full of rain and the mutter of thunder. Far below, the path was a faint zigzag rising to the base of the cliff. And on the path, little creatures crawled: German soldiers.

It occurred to Wills that while the Swallow's Nest might be an impregnable redoubt, on an island crawling with German soldiers it was also a blind alley.

For a very small moment after the steel door hissed shut, Miller and Andrea stood quite still, listening. There was in all conscience plenty to listen to.

They were standing in a corridor hewn from the basalt. The corridor was lined with doors, full of voices echoing from the hard surfaces of the rock, and the steel plate of the door, and the girders that supported the staircases and the lighting and forced-draught units, and the loudspeakers that at this very moment were squawking klaxon noises into the babel below.

There were men everywhere. There seemed to be a lot of *Wehrmacht*, and a sprinkling of camouflage-smocked *SS*, and civilian workers, some mechanical-looking, in blue overalls, and one man in a white lab coat with pen-clips showing in the breast pocket, and rimless glasses below a head like a pumpkin. A squad of Greeks marched past, dressed in the rags of peasant field clothes, under the guard of four *Waffen-SS*. Everybody was too busy scuttling to and fro to spend any time staring at a couple of filthy, bloodstained men in ripped camouflage smocks.

For the moment.

The moment did not last long. A *Wehrmacht* NCO came marching past. He stopped, stared up at Andrea, and said, 'What the hell do you think you've been doing, killer?'

Andrea stood to attention, eyes front, chin out.

'How tall are you?' barked the NCO. The man's eyes were small and evil. Any minute now, thought Miller, they were going to slide down Andrea's body to his boots, his British army-issue boots, and that would be that –

'Two metres, *Feldwebel*,' said Andrea.

'Never seen shit piled so high in my life,' said the NCO. Andrea's eyes had slid down the corridor. A door had opened. A wisp of steam floated into the corridor. A man with a drawstring bag came out, fumbling with his tunic buttons. 'You *Sonderkommando* cutthroats think you can march about the place with your arses filthy, you can –'

'Permission to take a shower, *Feldwebel*!' roared Andrea.

'Permission to take a shower, *Feldwebel*!' roared Miller.

Andrea turned left, cracked his boots on the concrete, and headed for the door. The *Feldwebel* turned away. If these Nazi animals wanted to take a shower during a general alert, then a shower they would take, *Herr Gott*. They were above the law, these brutes. The best you could hope was that they refrained from cooking and eating your men, and robbing the dead. God knew what the army was coming to. All mixed up with this *Sonderkommando*, and civilian labourers, and boffins, and God alone knew what other riffraff. Apparently some fool had crashed a train in the quarry, too. Beer, thought the *Feldwebel*. That was what you needed in a climate like this, at a time like this. He stumped off in the direction of the Sergeants' Mess.

The klaxons had stopped. *ALLES KLAR*, said the big metal voice in the corridor. ALL CLEAR. STAND DOWN.

Andrea shoved open the door of the shower room.

It was a big shower room, full of steam and the cursing of men who had stopped their showers and hauled their uniforms on over soapy bodies only to be told that the whole business had been in vain.

So now they stood under the showers, brown heads and arms and legs and milk-white German torsos, and washed. Miller and Andrea found a steamy corner, took off their tell-tale boots, and buried them and their battledress under the camouflage smocks. Then they stepped under the water.

'Most refreshing,' said Miller.

'Exactly so,' said Andrea.

'Murderers,' said a small man, presumably *Wehrmacht*, under the next nozzle.

Andrea reached out a huge hand, picked him up by the chin, and said, 'What exactly do you mean by that?'

The *Wehrmacht* man was very small and very frightened, but also very brave. 'What I said.'

Andrea gazed at him. Finally he said, 'You're quite right.' He grinned horribly. The little man ran away.

'Don't like each other, do they?' said Miller, in German.

'Sometimes,' said Andrea, grimly, 'life can be very beautiful.'

He looked around in the steam, scowling, a hairy giant with someone else's towel wrapped round his waist. Miller had a sudden mental glimpse of this shower room in a few hours: red gouts of flame shooting through the doors, the ceiling bulging in, dust and screams where the steam now hung . . .

If everything went according to plan.

Meanwhile, he knew what Andrea was looking for. Andrea was looking for someone in the shower with the same size feet as him.

Three hundred yards away, Mallory was thinking boots, too.

After he had jumped out of the train, he had hit the ground with his feet, cradling his Schmeisser. He had rolled, the para-trooper's roll, come back on his feet like a cat, and started running through the rain and steam and dust for the cliff face. There had been shouts. He paid no attention. Carstairs was up the face of the cliff, heading for the aerials. He did not trust Carstairs. Carstairs needed watching. So Mallory was going up the cliff towards the aerials, to keep an eye on him. He knew the face of that cliff, had summed it up in his mind the way a yachtsman sums up a chart or a fisherman a stretch of river.

He arrived at the locomotive, a crushed barrel issuing jets of scalding steam. He ran up the iron side, avoiding the geysers. The white fog was thick here. Suddenly he was at the rock wall.

Once, it would have dropped straight into the marsh. Since the reclamation of the land it now dropped straight into the platform where the railway and the road causeways arrived at the Acropolis. But there had been building inside the cliff, and ten feet above the platform, a drainpipe had been cemented in. Now, Mallory ran along the locomotive's boiler, jumped, locked his fingers round the drainpipe, drew up his legs, drove his bootnails into the rock, and straightened his knees. He got a foot to the top of the drainpipe, stood there a moment, perfectly in balance. The rain and steam were thick as porridge up here. Somewhere thunder roared, or perhaps it was the locomotive's boiler, mingled with the sound of the big concrete mixers.

He reached up. At fingertip height, an electric cable ran across the sheer face. He flexed his knees, and jumped. The cable came into his hands, fat and solid, anchored to the wall with good Ger-man steel. He drove his boots into the rock and walked his feet up. Tenderly, so as not to pierce the insulation, he got a sole to the cable. Then he shifted his weight, bending his knee. In a couple of seconds he was standing on the cable, walking to the right, northwards, twenty feet off the ground.

From his vantage point he saw grey rain thickening into a solid mat of vapour, from which rose a confused roar of noise. The hiss of escaping steam was fading. The sound of voices was louder; raucous voices, bellowing orders, and the churn of the big concrete mixers. He did not have long. He walked on along the cable, one foot delicately in front of the other, water streaming down the cliff to his left. He was concentrating on his balance, tiptoeing along behind the curtain of the rain.

The concrete mixers were still grinding away below him. You did not stop concrete mixers. You kept them turning, or they went solid. From high above there descended on a cable an angel of mercy in the form of a great steel bucket.

There now began one of the longest minutes of Mallory's life. He moved along the cable until he was standing on a concrete cornice directly above the concrete mixer. The cornice was eighteen inches wide. He lay along it, face averted from the yard.

Down below, men shouted and milled. The rain sheeted down, soaking Mallory to the skin. The bucket dropped, five feet from his right ear, clanked down into the enclosure in front of the mixer. He heard the flop of the concrete as the operator shot it down the pipe and into the bucket, the groan of the wire as it took the strain. Then the bucket was rising again.

Mallory got back on his feet. He saw the grease-black cable rise before him, no handhold there. He saw the battered steel rim of the big bucket. He knew it was now or not at all.

As the rim came up to eye level, he jumped.

His clawed fingers hit concrete-splattered steel, hung on. His toes found the flange at the top of the bucket.

Down below, someone started shouting. It was a new kind of shouting. It meant only one thing. Trouble.

He looked down. The reclaimed area was a mass of men, swarming around the wreck of the stone train like worker ants around a queen. Mallory scrambled on top of the bucket. His final glimpse stayed with him. Heads, helmeted or capped or just hairy, milling to and fro. And in the middle of all those heads, one face turned upwards into the rain, eyes wide, open-mouthed. *Wehrmacht*-grey shoulders. An expression of total shock.

Mallory sat on the handle of the bucket out of sight of the ground, and hoped that nobody would pay any attention to one man who had spotted something wrong with the concrete lifting gear. The cliff moved past fifteen feet away, sheer and black. Carstairs was up there somewhere; either that, or dead. Mallory would rather have been climbing. The bucket was a trap. There was no way off it –

The bucket stopped with a jerk, and hung swinging. Seven hundred and fifty feet below, little figures milled. Seven hundred and fifty feet is two hundred and fifty yards. At two hundred and fifty yards a human face is invisible, even if it is staring at you, or looking at you through binoculars, or aiming a rifle at you. Mallory drew his head back sharply. Then he looked up.

Some distance above – it was impossible to tell exactly how far, but it could have been a hundred feet – was a projection in the cliff face. A jetty or platform, crusted, by the look of it, with spilt concrete, and a crane jib. Not a crane, perhaps; a windlass. Call it what you liked, there were people up there. And the odds were that they had been warned by telephone that there was someone on the concrete bucket. So why would they halt the bucket in mid-ascent?

There were a lot of answers. The one that made the most sense to Mallory was that they were waiting for reinforcements.

Mallory looked at the cliff face. It had sloped gradually away from the bucket. Now it was a good twenty-five feet off through the rain, a wall of black basalt, but weathered up here, unsmoothed, pockmarked . . .

Only twenty-five feet. Too far to jump.

For a moment, Mallory watched that wall with the intensity of a falcon watching a pigeon. Then he unstrapped the lightweight rope from his pack, took a deep breath, and began.

He looped an end of the rope through the handle of the bucket, and hauled in until the two ends were equalized. He grasped the doubled rope, spat on his hands, and went over the side.

It was flimsy stuff, this silk rope, only one up from parachute cord. Harder to grip than the wire-cored Manila they had used on Navarone and in the Pyrenees; but lighter. Infinitely lighter. You could carry twice, three times the length for the same weight –

Comforting things, technicalities. They had brought him down hand over painful hand until he was hanging seventy-five feet below the bucket, like a spider on a thread, turning slowly.

He wound his left hand into the rope above his head, let go with his right. The horizon wheeled around him: clouds, the mountains on the far side of the valley, the sea, a ray of sunlight striking through the clouds making a sudden dazzling path; then the slopes and faces of the Acropolis, the cliff, twenty-five feet away, not far at all. His left hand was agony now, the rope biting like a cheese wire. His right fumbled with the rope, tying a double figure-of-eight as the world turned another forty-five degrees, ninety, to the lengthening shadows of the aeroplanes and the fuel dumps on the dim sward of the airfield. And directly below, spinning with wonderful slowness, the little corpse of the wrecked train.

The knot was finished. The two strands of the rope were tied together. Mallory jammed his right boot into the loop, and put his weight on it, and flexed his left hand to get the blood circulating again. He hung there and let the world turn another two hundred and seventy degrees. Nobody seemed to be shooting at him. When the spin had brought him face to the cliff again, he let his weight drop back.

Seven hundred feet above the wrecked train, seventy-five feet below the bucket, a hundred and seventy feet below the crane, he started to swing.

He swung like a child on a rope hung from a tree branch, except that he was a soldier an eighth of a mile from the ground. The arc grew. He could feel the air dividing in front of his face, smell, as he approached the cliff, that odd smell of hot wet rock, half clammy, half aromatic.

He started to analyse the place where he would land. His present arc would leave him somewhere too smooth. Over to the right, erosion had left a little hook, a semi-detached plate of rock with a tuft of sun-dried grass sprouting from the crevice above. It swept towards him. He reached out his hand, measuring. Just short. The next swing, he moved the axis, gave the rope a little extra pull, gained that extra ounce of speed; so that on the next swing he found himself at the top of the arc, weightless, standing for a split second on nothing, stationary at the apex of his swing. He put out his hand and grasped the little hook of rock, jamming his fingers into the crevice behind it. His weight came on to the flake. He heard his finger joints crack. His boot hit the rock. The nails found a hold. He stood for a second like a starfish, his right hand and right boot holding the cliff, his left arm and left boot engaged with the doubled rope. He shifted the foot. Now he had two boots on the face, his right hand on the flake, his left holding the rope. He would need the rope again –

The flake under his right hand gave way.

There was no warning. One second he was on the wall, getting balanced. The next he was out, falling, no holds anywhere except in his left hand, where the thin rope was sliding through his palm, and the ground far below was coming up to meet him.

He clamped his teeth and his fist at the same time. His fist slid to the knot he had tied in the end of the rope, the bulky double figure-of-eight. He stopped with a crack that tried to tear his arm out by the roots. Each swing tried to shake him off. He held on grimly. As the oscillations grew smaller, the centrifugal force was not so tormenting. He got his right hand on to the rope, then his foot. He manoeuvred himself into a standing position. He thought his knees into not shaking.

Then he started all over again.

This time, he left nothing to chance. He found a new handhold, and went for it. But this time, he committed himself only when he was quite sure. He found himself a place to stand, and he stood there, and methodically untied the figure-of-eight, and coiled the rope, and slung it, and started to climb up and to the left, into a sort of shallow gully or couloir, where he would be out of sight from below and above.

He went up hard and steady, climbing from the hips, his mind fixed on the next hold, never mind the top; the top was just another rest, and would look after itself. It was not until he got into the couloir that he started to shake.

Up in the Swallow's Nest, Wills' head was getting clearer by the minute. One of the things becoming clearest was that he was in a tightish spot, with a woman. He opened a tin of sardines, and looked at Clytemnestra, the olive curve of her cheek against the black fringe of her shawl; hard as a steel spring, light on her feet as a feather. The other thing he had noticed, now that his brain was working again, was that she was extremely beautiful. In Wills' experience of women, which was limited to a few devoted hours spent carrying the golf clubs of his cousin Cynthia, they were not to be counted on in tight spots. Well, not not counted on, exactly; but their place was not in the line of fire, but on the . . . well . . . home front. Clytemnestra seemed to be different. This had come as a shock to Wills, though not a disagreeable one. He ate another sardine.

Clytemnestra was peering down one of the spouts of the Swallow's Nest. As Wills watched, she took a German stick grenade, pulled the toggle, and dropped it through the spout.

Well, thought Wills, fitting her into a known structure. For Clytemnestra and the islanders of Kynthos, this is the home front. He watched the grenade fall, wobbling in the air. The little figures on the zigzag were bigger now, five hundred feet below. They did not look up.

It was a nicely calculated drop. The grenade burst in the air, at about waist height. Wills heard nothing that he could class as an explosion; a flash and a puff of smoke, and a split-second later a flat, ineffectual-sounding *whap*. Three of the little figures on the path were not on the path any more. The rest stopped and lay down; fifteen of them at the most, with more coming up behind. A lot more. They faltered, all of them. It must be unnerving to find yourself under fire from a place you could not see, on an island of which you were supposed to be in control.

After a while, small voices floated up from below, mingled with birdsong. The men below started to move in little rushes. If they had been on a plain or a hillside, they would undoubtedly have spread out. But this was a cliff, and the path was the only means of access. They were bunching again, directly below the Swallow's Nest . . .

'Thermopylae!' yelled Wills, and pulled the strings on two bombs, and let them go.

Again the flash and the puff and the *whap*. Again the little figures, flung off the path and vanishing over the horizon. Again the silence.

But in that silence, a single word. *Hoch*. Up. And all of a sudden, in that huddle of figures, a series of pale discs: faces. And after the faces, the small flicker of muzzle flashes, and the sting and whine of bullets beyond the Swallow's Nest walls.

Clytemnestra sat back, her legs out in front of her, and took a sip of water, and smiled at Wills, showing those white teeth and those fierce eyes, slapping the dirty floor-slabs as you might pat a horse. What she was saying was that there were six feet of good solid masonry between them and those bullets. Nothing was going to shift them, short of artillery.

Wills grinned back at her, feeling the stretch of burned skin on his face.

A shadow flitted across his thoughts. There were a lot of Germans out there. Up here in the Swallow's Nest there was food and ammunition for a couple of days, no more. Maybe they would be relieved. The men in the Acropolis were good men, they had proved that already. Four men, said the small, dark voice in Wills' head. Against a thousand or so.

He heard the scritch of grenade fuses, the *blat* of the explosions, Clytemnestra hiss a curse. A file of soldiers was running up the last zigzag and into the shelter of the cliff. The grenades knocked three of them down, but that left a dozen. Clytemnestra grabbed for her Schmeisser. The Swallow's Nest filled with its jackhammer clatter. She swore again, stopped firing. The range was too big. Wills found himself a loophole that covered the mouth of the path, and waited, sighting down the groove in the stone. Clytemnestra had shot the first lot. It was Wills' turn.

For twenty minutes, nothing moved out there except a lizard, hunting flies on the plates of rock at the mouth of the defile. Then the lizard became suddenly still, as if listening. A fly landed within six inches of it. It paid no attention. Fast as an eye blinking, it was gone.

After it there came, first of all, a boot. Wills rested the foresight of the Schmeisser on the place where the knee would be, and moved the v of the backsight up to cradle it.

A man came out, helmet down, like a rabbit with a ferret on its tail, slap into the sights. Wills fired a four-round burst. The man straightened up and fell backwards into the soldier who was following, stopping him. While he was stopped, Wills shot him in the head. He slammed back. Another man was behind him, and another. Wills fired a longer burst. Hands went up and legs buckled and somebody somewhere began shouting, whether from pain or shock he could not tell. The main thing was that nobody else came through the gap. Like pheasants, he thought. Like pheasants that you take out in front, one, two, except with a machine pistol you could take three, four, five. His head was light, and he thought that he might be going to laugh or cry, he could not tell which. 'Like pheasants,' he said.

'Like Nazi swine,' said Clytemnestra.

Suddenly, Wills was shaking. Clytemnestra put her hand on his shoulder, and made small, soothing noises. 'I'm sorry,' he said, when he could speak. 'I was in the Navy. It's a new way of . . . seeing men die.'

She smiled and nodded. She did not understand, though. She had seen her brother hanged for no reason except that he had been in the wrong place at the wrong time. She was not thinking about the way she felt. She was thinking about the enemy, hoping one of them would show himself and she would have a chance to kill him. Kill or be killed, thought Wills, a little wildly: that is the whole of the Law –

Outside, a machine gun started hammering. The bullets whanged off the stones. None of them found its way through the loophole. Clytemnestra was firing now, short bursts again. She must have learned from someone, thought Wills. Short bursts don't overheat, and guns that don't overheat don't jam. Andrea might have taught her –

'Four more,' she said, snapping out the magazine.

It was lives out there, Wills knew. Not weapons training. Seven men bleeding down that hillside. Five left.

The machine gun opened up again. Clytemnestra was still reloading. Wills popped up, saw two more men running along the groove, squeezed the trigger, tumbled the first one like a rabbit, cut the second one's knees from under him. Don't do it, you bloody fools, he was thinking. Christ, why am I saying this? I want to live. But now he could see these men, he wanted them to live too, to stop bursting out of the slot in the cliff and running down that gutterful of flying lead –

He got his wish. They stopped. Down below, the path zigzagged empty. Wills offered Clytemnestra a cigarette. She refused. He lit one himself. He could feel the pressure of the silence: fifty men, waiting in dead ground for the next thing to happen.

Whatever that was going to be.

'They're getting ready,' he said.

Clytemnestra showed her teeth. 'Soon, we kill them all,' she said; Helen, Medea, the whole vengeful regiment of Greek myth rolled into one and carrying a sub-machine-gun.

They waited.

Nothing happened.

They both watched the slot in the cliff, the things lying in the rock gulley that had once been men, but were now mere bundles of rags drowned in a long gutter of shadow. The sun was going down.

'What do we do when it gets dark?' said Wills.

'Leave,' said Clytemnestra. 'There is a way. A way beyond.'

'So what happens if the Germans find it?' said Wills.

'Nobody will find it who was not born on Kynthos,' she said, with a scorn so magnificent that it drove away the anxieties flocking round Wills, and really made him believe that there were things here invisible to normal eyes, things that only Clytemnestra could see.

'Top-hole,' said Wills.

Something that sounded like an express train roared overhead. There was a huge explosion. The floor of the Swallow's Nest shook as if in an earthquake. 'Christos!' said Clytemnestra. 'What was that?'

'Gun,' said Wills. 'Eighty-eight, probably.' Now that there was actually a military problem to engage his mind, he felt oddly better. 'They'll have them on the airfield, for flak. They'll be spotting it in, I expect. Chaps round the corner'll be on the radio.' His mind rolled on. There would be no radio to the airport gun emplacements. Telephone only. So the chaps round the corner would be transmitting to the big aerials on the top of the Acropolis, and someone up there would be calling the fall of shot to the chaps by the gun. Elaborate, but it seemed to work –

Another express train passed overhead and to the right. Another explosion pummelled their ears. Another earthquake shook the floor. Bracketed. Now all the gunners had to do was dot the i.

The sun was well behind the mountains, now. Far away across the valley, an edge of shadow was creeping up the sunlit crags of the Acropolis.

A great fist smashed Wills to the ground. He found himself lying

118

with his head on Clytemnestra's belly, his ears chiming like a belfry, bits of cement and chips of stone raining down on him. Overhead, where the roof should have been, he could see a patch of blue sky veined with little golden wisps of sunset cloud. There was a strong reek of burned stone and high explosive.

'Wait till they hear about that,' said Wills, in a voice that did not quite shake.

'About what?' Clytemnestra's hand was in his hair. She stroked it absent-mindedly, as if he was a dog.

'They're zeroed in,' said Wills. 'Hang on to your hat.'

EIGHT

Thursday 2000–2300

The rain had passed. From the west face of the Acropolis, the sun was a red-hot cannonball falling into a sea of ink. Mallory climbed hard and fast, staying in gullies, where the shadows lay like a dark liquid. He was not interested in the view. He was looking forward to the falling of night. Things were safer in the dark . . .

He paused, comfortable in his foot and handholds, and looked about him. He was on a vast, curved face, a sort of oil drum of rock. He had bypassed a couple of vents and entrances; the concrete crane was a thousand feet below him. The oil drum was the final peak on top of which the aerial array stood. He was tired. Fumbling in his pack he found the Benzedrine, popped out a couple of pills, swallowed them.

High on the curved face of the rock, something flickered across Mallory's vision. A mere speck, crawling from one gulley, across a sun-gilded ridge and into the next gulley. It might have been a bird, a bee, even. But Mallory knew that it was his quarry. Carstairs, climbing very fast, solo. He hoped the man's technique was up to it.

There was only one way to be sure.

Mallory went after him. The Benzedrine spread cool energy through him as he drifted up that cliff, keeping just below the line of shadow the sinking sun drove up the cliff from the mountains at his back, relying on the contrast between the light and the darkness to hide him. Ten minutes later, he was in the same chimney as Carstairs, an easy chimney, with a chockstone seventy feet up, and the summit just beyond the chockstone. He looked up, shielding his eyes against the grit coming down off Carstairs' boots.

If Carstairs wanted the aerials, two would do the job more easily than one.

Mallory whistled.

Carstairs had never done such a long solo. He was an expedition climber, a man used to ropes and sherpas and a glass of cold champagne at base camp. At first, his knees had shaken, and the loneliness had pressed in on him. But he was a good technical climber, so he had taken it easy, taken it slow, driven himself up all those vertical feet, safe as houses, accelerating as he got the hang of it until he was climbing at a pretty fair speed. Oh yes, he had begun to think, I'm good at this. Now, as far as he could see, he was nearly at the top. There would be guards at the top; after all this climbing, fighting . . .

He was up and under the chockstone now. The boulder jammed into the crack blocked his further progress. He would have to go out on to the lip of the crack, work his way round the boulder, then prepare for the . . . well, final assault. He belayed his rope. Then he reached up a hand, straining round the boulder for a crack, probing with the tip of a spike. Found a place. The spike went in. He worked it in further; worked it in by hand. There would be guards up there. The clink of a hammer on a spike would carry. The guard would look over . . .

That was when he heard the whistle.

His heart leaped in his chest. He glanced down, saw the figure in the SS smock. A German. His hands were engaged. He could not get a weapon. He did not know it was Mallory, following him. All he knew was that that figure down there would go for his gun, shoot him out of the sky. He needed to get out of the line of fire. Over the stone. He put his weight on his right hand, swung out of the chimney . . .

He was half-way out when he lost his grip and fell.

He saw the floor of the world turn under his eyes. For a split second he thought, this is it. Then the rope caught him. He swung wildly. Something smote him a wicked bang on the head, and everything went first red, and then black.

Mallory saw the foreshortened figure above reach out, grab, slip, fall, swing. He heard the wet smack of the head on the rock, saw him twitch, then hang limp on the rope.

He waited for the rope to stop swinging, the deadly swing that could work a spike loose. Then he went up, fast, out of the groove in case Carstairs fell, up the right-hand side on holds a fly would have despised. He reached the spike and checked it. It was deep in the crack, holding; a good belay in a difficult spot. Carstairs knew what he was doing, all right.

Once he had checked the belay, Mallory went to the body. There was a good pulse, a lump rising on the back right-hand bulge of the skull under the hair, sticky with brilliantine and stone-grit. The man would live. Mallory hauled the body up into a sitting position, looped the tail of the rope under its armpits and rolling-hitched it on to the standing part. Now Carstairs was sitting on the end of the rope like a drunk on a bar stool, dangling over a thousand feet of nothing. Perfectly safe.

Mallory went through his pockets, found the cigarette case, the knife, the silenced Browning automatic in a shoulder holster; a murderer's weapon. In the waist pouches, he found what he was looking for: two blocks of a substance like putty, wrapped in greasy paper. Plastic explosive. But no time pencils.

Mallory stood wedged in the chimney, sweating. Plastic explosive was funny stuff. You could burn it. You could spread it on bread and eat it, if the worst came to the worst. And of course you could blow a hole in steel with it. But only if you had some fulminate of mercury to start it off, in those little colour-coded pencils, the size of a long cigarette.

Mallory went back to Carstairs' pockets. The gold cigarette case came out. There was lettering on it: 'Darling Billy, from Betty Grable – What a night!' Mallory opened the case one-handed.

Turkish this side. Virginian that. And in the middle, the time pencils.

Mallory shoved the case in his breast pocket and climbed on. The cliff face was curving away from him now, becoming less a precipice, more a slope. He could see the aerial pylons glowing as if red-hot in the last rays of the sun. He stayed low, creeping on his belly until he could see the whole dome of the summit. The pylons stuck out of the naked rock, a hundred feet apart, supporting a web of fine wires. There seemed to be a lot more wire than was required for normal short-wave apparatus. Mallory supposed that if you were shooting things into space, you would need some sort of sophisticated radio to find out what was happening to the machinery. Not that he cared. It was as much part of a weapon as a sight was part of a rifle. His job was to destroy it.

He made a circuit of the mountain top. It had the look of a place untrodden except by maintenance engineers. There was a trap door at the far side, a hefty steel object set in concrete. To the east, the Acropolis continued as a series of lower peaks, a series of plugs like the noses of a clip of giant bullets, a hot wilderness of shale and sun-scorched shrubs, its declivities filled with the violet shadows of evening; a hard place, with a sense of pressure underneath it. Mallory was a New Zealander. He knew the sensation of standing on a volcano; the feeling that the ground under his feet had once been a white-hot liquid, pushing to get out into the air, burn and destroy. No change there . . .

He found himself peering into the deepest of the valleys: more a hole than a valley, really. And in its bottom, instead of the usual dried-up pond with a patch of thorny scrub, was something else. No vegetation: a smooth, dark bowl. It was as if the hole was a deep one, made shallower with carefully-slung camouflage nets.

Mallory filed the information away in his Benzedrine-sharpened mind, and trotted up the dome to the base of the aerials.

There was a faint hum up here, a sense that the ether was troubled by invisible forces. Mallory crouched and wrapped a charge of plastic explosive round the base girders of one of the pylons, making sure it was good and close to the wrist-thick wire that snaked along the rock from the hole by the trap door. Should bring one pylon down, break that cobweb of wires. Mending them would take time – time during which the Acropolis would be dumb and deaf.

He packed on the charges, pushed in two black time pencils, crushed them and pulled out the safety tags. The electrolyte began eating away at the corrosion wire that held back the spring-loaded plunger from the blasting cap. Ten minutes, perhaps less on a warm evening like this. The sun was balanced on the horizon. Time to get clear. He went down the slope until the slope became a cliff. He doubled his rope around a projection of the rock, looped it over his shoulder and up between his legs, and walked backwards out and down, casting left and right for the chimney where he had left Carstairs.

He found it on his left, saw the chockstone coming up, slowed his descent. He would need to get the Englishman on to a ledge, keep him warm, get a briefing from him, leave him to recover –

He stopped next to the chockstone. Somewhere behind him and below, deep in the gulf of shadow that was the marsh and the valley, a gun fired: the peculiar flat crack of an 88. Normally, Mallory would have pitied the poor devil who was on the receiving end of that high-velocity, flat-trajectory packet of death. He would also have asked himself who, on this German-controlled island, was shooting at whom.

But he did not ask himself any of this, because he had other things on his mind.

He had left Carstairs unconscious, trussed into a sitting position, hanging from a piton over a thousand-foot drop.

Now, Carstairs was gone.

Mallory looked down. On the floodlit platform three hundred yards below his feet, people were moving, vehicles crawled, a gang was clustered round the engine. (*Crack*, said the 88 again, down in the valley.) There was none of the ants'-nest activity you would expect if the body of a commando with a Clark Gable moustache had plummeted out of the sky and into their midst.

Mallory thought for a moment.

There was no telling where Carstairs had gone. The only certainty was that in (he looked at his watch) four minutes, anywhere near the aerial site was going to be a very unhealthy place to be.

Hauling down his rope from the summit belay, he made it fast again, wrapped it round himself, and slid rapidly into the thickening shadows below.

For Miller, the shower he took in the entrance lobby of the Acropolis V4 complex was not the most refreshing in living memory. The water was hot, the soap plentiful, the hygiene nothing to complain about by the standards of twenty-four hours on a Sporadic mountainside. It was the company Miller objected to. Mixed at best, he thought gloomily, watching a rat-faced *Wehrmacht* private disrobe, pick his nose, and waddle under the showerhead. At worst –

'Scrub my back?' said a voice behind him. He turned to see a large blond individual with no neck and a crew cut smiling upon him tenderly.

'Can't reach,' said Miller. The blond man pouted, and started to lather his vast acreage with violet-scented soap. He was about the same size as Andrea, something (Miller observed) that Andrea had not been slow to notice. Andrea was out of the shower, had dried himself on someone else's towel, and was sidling towards the locker where the blond man's clothes were hanging.

The blond man finished soaping himself. He had a disappointed air. He put himself under the jet of water and rinsed off the lather. There were SS lightning-flash runes tattooed on his mighty bicep. Miller could see Andrea struggling into a pair of jackboots. It looked as if he would be some time. The outside door opened. A man came in, lanky, about Miller's height, with a brown engineer's coat and a clipboard. The coat would be useful. The clipboard was a blessing from God. Miller said to the blond man, 'You off, then?'

'Not much happening here,' said the blond man, sulkily.

'Ah,' said Miller. 'Well I think this is your lucky day. See that guy just come in?' He pointed at the man in the engineer's coat. 'Very nice guy,' said Miller. 'Likes a bit of fun.'

'Zat so?' said the blond. 'Thanks, friend.'

'Any time,' said Miller, and sashayed rapidly on to dry land.

As he dried himself, he watched the lanky engineer hang up his overall coat with finicky precision, put his trousers on a hanger, arrange on the floor of the locker a pair of brown suede shoes, become indistinct in the steam, and start soaping himself. Miller saw the large figure of the blond SS man start making his way casually towards him. He tweaked open the locker, removed the engineer's clothes and marched over to his own untidy pile. He put on his own undergarments and the engineer's overalls, slung his pack on his back, and bundled his own clothes up inside the scarf so they looked like washing. When he turned he found himself looking at an SS *leutnant* with Andrea's face and a washing bundle of his own.

'Come,' said Andrea. 'Quick.'

Some sort of fight seemed to have broken out in the shower. '*Ja, Herr Leutnant*,' said Miller. They walked out of the door, an SS man and an engineer, the engineer carrying a load of laundry, the SS man talking to him with earnestness and concentration.

'What now?' said Miller.

'Find out the geography. What's on your clipboard?'

There was a list of bolt sizes, with under it some blank paper. Miller shuffled the blank paper to the top. The pair of them walked off, Andrea chin up and arrogant, Miller trailing behind doing his best to look dazed and acquiescent, struggling under the awkward load of clothes and explosives.

'Hey!' said Andrea. 'You!'

A small *Wehrmacht* man had been passing. He said, 'Me?'

'None other,' drawled Andrea. 'Take these clothes. Throw them away.'

'Away?' The man's eyes were dull and stupid.

'A tubercular patient in the village,' said Andrea. 'They are to be burned. Now. Where is the hospital?'

'Third level,' said the soldier.

'Remember this,' said Andrea. 'The faster you go, the more likely you are to live. And don't tell anyone, or they'll give you the treatment.'

'Treatment, *Herr Leutnant*?'

'Paraffin enemas,' said Miller, with a ghastly grin.

The private gulped and scuttled off, holding the bundles as far away from him as possible.

'Now,' said Andrea. 'Let us see to the state of the wiring in this pest hole.'

'Yes indeed,' said Miller, bowing his head over his clipboard and writing diligently. 'After you, *Herr Leutnant*.'

They walked up the steel stairs, slowly, but putting distance between themselves and the crisis that would be developing in the shower. The base level seemed by a thrum in the rock to consist of machinery and shelters. Above were living quarters: they passed rooms in which double-tiered bunks stretched away to impossibly distant vanishing points, a couple of mess rooms wafting the sour smell of boiled sausage and fried onions. A *Wehrmacht* major was marching towards them. 'Two hundred and ten,' said Andrea. Miller scribbled on his clipboard. The *Wehrmacht* major stopped, frowning. Miller felt his stomach hollow out.

'What are you doing?' said the major.

Andrea crashed to attention. '*Heil Hitler*!' he yelled, shooting out his right arm.

'Oh,' said the major, who had a mild, clerkish, non-Nazi sort of face. '*Heil, er, Hitler.*' He gave the army salute. 'What are you doing?' he said again.

'Light bulb audit,' said Andrea, with a face like granite.

'Light bulbs?' said the major, frowning at the *SS* runes on Andrea's smock.

'Those are my orders,' said Andrea.

'*Jawohl*,' said Miller, squinting furiously at the bridge of his nose and trying by willpower to stop the sweat running down his face.

The major sighed. 'So they fly you from the Harz specially to count the light bulbs,' he said. 'Shouldn't you be torturing women or something?'

'*Herr Major?*' Andrea's face was as stiff as a poker.

The major shook his head. There was drink on his breath. 'Oh, hell,' he said. 'I suppose someone's got to do it.'

'*Jawohl, Herr Major,*' shouted Andrea.

'Carry on,' said the major. He walked away, muttering.

They carried on. They went up more stairs to something that seemed from the smell of antiseptic to be a hospital level: though there was no hospital to be seen, merely a horizontal corridor with a steel catwalk suspended over a rough floor of volcanic rock. The hospital was an opening off the tunnel. At the tunnel's end was a concrete doorframe with a lift inside it. On the right of the lift was a small wooden structure, like a sentry box, but bigger.

There were fewer people up here. A couple of men walked past, deep in conversation, wearing engineers' coats like Miller's. They looked at him as they passed. He nodded. They nodded back and walked on without altering their step. At the end they paused by the sentry box, fished out passes of some kind. An *SS* man came out of the sentry box. He looked at the passes, the engineers, back at the passes, the engineers again. Then the engineers signed a book, and moved on to the lift.

'They've got keys,' said Andrea.

'You would almost think,' said Miller, 'that they did not want anyone to get in.'

As he spoke, there was a small, distinct bump that seemed to come not down the tunnel but through the rock itself. Miller felt a twinge of significant happiness. He was always suspicious of the ability of anyone but himself to use explosives. But it seemed likely now that Mallory had managed to make the stuff go off. And knowing Mallory, he would have put it in the right place.

All this he thought very fast indeed. There were klaxons moaning again, and he found that he was walking, walking alongside Andrea – not into the great mass of people seething and swirling behind them on the lower levels, but forward; forward towards the sentry box at the foot of the lift shaft.

Up in the Swallow's Nest, Wills lay with his head on Clytemnestra's belly and dust in his eyes and wondered why he was not dead yet.

He did not lie for long. He got up and grabbed at a Schmeisser and went once again to the loophole. The sun was all the way down now; outside, the world lay in deep shadow, deepest over the bodies crumpled in the gulley of the path. The killing ground was quiet, empty of living things. The last ray of sun lit the summit of the mountain above the Acropolis, where the aerials were.

From that summit there came a small, brilliant flash, followed some time later by the tiny thump of an explosion.

He raised his glasses to his eyes.

A black smear of smoke drifted in the light. The aerials had gone.

Down in the valley, the 88 crashed again. The shell smashed into the cliff, miles above their heads. Wills thought for a moment, then went back to Clytemnestra. He wanted to talk; but he found himself grinning too hard.

'What is it?' she said. She was picking herself up now.

'They were talking to the radio room on the mountain,' said Wills. 'Someone was spotting for the 88. The aerials have gone. They're firing blind.'

Clytemnestra got up and reeled to the loophole. She pushed the hair out of her eyes. Wills gave her a water bottle. She spat out the first mouthful, then drank deeply. 'Fine,' she said.

Wills had stopped grinning. The immediate danger was past. Longer-term, the situation had not changed. 'We're still stuck,' he said. 'All they've got to do is wait there till we starve.'

'Oh, no,' said Clytemnestra. 'Not true, my sad English friend. Now it is dark.'

'Can't eat dark,' said Wills.

She laughed. It was a confident laugh, most encouraging. 'Tonight,' she said, 'we eat not dark, but sheep.'

Concussion, thought Wills. Poor girl, what the hell will I do with her now? 'Sit down,' he said. 'More water.'

'I have sat down enough,' she said. 'Also, I have drunk all a woman needs to drink, who is about to take a journey.'

'Journey?' said Wills, fogged.

'We are leaving,' said Clytemnestra, shouldering her pack. 'Follow me.'

'Top-hole,' said Wills. He strapped on his pack and slung his Schmeisser. Once, before he had started skulking in the mountains with beautiful Furies, he had been the commander of an MTB. That had been in another life, over twenty-four hours ago. He squeezed a burst out of the loophole at the slot in the rocks, the muzzle flash making blue lightnings in the dark. Then he was jogging down the stone stairs into the mould-smelling lower room of the Swallow's Nest, out into the warm night, up the alley that did duty as this hamlet's main street, his back crawling with the expectation of bullets, through a passage so narrow he had to turn sideways, following the faint scuff of Clytemnestra's boots in front. The passage became a path. Thick bushes brushed against his legs, and once something that looked like a wall of trees reared up in front of him and whipped his face, and he knew he had gone through a curtain of some kind. Then they were climbing athwart a slope so steep he could touch the ground with his right hand, while on his left he felt the presence of a dark and mighty gulf. At last, the voice in front said, 'Stop.' He groped his way along until he found an opening, and slid in. There was a scrape and a flare of light as Clytemnestra lit a match. She ran her hand along a ledge, and came down with a stub of candle. They were in a cave, square-sided: another tomb. 'They won't find us here,' she said. 'Not without dogs.'

There had been dogs everywhere. But Wills found himself so tired that he would not have batted an eyelid if the whole pack of the hounds of Hell had been baying at his heels. Tired or not, Wills had been decently educated at public school, and he knew how to treat a lady. 'Are you quite comfortable?' he said.

Clytemnestra yawned, the yawn of a sleepy cat. 'I have killed some Germans,' she said. 'I am free in my country. How should I not be comfortable?'

'You might have a nice armchair,' said Wills. 'Dinner at Ciro's.

Bottle of Romanée-Conti. Nip along to the Mottled Oyster afterwards –'

'Mottled Oyster?' said Clytemnestra.

'Night club,' said Wills. 'Dancing.'

'And you would need a woman,' said Clytemnestra. 'A beautiful
girl.'

There was a short silence. Then Wills said, 'No shortage here,'
and lay back, head on pack, so that even in the candlelight there
would be no chance of her seeing the crimson in his face. When
he glanced furtively across at her, he saw that she was smiling a
small, contented smile. It suddenly struck him that he had been
manoeuvred into saying what he had just said. Hello, he thought.
Hello . . .

But before his thoughts could develop further, he was asleep.

Mallory welcomed the darkness as if it had been a long-lost brother.
What he did not welcome was the fact that he had lost Carstairs.
If he had fallen, that was very bad. If he had not fallen, then
knowing Carstairs that was probably even worse.

He scrutinized the face of the cliff with a pair of small but powerful Zeisses that he had removed from a Panzer general, the Panzer
general being at the time *en route* for a British prison camp having
been plucked from the Cretan mountains by Mallory and his comrades. In the disc of his vision, Mallory saw the corrugations of the
cliffs, ridge and gulley, boulder and boiler plate, precipice and
ledge –

The disc stopped. Mallory balanced on two toes and a hand, and
moved the focus wheel as gently as a biologist focusing on a new
bacillus.

Across the cliff wall two hundred yards to his right, a shadow
was moving – a shadow like a four-legged spider, scuttling and
pausing.

Mallory shifted the disc of the glasses ahead, in the direction
Carstairs was travelling. He saw a ledge; a ledge too sharp and
clearly-defined in construction to be altogether natural. A way
into the mountain. A way through to the *Kormoran* survivor. His
objective.

But as Mallory started once more to watch him move across the
cliff, he frowned. There was something wrong with the way the

man was moving. He watched the right hand, a pale crab against the dark rock. It scuttled, then paused, patting the surface as if the mind guiding it was working in short bursts, going numb between bursts of lucidity. The mind, Mallory realized, of a man who had recently hit his head very hard on the side of a mountain.

Something on the ledge caught Mallory's eye: a sudden flare of light, a face and a helmet-brim suddenly glowing sharp and clear as a soldier sheltered a match in cupped hands to light a cigarette.

Carstairs kept struggling on, as if he had not noticed anything. Perhaps he had not. Mallory would have cursed if there had been time for cursing. Instead, he took his boots off and hung them round his neck. Then he stepped across on to the wall and started climbing, fast and smooth.

He was travelling four feet to Carstairs' three, but Carstairs had a long start. As he climbed, Mallory saw with increasing clarity that to Carstairs, the ledge was simply a way in, and that his brain was not working well enough for him to be cautious. What was going to happen was that he was going to blunder straight into the guard, who would have the advantage of surprise, and a clear head. If Carstairs was captured alive, Dieter Wolf would have him answering questions in about ten minutes. If the sentry killed him, the word would be out that the partisans in the mountains were now inside the Acropolis defences. Presumably, the Germans would have been relying on their security at the gates, rather than running checks inside the Acropolis. But that would change in a moment, and life would get very difficult for anyone who was inside.

Perhaps it already was.

Mallory climbed on, eating up the traverse. Holds were plentiful. Many men might have been made nervous by the six hundred feet of nothingness below. But Mallory had slept on the west face of Mount Cook, in a sleeping bag hung from two pitons over five thousand sheer feet. He climbed carefully, but with nerves untroubled by altitude.

What was preying on his mind was Carstairs, now thirty feet below and twenty yards to the right. Mallory could hear him: the scritch of nails on rock, the harsh gasp of his breathing. And if Mallory could hear him, so could the guard . . .

Carstairs was a biscuit toss from the ledge now. With his dark-adjusted eyes, Mallory watched the dreadful story unfold.

The guard had been smoking his cigarette and humming, gazing, no doubt, upon the beauty of the sea, now a silver-paved floor under the vault of the stars. Then suddenly he stopped, dropped his cigarette, unslung his rifle, moved right to the back of the ledge, and plastered himself against the cliff wall.

Carstairs' boots sounded like a marching army. Mallory knew what was going to happen. There was a low parapet around the ledge. As soon as Carstairs' head and shoulders came above it, the sentry would open fire, secure in the knowledge that Carstairs' hands would be fully occupied with climbing.

Mallory as good as ran across the cliff. He could feel the stone tearing at his stockinged feet, but he paid no attention. As the ledge arrived twelve feet below, he began to move slowly. The cliff was gritty up here, and dislodging the smallest pebble could lead to disaster.

Very slowly, he moved across the face until the sentry's steel helmet was a metallic egg below, the barrel of his rifle trained on the right-hand end of the parapet. If only he had had a silenced Browning, thought Mallory, like the one Carstairs carried, and Miller . . .

But all Mallory had was a knife.

He moved the last six inches to the left. Now he was in position directly above the sentry. He took the knife from its sheath and gripped it in his hand. He looked down at that steel helmet, and for a fraction of a second there flitted across his mind pity for this boy who was just doing his duty, and disgust at himself, washed by the current of war against this man, now the agent of his drowning.

He shifted his foot half an inch to give him a purchase, and prepared to jump. He felt the pebble roll, and stopped, knowing it was too late. He felt it escape, saw it fall, a tiny crumb of stone, heard the small *plink* as it hit the brim of the soldier's helmet. The soldier looked up: a young face, shocked, mouth open. The last thing he saw was Mallory, falling like a thunderbolt, hands down, knife out, felt the crushing weight, the terrible sting of the razor-sharp steel.

Then he saw no more. He struggled for a moment, though: the wild, reflex struggle of an organism already fatally wounded, going through the motions of self-defence, to the limit of its dying strength.

Mallory was not prepared for it. The knife had gone in hard and deep, and he had expected the man to collapse. Instead he found the dagger torn from his hand and the man's tunic rent away from his fingers as the spasming muscles jerked the man out of his grip and away, over the parapet.

And the ledge was an empty slice of rock, with a steel door concreted into the cliff at its back.

'Carstairs,' said Mallory, low-voiced.

Carstairs hauled himself over the parapet. He sat down, and let his head hang, and said, 'What the hell happened?'

'You tried to commit suicide,' said Mallory, cold. 'You nearly succeeded.'

'Wha?' said Carstairs, uncomprehending. 'Oh, I see. Joke.' He fumbled in his breast pocket. 'Cigarette? Virginian this side, Turkish tha – Oh, God. Lost me case.'

'Here,' said Mallory, and gave it to him. 'No smoking.'

'Oh, I say,' said Carstairs, frowning. His brain was not working. 'Sentry's gone. Relax, eh? Nobody knows we're here.'

Mallory shook his head. He walked over to the steel door, and shoved it open. 'They will,' he said. 'They will.'

Private Otto Schultz weighed eighteen stone, and this evening every single ounce of him was completely fed up. Some fool had crashed a locomotive, and Schultz had spent a miserably sweaty hour with winches and levers and NCOs screaming at him. Then he had gone for his dinner, and half-way through his fourth sausage all the aerials (someone had said it was the aerials, anyway) had been bombed or shot up, nobody knew which, so they had all had to go and sit in the shelters. And then, before he had had time to finish his food, he had been told to report for duty in the guardhouse with two of those *Sonderkommando* thugs. They had spent the last half-hour reminiscing about some place called Treblinka, about which Schultz had no desire to hear. Then one of them, Putzi he seemed to be called, had beaten Schultz at chess. Schultz was pretty sure Putzi had cheated, but that was not the sort of thing you accused a *Sonderkommando* man of, if you wanted to keep your head on your shoulders. Putzi had high cheekbones and hard blue eyes and a smile that never faltered. But sitting there across the table from Schultz, you could see he was just a piece of vicious scum, like all the rest of them. Schultz had been a mathematics teacher, and he did not enjoy being trounced at chess by thugs.

'Your move,' said Putzi, as if Schultz did not already know. Schultz moved. Putzi's grin became more scornful. He moved his bishop. 'Checkmate, fatso.'

'Rubbish,' said Schultz. But Putzi was right. He opened his mouth to concede.

But he never said it.

There was a crash like a bomb going off. Something fell on to Putzi from the sky, and he vanished, the table with him. Splinters of wood flew around the guardhouse. Schultz leaped to his feet and hit the red general alarm button.

Sigmund, the other *Sonderkommando* man, was bending over the mess on the floor. 'Dead,' he said.

Schultz gave the subject ponderous but methodical thought, and arrived at an understanding. A human body, by its uniform a member of the *Wehrmacht*, had fallen through the asbestos roof of the guardhouse with enough force not only to kill Putzi but to drive his corpse some distance into the floorboards. This implied that he had fallen from a considerable height – one of the lookouts on the cliff face above, no doubt. A tragic accident. Schultz wagged his head on its great rolls of neck.

Then Sigmund rolled the sentry's jellified body off the crushed corpse of Putzi. It was at that point that Schultz sat down heavily, and started to shake.

For there was no part of Schultz's imagination that could explain what kind of accident it was that had sent a *Wehrmacht* private plummeting out of the heavens with a British Special Forces-issue dagger driven to the hilt in its right eye.

When the charges on the aerials went off and the air-raid klaxon began to sound, Miller and Andrea had a short discussion. Men were still strolling in the corridor, unmoved by the moaning of the alarm. Presumably, they were far enough into the mountain to be safe from bombs. So they walked briskly down the steel staging to the sentry box in front of the elevator, and came to attention in front of the guardhouse. There was a *Feldwebel* and a private behind an armoured-glass window, wearing camouflage uniforms. They looked at Andrea. The *Feldwebel*'s eyes flicked from his dark Mediterranean features to his badges of rank. Miller saw the man start to frown, then deliberately smooth his face out. There was a fixed number of huge *SS Leutnant*s on Kynthos. It looked as if this might be a *Feldwebel* with eyes and a memory. Look out, he thought: trouble.

Andrea said, 'I want to look at your records.'

The sergeant said, 'Records, *Herr Leutnant*?'

'The pass records. There may have been a breach of security.'

The sergeant stiffened. 'I can assure the *Herr Leutnant* that –'

'Let us in.'

'The *Herr Leutnant* will excuse me,' said the sergeant. His hand went for the telephone.

Miller started to cough. He coughed very badly, doubling up, out of the vision of the men in the guard hut. He had his knife out, and as he doubled up he hooked the blade under a cable that ran out of the hut and away down the tunnel, and cut.

Inside the hut, the sergeant jiggled the cradle furiously.

'Let me in,' said Andrea, low and dangerous.

The sergeant was looking ruffled now. 'But I do not . . . that is, I am not acquainted with the *Herr Leutnant*'s face.'

'This is of no interest to me,' said Andrea. 'You will however remember the *Hauptmann* Wolf, with whom you will renew your acquaintance very speedily unless you open up as instructed, immediately.'

At the mention of Wolf's name, the sergeant's face turned a nasty grey, and his memory apparently lost its influence. 'Open the door,' he said to the private. The door opened. Andrea walked in. 'The books,' he said.

The sergeant handed over a large ledger. Andrea put it on the desk, leafed through the pages. 'Excuse me,' said the sergeant. 'The telephone is *kaput*. I must arrange for repairs. Schmidt –' he looked at the private '– fetch a maintenance crew.'

Andrea slammed the book. 'All seems to be in order,' he said. 'But Schmidt, stay here. There is a general alert. Maximum vigilance. Now, give me the key.'

The sergeant snapped to attention. '*Herr Leutnant*?'

'The key,' said Andrea. 'To the lift.'

'The *Herr Leutnant*'s pass?'

Andrea said, patiently, 'My pass is being renewed. Now my duty takes me into that lift.'

The sergeant's face turned to stone. 'I am sorry,' he said. 'No pass, you cannot. It is not permitted.'

'I am sorry too,' said Andrea, in a low, dangerous rumble. 'And you will be sorrier, I promise you.'

The sergeant stared straight ahead of him, the impassive stare of the German NCO who knows he is obeying orders, that the chain of command is complete, that his position is unassailable and his duty done.

Two engineers stopped at the window. 'Carry on,' said Andrea. The engineers signed their names and the time in the book. 'You will please report this telephone out of order,' said Andrea to the engineers. The private escorted them to the lift door. One of them opened it with his key, pulled back the inner door, slid the outer door into place. The lift machinery hummed.

'Very good,' said Andrea. 'You have made a note, *Herr Doktor* Muller?'

'I shall get my notebook,' said Miller. 'One moment.' He crouched, opened the pack he had been carrying. The sergeant moved suddenly, and looked over the lid and inside. His eyes widened and his jaw dropped, and he raised the Schmeisser in his hands.

But Miller had a hand of his own, and in it was a Browning automatic with a long cylindrical snout. The snout coughed flame. The wall behind the *Feldwebel* turned red. He slammed backwards into the wall, eyes blank, a new eye in the middle of his forehead. The private ran out of the shed and started to run, unlimbering his own Schmeisser as he went. Miller went after him. The man turned. Miller raised the Browning two-handed. The private went down.

'Hide the bodies,' said Andrea, dragging the *Feldwebel* out of the shed and round to the back.

Miller nodded. He looked whitish in the face, and his hands were shaking. As he hauled the private back to the shed, the man's heels clattered on the grating. Andrea bent, and retrieved a key from the ring on the man's belt.

'Signature,' said Andrea, pushing the book at Miller. Both men signed the register. 'Key,' said Miller.

Once you had turned the key in the lock, it was a lift like any other lift. The motor hummed. Outside the concertina inner door the wall went by, a rough-hewn shaft that seemed to go on for ever, with iron step-rungs inset. It was an unpleasant sensation, Miller found, standing in this lattice-sided can with rock all around you, two bodies by the downstairs exit, God knew what waiting upstairs –

The lift stopped.

It did not stop at a floor. It stopped between floors. There was nothing to see except the walls, and the steps, and Andrea. 'I am afraid,' said Andrea, 'that someone has found some bodies.'

'The steps,' said Miller. He hated this elevator. He wanted out as fast as possible.

'They will be expecting that,' said Andrea. 'We will stay here, my friend. More or less.'

Well, thought Miller, what can you do, Andrea being a colonel and all, God damn it.

'Up,' said Andrea, and pointed to the escape hatch in the roof.

Oh, no, thought Miller. Not again. Not standing around waiting to be torn apart by machinery again. Nor waiting for a wire rope to break and the plummeting to start –

But by this time his head and shoulders were already through the trap door, and Andrea was shoving hard from below. Miller found himself standing in darkness on top of the lift, next to an oily cable. Andrea shoved up the pack, then came up himself, and sat on the trap door.

There was a jerk. The lift started upwards. It went up a long way. Miller could hear the engine. He started to sweat. To distract himself he examined as much of the machinery as he could. 'This is a piece of cheap Kraut rubbish,' he said, 'not an Otis.'

'What?'

'Nothing,' said Miller, rummaging in the pack.

Then Andrea said, 'Quiet.'

They froze. The sound of the machinery was very close above. Out of the corner of his eye, Miller could see a streak of light gleaming on the flange of a huge wheel spinning in the obscurity above. The streak of light from the upper door.

The lift rose past the streak, and stopped. The machinery was close overhead; close enough to touch. Many boots crashed into the car. 'The ceiling,' said a German voice. There was a grunting, as if someone was trying to push. Andrea stood on the door, braced against the axle of the winding drum above his head. 'Help me,' said the voice below.

Someone presumably helped him. Tall men, they must be, and big. Sweat rolled down Andrea's face, and the veins in his neck stood out like hawsers. 'Some fool's welded it shut,' said a voice from below. 'Some bloody Greek.'

Which was not, thought Miller, as he worked at what was in his hand, so far off the mark.

'No good,' said a voice with the bark of authority in it. 'They must be on the steps down below.'

Under Miller's feet, the lift lurched, and started downwards. Miller and Andrea just had time to grab the axle overhead. It was turning, the axle, but it was greasy. The lift dropped away below, leaving a shaft like a well. Andrea heaved himself over to the wall and hung on to the first of the steps. Miller reached a hand towards Andrea. The big Greek caught him just as his fingers let go. Miller slammed into the ladder, grabbing the cold metal. 'Out,' he said.

'There'll be a guard –'

'Out. There's no safety lock.'

Andrea heard real urgency in his voice. He did not know what Miller was talking about. But he had worked with Miller long enough to trust his instincts.

Miller was right. The door slid open. Andrea and Miller stepped on to the threshold, blinking in the sudden light.

The eight *Wehrmacht* soldiers outside raised their Schmeissers to belly height. '*Hände hoch*,' said the officer in charge. '*Ausweis, bitte*.'

'For Christ's sake,' said Miller, in his excellent German. 'It's one or the other.'

'*Hände hoch*,' said the officer. He had an efficient look that Miller disliked intensely. The lift was in a sort of lobby, shielded by concrete walls from whatever took place beyond. Andrea and Miller separated, standing one on either side of the door. The officer started rummaging in Miller's pockets. It was evident to Miller, with four Schmeissers trained upon him, that he and Andrea were in big trouble. But then again, the only thing that really amazed him was that they had got this far.

Andrea had a look of great stupidity on his face. He rolled his eyes towards the empty door of the lift shaft, and gave Miller a wink cunningly judged to be both conspiratorial and obvious. 'You bloody idiot,' said Miller, with venom. 'They've had it now.'

The German officer frowned. He said, 'Cover me,' to his men. Four of them went to the lift door, and peered down the shaft.

'Nobody,' said the officer.

Miller glanced at his watch. 'Now, boys!' he said.

From the lift shaft there came the sound of a large, hollow boom, followed by a twang of breaking cable, screams, and a crash. The men at the door were blown backwards by a blast of hot gas. The men covering Andrea and Miller clapped their hands to their scalded eyes. One of them fell into Andrea, who heaved him down the shaft.

Miller felt quietly proud. It was not everyone, he considered, who would, under the kind of pressure he and Andrea had suffered on the lift roof, have noticed that it was a device with neither a safety wire nor a shaft brake. Nor would it have been just anybody who would have taken the time to wrap half a pound of plastique round the cable, with a five-minute time pencil.

Miller flattered himself that it had all gone rather well.

But he did not waste time feeling smug. He pulled a fire extinguisher out of its clips, smashed the button in, and started spraying the men staggering about by the lift gate. '*Hilfe!*' he yelled. '*Feuer!*'

When the first reinforcements came round the corner, they found a huge SS man and a lanky engineer in a cloud of evil-smelling smoke, dousing the fuming lift shaft and half-a-dozen smouldering soldiers with foam. The reinforcements started yelling as only German reinforcements can yell. More fire extinguishers started going off. And nobody paid any attention when the SS man hefted his pack and vanished into the workshops, accompanied by the engineer.

NINE

Thursday 2300–Friday 0300

Herr Doktor Doktor Professor Gunther Helm was a neat man. His brown overall was sharply pressed, his black shoes polished to a mirror-like sheen, and his dark, narrow moustache trimmed with mathematical exactness below his long, mobile nose. Helm was a specialist in inertial guidance systems. It had been bad enough to be removed from his comfortably ancient rooms above the river at Heidelberg University to a shed on a Baltic sand-flat at Peenemunde. This place, this hideous warren of black rock and bare cable and improvised factory space, was unpleasant. Worse, it was untidy.

Boots were crashing in the tunnel ahead. They belonged (Helm saw, as they rounded the corner) to two SS men. To two of the untidiest SS men he had ever seen. For one thing, neither of them seemed to have shaved for at least twenty-four hours. For another they were filthy dirty, smeared with white clay and blood, and unless he was gravely mistaken, wearing non-regulation boots. In addition, one of them had a moustache not unlike his own, but (*Herr Doktor Doktor Professor* Helm was compelled in all frankness to admit) considerably blonder and more lustrous. They had a wild look, as if they had been outdoors. They took up more room than seemed necessary. Frankly, Helm found them intimidating.

'Where's the hospital?' said the one without the moustache.

'The hospital,' said Helm, flustered. 'You proceed down this corridor. You will see three fire extinguishers on the wall, then a steel staircase. Ignore this. Proceed until you see a sign saying *Ausgang* – no, I am wrong; *Eintritt*, it says –'

'What level?' said the SS man, who was Mallory.

Helm was notoriously a hard man to stop, but there was enough violence in the voice to stop him. 'Third level,' said Helm, and found himself flung back against the wall by the breeze of their passing. Breathing heavily, he returned to his desk, picked up his slide rule, and re-entered the calm, ordered world of numbers. Somewhere at the periphery of his attention, he heard the klaxons going again. The klaxons were always going in the factory. It was part of the general untidiness. Since there was no way of controlling it, it was in the view of *Herr Doktor Doktor Professor* Helm best·ignored.

He therefore ignored it.

The klaxons started as Mallory and Carstairs clattered down a steep set of spiral stairs. There was the distant crash of steel doors slamming, the bang of running feet. A squad of men ran up the stairs. Mallory braced himself. The squad ran past. Mallory started running again, full-pelt, down the endless latticed-steel corkscrew of the stairs. Endless stairs, in a vertical tube through the solid rock –

Carstairs was right behind Mallory now. Uniform or no uniform, thought Mallory, it was a nasty naked feeling to be inside this hollow mountain, knowing that one look at your papers –

Something hit him in the small of the back. A boot, he had time to think: whose boot?

Then Mallory was down, off balance, diving forwards, his shoulder driving into the sharp steel edge of the step, steel helmet (thank God for the helmet) ringing like a gong against the stair treads. Mallory bunched up and rolled, the way he had been taught to roll in his parachute training, tucking in his hands, protecting his fingers and his elbows and knees from the hammer of acute-edged metal. He went down twenty steps before he hit the wall. He lay there, ears ringing, winded. Carstairs ran past. Carstairs pushed me, he realized. Carstairs wanted time on his own. What for? To find the survivor of the shipwreck. Mallory remembered the grenade, pin out, above the ambulance in the gorge. Not to debrief the survivor. To do something more final than that . . .

A couple of *Wehrmacht* privates rattled down the stairs. One of them aimed a kick at his *SS* ribs. It hurt. But Mallory grinned. Dissension in the enemy camp was truly a marvellous thing.

Dissension in his own was a different matter. He spat blood, and hurried stiffly down the steps. Three minutes later, he came to a door. On the rock above the door was stencilled a broad black number three. Mallory went through it.

He was at the opposite end of the long, steel-floored corridor from the place where Andrea and Miller had taken the lift. 'Papers!' screamed a voice. It belonged to a *Wehrmacht Leutnant*, white in the face and greasy with sweat. Behind him, at the far end of the corridor where the lift doors had once stood, there was a throng of men, noise and smoke and shouting.

'Papers!' screamed the *Leutnant*, again.

Mallory gazed upon the man with freezing eyes. 'There are wounded men down there,' he said. 'They need you.' Then he walked straight through him. The *Leutnant* reeled back into the wall. His hand went to his holster flap. Mallory allowed his own hand to stray to the grip of his Schmeisser. The *Wehrmacht* officer thought better of his move, and hurried towards the lift door. Mallory walked through the doorway with the red cross above it. An orderly looked up from a desk. 'The man from the shipwreck,' said Mallory.

The orderly looked nervous. There had been too many alarm bells, and he really hated these *SS*. 'Down there,' he said, pointing down the corridor. 'Your friend's already with him.'

'When I want your conversation I'll ask for it,' said Mallory, to pour oil on the flames. Then he crashed off down the corridor.

The door the orderly had indicated was closed. Mallory twisted the handle. It was locked. It was a hospital door, not a military door; a flimsy thing of cheap deal. Mallory hit it with his boot, hard, next to the handle. The orderly had been watching him. When he caught his eye he quickly looked away. The door held. Mallory knew he was on the edge. Never mind how much trouble there was between *Wehrmacht* and *SS* and boffins, there came a time when he would no longer get away with disobeying orders and wrecking government property. But Carstairs was behind that door, with a man Mallory was interested in, and who would not be alive for long, unless –

His boot hit the door again. This time it burst open with a splintering crash.

It was a small, green room, with a smell of cleanliness, a bed and a chair. There were two men on the bed: one lying down, legs thrashing, the other bent over him. The bending man was Carstairs. The reason for his bending was that he had a pillow in his hands, a pillow he was pressing over the face of whoever it was that was lying on the bed. The survivor of the *Kormoran*, at a rough guess.

Mallory could kill, all right. But he was a soldier, not an assassin. There was a difference between killing and murder.

He said, 'Stop that.'

Carstairs did not answer. His face was set and ugly, ridged with muscle, holding the pillow down. Mallory lifted his Schmeisser. 'Stop it now,' he said.

Carstairs raised one hand to swat the barrel aside. 'No noise,' he said. 'Quiet, you idiot.' The assumption that he would not use the weapon fed Mallory's irritation. He jabbed Carstairs on the arm with the barrel. The flapping of the supine figure's legs was weakening. 'All right,' said Carstairs, face twisted with effort. 'So fire.'

Mallory did not fire. Instead, he kicked Carstairs very hard on the bundle of nerves inside his right knee. It was a kick that would hurt like hell, but do no permanent damage.

It worked.

Carstairs crashed to the ground, grabbing for his dagger. Mallory stamped on his hand and let him look down the black tube of the machine pistol's muzzle.

The man on the bed said, 'Jesoos.'

'Shut up!' hissed Carstairs.

'Hold your tongue,' said Mallory.

The man on the bed was small and stout, with curly black hair and a thick black moustache and a very bad colour. 'Don' kill me,' he said. 'Don' kill me. For why you want to kill me?'

Mallory looked at Carstairs, then at the black-haired man. He said, in English, 'What happened to you?'

The small man's eyes narrowed. He said, in German, 'Why are you speaking English?'

Mallory lay wearily back in the chair. Carstairs was spluttering like an unexploded bomb on the floor. 'Because I'm English,' he said. 'Who are you?'

'Shut your bloody mouth,' said Carstairs, frantic. 'I forbid you to speak.'

'So,' said the short man, indignation getting the better of

suspicion. 'I answer your damned question, and you tries to suffocate me. And now there is another German *SS* who talk English and want to know. Is it for this that I swim, I paddle, I bring –'

'Start at the beginning,' said Carstairs, wearily. 'Go on.'

'How do I know who you are?' said the Greek.

Mallory offered the man a cigarette, lit one himself, closing his mind to the idea that outside that door was bandit country, crawling with people who would kill him as quick as blow their noses. Carstairs had had orders from Admiral Dixon to assassinate this man. Mallory had countermanded them. There would be trouble in England, too. Wearily, he took off his helmet.

The Greek made a sound half-way between a gasp and a squeak. 'Mallory!' he said. 'Is no possible.'

Mallory looked at him, one eyebrow up.

'Mount Cook,' said the Greek. 'My cousin Latsis he went to New Zealand for the farm. But the farm no work out good so he get work with expedition, because he know how make food in fire far from roof. He cook with you. He send me photograph, newspaper story. You and Latsis. You remember? My cousin Latsis. Sure you remember. Yes, yes, you remember.'

Mallory remembered, all right. He remembered the Mount Cook expedition, the first and last major expedition he had led in the Southern Alps, after his lone climbs. He remembered far too many people, far too much organization: the green New Zealand sky over the white prisms of the mountains, the crisp new air, the sound of too many voices; the taste of burned beans. He remembered a charming Greek with a huge nose, a ready smile, and absolutely no talent in the kitchen.

'Big nose,' said Mallory.

If there had been wine in the little hospital room, someone would have opened it. As it was, the Greek seized Mallory's right hand in both of his and shook it furiously. 'I am Spiro,' he said. 'And I must tell you what I told your . . . this man.' Here he narrowly failed to spit on Carstairs. 'I have got the machine.'

'The machine?'

Carstairs said, 'Now look here –'

'The seven-rotor Enigma,' said Spiro. 'Of course.'

'What is the seven-rotor Enigma?' said Mallory.

'Nothing,' said Carstairs. 'Spiro, I should warn you –'

'Shut the mouth,' said Spiro. 'I am tired. So bloody tired you would not believe. Always I keeps my mouth shut –'

'A little longer,' said Mallory. 'First, we must get you out of here.'

'So let's get out,' said Spiro. 'And then I show you machine.'

'Show us?' said Carstairs. 'You don't really mean you've got it?'

'Yes,' said Spiro. 'What did you think?'

Carstairs' face had gone a nasty shade of grey. 'They told me you knew about it,' he said. 'That you had been sent to steal it. But that there was no hope, what with the shipwreck. I was to . . . silence you before you were tortured. If I'd known . . .'

'Of courses,' said Spiro, nastily. 'First murder, then asking questions. Fool.'

Carstairs gave him a sickly smile. 'Awfully sorry,' he said, 'but I'm sure you understand, what? Now, then. This is marvellous. Exactly where is it?'

Spiro turned upon him a puffed and hostile gaze. 'I tell your friend when we are out,' he said. 'Just for now, it is in a safe place. Okay?'

'Where?'

'Out first,' said Spiro. 'Where later.'

Miller found the workshops most impressive. In the lava bubbles of the cold volcano, the Germans had built a fair-sized factory. There were machine shops and an assembly line staffed by brown-coated engineers, with Greek slave labourers in blue boiler suits wheeling racks of parts and tools. The air was full of the limey reek of wet concrete. Someone somewhere was building something. Miller found an abandoned trolley and loaded in the explosives pack. They trundled it along the lines of benches, through tunnels into new caverns, with curved alloy castings and cylindrical motors of huge complexity with nozzles and no driveshafts, fuel and lubricant tanks, steel doors marked with skull-and-crossbones stencils, until at the end they came to a series of concrete baffles built out across the passage. Standing in front of the baffles was an SS man with a Schmeisser. Above his head, a large sign said: *Eingang Verboten*.

'Looks like it,' said Miller. 'Plan?'

Andrea did not answer. But Miller saw from the corner of his eye the huge Greek's right hand go to the place on his belt occupied by his knife. And not before time: from behind, there was the sound of shouting and running feet. The confusion by the lift seemed to have sorted itself out.

Somewhere ahead, a field telephone rang. The SS man picked up the receiver and gave what must have been a password. Then his eyes bulged out of their sockets and his mouth opened and no sound came out, because Andrea had walked straight up to him and slammed his knife between his fourth and fifth ribs and into his heart, and as he slid to the ground had plucked the telephone from the dead fingers. '*Bitte*?' said Andrea.

'Intruders,' said the voice. 'Two men.' The voice gave a fair description of Andrea and Miller. 'Shoot on sight,' it said. 'Tell *Hauptmann* Weiss.'

'*Zu Befehl*,' said Andrea. He put the telephone down and tore the wire out of the junction box.

Miller had dragged the corpse out of sight. They walked round the baffles, and found themselves confronted by a huge steel door. Andrea rapped on it with his gun-butt. '*Hauptmann* Weiss!' he said.

A slider on the door went back. 'Who wants him?'

'Wolf. Immediately.'

There was the sound of grumbling. A wicket opened in the steel door. A man in SS uniform started through. The silenced Browning jumped in Miller's hand. The SS man fell back. The two men ran in, and shut the door behind them. Two SS privates were hauling their Schmeissers into firing position. Miller shot both of them.

'Christos,' said Andrea.

It was the first time Miller had ever heard him blaspheme. But he could see why.

They were on the concrete floor of an enormous yard. There were very few people. In the middle of the area, a hundred yards away, stood a cylindrical object painted in a black and white checkerboard pattern that gave it the look of an obscene toy made for the children of giants.

But it was not a toy. It was a rocket – a rocket so much bigger than any other rocket Andrea or Miller had ever seen that it removed the breath from their lungs.

It was standing in a framework of gantries. High above, a roof of camouflage netting billowed gently in the night breeze. From connection points on its bulging flanks, hoses snaked away to doors behind blast-deflection baffles in the sides of the . . . hole, was what it was, thought Miller; not a crater, but a hole left by the parting of the ways of three magma streams in three different directions.

'Most impressive,' he said.

Andrea just shook his head.

Behind them, someone was hammering on the steel door.

Miller rubbed his hands. They had now entered his area of special expertise. The gentle art of destruction, of which Miller was one of the world's great exponents.

'Now listen here,' said Corporal Miller to Colonel Andrea, and opened the big wooden pack. Andrea listened. After a couple of minutes, he stowed four packages in his haversack, walked across the concrete to the gantry. Whistling, he trotted up the steps until he came to the level just below what he presumed was the business end. Here he paused, and moulded the putty-like explosive to the surface, leaving a thickness in the middle. Into the thickness he pushed an eight-hour time cartridge, crushed the tube, and withdrew the tag.

When he turned, a scientist was staring at him. 'Monitoring,' said Andrea. 'Telemetry.'

The man pointed at the charge, mouthing. 'Oh, all right,' said Andrea, and kicked the man off the platform and on to the concrete. Then he started down.

Miller was nowhere to be seen.

He had strolled across to the baffles in front of the place where the pipes came out of the wall. *Brennstoff*, said stencilled letters. Fuel. He unlatched the door. There were no guards: nobody except another engineer in a brown coat, who simply nodded at him as he let himself into the chamber.

It was a squared-off cave, lit with harsh fluorescent lights. On the concrete floor, rank after rank of huge steel tanks lay like sleeping pigs. Half of them were thick-walled, pressurized: liquid oxygen. The rest were of riveted steel. Miller felt a momentary gloom at the thought of all that good alcohol going to waste. Then he sighed, took a little toolkit out of his pocket, and followed the hoses to their starting point. There were two tanks, one of oxygen, one of alcohol, the one next to the other. As he had hoped, their contents were indicated by ordinary *Luftwaffe*-pattern flow gauges downstream of the outlet valve. Humming, Miller pulled a tub of grease from the pocket of his overall. He unscrewed the cover of the valve, scooped some of the tub's contents out with a wooden spatula, and greased the innards heavily.

'*Wer da?*' said a voice at his shoulder.

Miller turned to see an *SS* man pointing a machine pistol at him. 'Maintenance,' he said.

'*Vas?*'

Miller shoved the grease under his nose. 'Slippery stuff, cretin,' he said. 'Feel.'

But the soldier, thinking perhaps about the cleanliness of his uniform, said, '*Nein,*' and pushed the tub away.

'Suit yourself,' said Miller, under whose arms the sweat was falling like rain. 'Only twenty more to do.'

The soldier grunted. The rifle muzzle dropped. 'Get on with it, then,' he said.

'So what's all the fuss about?' said Miller.

'Someone's stolen some uniforms in the showers,' said the *SS* man. 'So they're all going crazy. Now the telephones are dead.' He yawned. 'So they panic, these *Wehrmacht* bastards. Some of us have got work to do. No time to panic.'

Miller grunted, took himself along to the next tank, unscrewed the gauge cover, smeared on the paste from his tub: his own patent paste, compounded of carborundum powder, magnesium, iron oxide and powdered aluminium. When the gauges started to spin, the carborundum would heat up. When it reached the right temperature, the magnesium would ignite and start the aluminium powder reacting with the iron oxide: an exothermic reaction, they called it, meaning that it got hot as hell, hot enough to melt iron and burn concrete. Certainly enough heat to ignite alcohol. And if by any chance an oxygen tank should rupture, well, the structural integrity of the entire V4 plant would be severely compromised. If not destroyed.

Personally, Miller was betting on destruction.

He did a couple more valves, for luck. Then he shoved his hands into his pockets and strolled, whistling, out of the fuel store.

Andrea was standing by the door, Schmeisser at the ready, as if on guard. 'Hey!' said Miller. 'You!'

Andrea snapped to attention.

'Follow me!' Miller started up the wall of the crater. He marched quickly, though his leg muscles were suddenly cracking with weariness, the blood pounding in his skull and his breath rasping in his throat. They scrambled from rock to rock, pushed under the edge of the roof of tarpaulins and camouflage nets. Behind them, the crater glowed under its blue floodlights. They began to scramble over the rocks towards the rendezvous.

Outside the hospital, the corridor was an ants' nest. Nobody paid any attention to two SS men with a stretcher. Mallory and Carstairs carried Spiro down two flights of steel stairs. The shift was changing. Greek workers were shuffling down a corridor Mallory had not previously visited. There were few light bulbs, and a smell of cheap rice cooking, and latrines badly cleaned. A hundred yards later they rounded a corner and came to a wire-mesh fence with a gate, beside which stood a bored-looking SS man. 'Throw it into the sea,' said the sentry, when he saw the stretcher.

'First, it has work to do,' said Mallory. The sentry laughed. 'We'll be a while.'

'Long as you like,' said the sentry, heaving the gate open. 'Don't touch the women, though. They'll claw it off.'

Mallory could feel Spiro's shivering transmitted along the handles of the stretcher. He walked on.

The camp was no more nor less than the old village of the Acropolis, cordoned off from the rest of the island by a wire fence, so the precipices and fortifications that had once kept out the Turk now served to hold prisoner the Greek. It was a depressed, ruinous place, harshly lit by the floodlights set in the cliff face above. They carried the stretcher into the shadows of Athenai Street, and set it down.

Mallory lit a cigarette, drawing the harsh smoke into his lungs. In the blue-white streets, black-overalled figures came and went. There was no curiosity. A village without curiosity, thought Mallory, is a village that is dead: and for a moment he felt a pure, clear disgust for the men who had killed it.

Then he said, 'This machine.'

'Po!' said Spiro. 'Po, this machina!' The words began to pour out of him in a torrent.

'Steady,' said Mallory.

149

'Okay,' he said. 'Okay. Only when they have you in this place, you keep your eyes shut one, two days, breathe slow, they say *Ach Gott* he sleeps still, they stick in you pins and needles, you do not twitching, wait for you do not know what, then when you think, well, now I will have to be awake but when I awake I will be fear and tell them all about everythings and they will kill me real slows real slows, the hell with it I will rather die than sleep no more, then sudden you get the angels down flap flap.' Here he cast himself upon Carstairs and began to cover his face with wet kisses.

'Ugh,' said Carstairs.

Mallory watched with some enjoyment as Carstairs disentangled himself. 'So what's the story?' he said.

'The machina –'

'From the beginning.'

'Yais,' said Spiro. 'Give me cigarette.'

'Turkish this side, Virginian that,' said Carstairs automatically, proffering his case.

'I spit on your Turkish,' said Spiro.

'The story,' said Mallory.

'Okay, okay. So I am in Trieste. In Trieste I am cook in café by docks, everything nice, when they tell me, Spiro, go on ship.'

'Who tells you?'

'SIS. Peoples in London. Spying peoples. They say Spiro, the King of Britains, big friend of the Kings of Greece, he need you stop listening to German mens talking in cafés, go to find cooking mans on *Kormoran*, arrange bad things. Then get on *Kormoran* and find out what goings on. So I find cooking man on *Kormoran* and give him accidents with open window and broken leg, and look at Spiro then, cook on this lousy God damned pig bastard ship *Kormoran* God rest his poor soul if his mother could see him now –'

'The story,' said Mallory.

'The story, hokay. So I am working in the café with SIS and this guy, my contact, he say, get on this pig bastard ship *Kormoran*. So I go down to the port and it is a mess, you know, they are bombing him, and all the way down the back end there is this ship, this dirty little ship, and they say sure, the cook's mate has fell down and broked his leg so we needs a cook's mate and Spiro we know you are not a cook – normally,' said Spiro, 'I working as a thief, but the war, you know. So come aboard, they say. Well

150

me I say I must go and kiss my girl goodbye, nice girl, very big moustache, but they say, no, come aboard now, so there I go, and they put me on that ship, slam door. Very strange ship. Outside dirty filthy like a latrine. Inside more tidy, clean, like German ship. And captain and officers stand-to-attention *Heil Hitler* sort of mens, must have all things regular and particular. Then big crateses arrives on an army sort of train, and more, gas bottles, I don't know. Spiro had thinked, oh ho, stupid SIS peoples, false alarm. But then Spiro thinked, oh shits, if it ain't a false alarm what in hells kind of alarm is this? But I carries on washing up, bringing bridge coffees, all that. Then,' said Spiro, his vast black pupils swimming with sincerity, 'come the miracles.' He drew breath. He was panting. He was also, Mallory realized, very frightened.

'It was morning,' he said. 'I took coffee to bridge. Ten fifty-five hours precisely. *Kapitän* Helmholz insist, exactly that time, no seconds before, no seconds after. Stupid bastards, dead now. So I get off bridge fast. And I am a little way down the stairs when bam! Something hit ship, then bam! Something else, and I can tell that all this is turning higgledy turvy and it is hot like hell and peoples screamings. So then I see the man go out of the radio rooms and up to the bridge, then one more bang and more broken glasses and he roll down stairses, head gone. Well I have seen before, bringing coffees to Sparks, that code machina, this seven-rotor Enigma, is in radio room, and SIS always pay good money for code machina. So I go quick double quick into the radio rooms and catches up the machina in his cases and jumps overboard double quick, big wind, everything terrible bright, and the case is a heavy thing and she wants to sink and it try to kill me but I do not let him. Well by the mercy of God the Creator the Redeemer may His name be blessed for ever and ever amen and also His holy saints' – here he caught Mallory's eye – 'I am finding a big broken crate of wood, a hatch, who knows? And there is a great wind blowing. And it blow me far and away, and on to the shore of Kynthos. Now you tellings me, is that or is that not a miracles yes or no?'

'Miracle,' said Mallory. 'Definitely.'

'And the machine,' said Carstairs. 'What about the machine?'

'Hah!' said Spiro. 'Well. I got him on beach. Very ill, I was. Lying with him, sleeping, very thirsty, sand in face, no move. Then a chap I think is there, speaking Greeks, give me drink of water.' He was frowning, as if he did not remember properly. 'Like dreams. Like dreams. Then I hear his voice loud, and other voices, not so loud, further away, and they are speaking Germans. I trying to get up, but no luck, fall on face bang, pass out again. And when I wakes up again I am in some ambulance, on some bed, and there are Germanses everywhere, but no machina.'

'No machine,' said Carstairs. 'Then they've got it.'

'Greeks man got it,' said Spiro. 'I spose. I never seen it no more. But I worry, I worry. I am thinking, if I wakes up, then they ask me questions, so I will be asleep and they will not ask me no questions and I will not be frightened. Because I am weak, you know, when I am tired like this, and I will tell anybody anything. So I make out I am knock out. So there.'

'You pretended to be in a coma for a week?' said Mallory.

'Just about. Yes,' said Spiro, with some smugness. 'Eat, drink when nobody lookings. When you are very very frightens you can be very very brave.'

Carstairs said, 'You are very brave and we admire you like hell, but we will tell you all about that later. Where is the machine?'

'I remembers,' said Spiro. 'This chap who give me drink of water on beach. He said he was hiding this thing in a place that only he know, nobody else, ever. So is okay. He is a good guy, I think: hate Germans scums, fight for us, our side. And he give me his name. So now we go find him, tell him, British armies arrived, hand over, me old cocky. Everything hunky-boo.'

'So what was his name?' said Carstairs.

'Achilles,' said Spiro. Then, by Mallory's computation about a thousand years later, 'What wrong? You get problem?'

'Yes,' said Mallory. 'Just a bit.'

Because Achilles was the name of the brother of Clytemnestra, who had been hanged in the Parmatia razzia. So it seemed very much as if the seven-rotor Enigma machine was somewhat lost.

In the dark very close behind them, someone cleared his throat. Mallory's hand jumped automatically on the cocking lever of his Schmeisser.

'Not today, thanks,' said a voice. And Miller stepped into the lamplight, with Andrea close beside him.

'I'll go and find her,' said Andrea.

'Find who?' said Carstairs.

'Clytemnestra. Achilles' sister.'

'You heard.'

'He wasn't exactly whispering.'

Carstairs laughed, his short, patronizing bark. 'Clytemnestra could be anywhere.'

'We have a rendezvous,' said Andrea. 'The road's open, again. We'll take transport. We'll find this machine.'

Carstairs nodded his head, wincing slightly. 'I expect you will,' he said. Then he swayed and lay down, suddenly.

'What is it?' said Mallory.

'Giddy,' said Carstairs. He tried to sit up, fell down again. 'Christ.'

'Stay there,' said Mallory. You could not expect a man who had smashed himself unconscious on a rock to laugh lightly and carry on as if nothing had happened. 'Andrea, get going. Miller, what's your timing?'

'Eight-hour fuses,' said Miller.

'Yes,' said Mallory. 'And the rest of it?'

'Depends when they start pumping fuel,' said Miller.

'Any sign of anyone doing any rocket firing?'

'Dunno,' said Miller. 'They've got one standing right there, pointed out of the roof. There weren't no action we could see. But I guess they could have that sucker ready to go in, what, two hours, from a standing start?'

Andrea said, 'I'll be at the jetty by sunrise.' There was no sound of movement. One moment he was there; the next, the darkness had flowed in to occupy the place where he had been standing.

'Well,' said Miller. 'This is real nice.' Miller was a man who believed in reconnaissance. On the way to the village, he had checked the place out. Once, it had probably been a thriving little community. Now, by the look of it, the original inhabitants had been displaced, the houses turned into dormitories for the men who worked inside the mountain, the church desecrated, a field kitchen on its mosaic floors turning out coarse bread and a soup whose smell did not inspire Miller to make its further acquaintance.

There was one bonus. The village was a prison, with the guards on the outside. The Germans would be looking for escapers, not intruders.

Miller left Mallory with Carstairs and Spiro, and went scouting.

He walked quietly among the little knots of men in the village square. Soon, he observed a man with a disc-shaped loaf of white bread and a bottle of wine. Miller had lived through Prohibition in the States, and his nose for a bootlegger was practically supernatural. So he followed on down a narrow alley, and found a lamplit door and inside it an old man with a white bandit's moustache, who looked at Miller's gold drachmae with a face that did not budge an inch, but was still extremely impressed. 'Where you from?' he said.

'Crete,' said Miller.

'How did you find me?'

'I found you,' said Miller, dour. He did not want to be gossiped about. 'What you got?'

The old man hauled bread, wine and olives from a wormy wooden box. Miller blessed him, and walked out.

At the back of the church was a little house; the priest's house, perhaps, built right up against the wall. It was dusty and cobwebbed, and had an odour suggestive of graveyards, and its floors were connected not by stairs but by a movable ladder, somewhat worm-eaten. But it was dry and secure, and to Miller it looked better than the Waldorf Astoria. He went back for Mallory and Carstairs and Spiro. Inside, he took out sardines and chocolate, and the bread and olives, and the wine. They ate like hungry wolves, tearing great lumps of bread and washing them down with draughts of turpentine-flavoured retsina. It seemed to Miller that for a man suffering from delayed concussion, Carstairs seemed to have a hearty appetite; a very hearty appetite indeed. Miller had taken a good few knocks on the head in his time as gold-miner and bootlegger. As far as he remembered – which was not, admittedly, very far, given the nature of the injury – for some weeks afterwards the very thought of food had been enough to make him spew his guts up . . .

Different strokes for different folks, thought Miller, watching Carstairs tap a cigarette on his gold case and light up. Very different folks. Carstairs was very different indeed.

Soon after this, in fact about ten seconds after this, he left his body behind, the sore eyes and the aching bones, and drifted down and down into a soft void, a place of no pain and total rest –

Then someone had hold of him and was yanking at his shoulder, and the softness was gone and the soreness in his head and his bones was back at double strength, and he was awake, looking at his watch. The watch that said he had been asleep for only ten minutes.

But during that ten minutes, the world had changed completely.

The crack under the door of the house had become a white-hot bar of light. Outside, there was noise; the noise of sirens squawking, of feet running; jackbooted feet. German feet.

Miller grabbed his thoughts by the scruff of the neck and told them to get themselves organized. They resisted, floating in and out of focus. Perhaps Andrea had got himself caught. Perhaps the Greek with the white moustache had reported that a stranger with a Cretan accent had paid him in gold. Perhaps they had found the plastic explosive charges on the rocket . . .

Or perhaps they had discovered all these things.

Mallory's voice came out of the darkness by his ear. 'Look after these two,' it said. 'I'll do the rest.'

Miller opened his mouth to complain. But the words never came out. For at that moment, there was a thunderous knocking on the door.

'The ladder,' said Mallory.

The knocking ceased, then came again. This time, it did not stop.

Andrea had had no trouble so far.

He had left unhindered by the gate. From there he had walked down to the transport compound, drifting through strips of shadow, a darker patch of the general darkness. He watched a truck come in over the causeway, unload, reload, heard the driver receive his orders in the traditional *Wehrmacht* bellow. The truck was returning across the causeway to the aerodrome. Andrea crept up to it, attached two rope slings to the back axle leaf springs, and lay across them as another man might have lain in a hammock. The truck started up and roared across the causeway. The driver showed his pass, and was allowed into the aerodrome. The truck rolled to a halt by a group of sheds; by the sound of voices and crockery, a mess room.

Andrea waited for the driver to get out, then dropped to the ground. Two pairs of boots were walking away towards the Acropolis. Otherwise there was nobody in sight.

Staying in the shadows, Andrea walked quickly into the open darkness of the airfield, heading for the far side of the perimeter. Once the runway lights flicked on, and he lay flat as a twin-engined plane landed and taxied to the dispersal area. Otherwise the world seemed quiet, out here in the warm breeze and the smell of dust and bruised dry grass. He accelerated to a trot, came to the fence, took out the little wire-cutters from his pack, and made himself a small trap door in the mesh, a door just big enough to squeeze through, its lower edge camouflaged in the dirt. Against the sky he could see the leggy alien form of a guard tower. There would be sentries –

There was a sentry.

The man strolled by. Andrea smelt the smoke of the cigarette in his cupped hand. This was not a sentry on lookout; this was a sentry going through the motions. If he was looking for anybody, he would be looking for people trying to break in, not out. The sentry passed. Andrea moved on, keeping very low.

Suddenly the night turned white.

Andrea saw his hand in front of him, a great brown spider on the bare, gravelly soil. He saw the guard tower, every plank and strut lit in remorseless detail; he saw the sentry, half-turned, mouth open, eyes round with fear.

For a moment, Andrea thought they had turned on the searchlights, and braced himself grimly for the shouts, the thwack of bullets. Then he realized that the light was not coming from close at hand, but from behind him, beyond the marshes. He turned his head, glanced over his shoulder. The Acropolis was lit up like a wedding cake. Klaxons whooped in the night. Whatever was happening, it seemed unlikely to be an air raid.

In the tower a telephone started ringing. The sound broke the sentry's trance. He trotted up the ladder. By the time Andrea heard his voice he was already moving on hands and knees across that flat gravelly stretch.

Then he was on his feet, loping away into the darkness. Behind him the perimeter lights jumped into life. But by then, he was far into the dark fringes of the night, less than a shadow against the loom of the mountains.

He was running across a checkerboard of fields, splashing through little irrigation gulleys, his feet brushing wheat and carrots, clogging with the rich volcanic soil of the plain. After a while, the ground began to rise. He was approaching the mountains.

Wills was in a churchyard. He seemed to be spending most of his time among the dead, nowadays. He hoped it was not an omen.

He had woken two hours ago, in the tomb above the Swallow's Nest. There had been something on his face: Clytemnestra's hand. 'Come,' she said. 'We must go.'

He was groggy with sleeplessness. For a moment he did not want to go anywhere, except back into the comfortable dark. Then he remembered about Clytemnestra, and he got his feet under him, and told himself that there was a reason for moving, and that was to go wherever Clytemnestra was going . . .

Then he was out again in the soft night, climbing something that he knew in daylight would have scared the wits out of him, but which at this hour was merely a near-vertical wall of rock with foot and handholds at strategic intervals; a path, in fact; a vertical path.

They went up it and on to a flat place. Clytemnestra took his hand and squeezed it, signalling silence. They walked past the dark shape of a German sentry, all the way past until he realized that she was still holding his hand and he hers, which he put down to forgetting to let go. Then they were off, heading north, as far as he could tell, over a dizzy and bewildering series of paths and precipices, tending gently downhill. After perhaps two hours they burst from a maze of boulders on to a ledge or cornice of rock, spiked with black cypresses. They walked through a small area of grass, on which daisies glittered faintly under the stars, and into a plain white building. Nailed double doors swung open as they approached a church. A small figure, black as the sky and wearing a hat like a pygmy oil drum, flitted away into the night without speaking.

'What was that?' said Wills, unnerved.

'The Patriarch,' said Clytemnestra, and drew him in through the door, and closed it.

At first, there was darkness, musty with incense. Then there was the little yellow glow of a sanctuary lamp. Clytemnestra had taken her hand away from his. As his eyes got used to the gold-tinged gloom, Wills saw that she was kneeling, head bowed in prayer.

Wills had done a bit of praying himself, in chapel at school with the other chaps, and then less formally but more sincerely on lonely nights at sea with the E-boat tracers floating out of the dark at him. But up here in this strange, musty place, he felt there were more important things to do than pray.

He opened the door and slipped out.

There was a low parapet around the churchyard. Below it, the valley lay spread like a dark map. There were lights down there: runway markers flicking on, the roar of a plane landing, the markers flicking off again. The village on the Acropolis was lit, too, with the smaller yellow lights of candles. Then suddenly the airfield had become a blue-white square, dazzling in its intensity, and all over the Acropolis floodlights had leaped into being. And floating across the intervening gulf of air there came the sound of klaxons.

Something was happening.

Wills checked the clip in his Schmeisser. Then he hunkered down in the black pit of shadow between a wall and a cypress tree, and waited.

Time passed. There was only the thyme-scented breeze, and the night, and whatever devilry they were hatching on the other side of the marshes. Earlier, in his dazed wanderings, Wills had not cared whether he lived or died. He had lost his ship, and his men, and he was far, far out on the most precarious of limbs.

But since he had recovered enough to notice Clytemnestra, he was interested in living again. Of course it was never easy to work out how women thought, not if you had gone straight from Wellington to Dartmouth and then active service. But he did have the definite impression that she was not ... well, averse to his company. She was a remarkable girl. A really spiffing girl –

Something descended on his mouth like a huge, soft leather cushion. A hand. Another hand came on the nape of his neck, and his chin was lifted until it would lift no further, and it dawned on Wills in a spasm of absolute horror that these hands did not care that this was as far as the chin went, they were going to go on lifting until his neck broke, and that would be the end of him –

'Hands up!' said a voice in Greek. A woman's voice. There was the metallic sound of a cocking lever. The hands relaxed.

Wills fell forward on to the parapet, groping for his Schmeisser. 'Back off,' he said. Then, remembering, 'Jolly boating –'

'Captain Wills,' said a voice he recognized: a soft voice that might have been a purr or a growl, there was no way of being sure. Andrea's voice. 'Captain Wills, you should not sit in a place where you can be seen against the sky.'

'Go away,' said the woman's voice. Clytemnestra's voice. 'Leave him alone, you great stupid ox.' She was beside Wills now, cradling his head in her hands. 'Can't you tell who is on your side and who isn't? Are you blind?'

'Understandable error,' said Wills, checking that his head was still there. 'Bit of luck you were coming out of the church, though.'

Clytemnestra snorted. 'Do you think I would leave you alone in the night?' she said. 'I have been watching you for the past two hours.' She put an arm around his waist. 'If you can't look after yourself, someone else will have to.'

Andrea cleared his throat. 'I hate to interrupt,' he said. 'But tell me, how much did you know about the life and habits of your late brother?'

In the view of Josef Koch, this island was a filthy place. Only a week ago, he had been pleased. After a winter chasing partisans around Yugoslavia the prospect of a little sun, sand and sea had been very enticing. But once he was actually here it had all gone wrong, thought Koch, hauling at the wheel, dragging the lorry's bonnet round yet another hairpin bend. The people on this island had the temperament of angry hornets, and most of the women had moustaches. If they were not fighting you, they were fighting each other. The *Wehrmacht* were bloody useless. The boffins were boffins: bloody useless too. Josef Koch's mind floated back to happier times: Bosnia, a wood with half-a-dozen partisans wired to the trees, him and a couple of privates slinging a rope over a branch, setting up the seesaw: a novelty, the seesaw, a thing of Josef's own invention. The idea was that the terrorist stood on one end of the seesaw, and Josef stood on the other. Josef was a big man: fat, some called him, if they dared. The terrorist, of course, had a noose round his neck tied to the branch above. The idea was that the private soldiers would tell Josef jokes, and try to make him laugh so he lost his balance, and the terrorist's end of the plank went down, leaving the terrorist kicking, but not alive, not after five minutes, anyway. The other thing Josef liked to do was walk towards the terrorist, so the terrorist's weight brought the plank down slowly, slowly, tightened the noose round the neck, while all the while Josef explained the error of the terrorist's ways, and the terrorist died, twisting and jerking on the rope, looking into Josef's thick-lipped grin and bulging, pink-veined eyes. It was fantastic, the fun you could have with a simple plank. Though obviously the terrorists did not enjoy it so much.

Josef sighed. He liked hanging people. He had had a goodish time in Parmatia last week, but that had been a small-scale operation. It sounded like there would be more such work soon, though. There had been fighting in the mountains, and trouble at the works, and . . . well, the Boss was severely ticked off, and when the Boss was ticked off, the best place to be was far away. So it was absolutely no hardship for Josef Koch to be driving this truck, on the Boss's orders, down the coast road to Parmatia to bring back some suspected partisan sympathizers from the lockup.

Next bend. Haul the wheel, change down a gear, foot flat on throttle –

There was a stone in the road. More a boulder, really. Josef stamped on the brake. The lorry halted. That was another thing you got, on this island. Lumps of mountain all over the road. There was a crowbar in the back. Sighing, Josef opened the door, swung his legs out, and slid down from the cab.

That was when the peculiar thing happened.

As his boots hit the road, he found himself grabbed from behind, scruff of neck and seat of pants. All of a sudden he had no control over his own destiny. A boot landed with shattering violence on his back, and the dark ground was passing at horrid speed under his eyes as he headed for the verge.

Not that there was a verge.

At the edge of the road was a strip of loose stones, on which the *Feldwebel* bounced once, face first. Beyond the strip of stones was silence, moving air, and far below, the shift of the sea.

The *Feldwebel* found that he was falling down a cliff. He screamed. The scream lasted exactly the time it took to fall two hundred feet on to sharp rocks.

On the road, the lorry stood, engine purring. Andrea helped Wills drag the driver's mate to the side of the road and roll him over into the dark, while Clytemnestra wiped the blade of her long knife on a tuft of dry grass. The driver's mate had bled surprisingly little. Wills possessed himself of the man's camouflage smock and took the wheel. Clytemnestra climbed into the middle, and Andrea squeezed his mighty bulk in next to her, lit a cigarette, and slumped back, hands on the grips of his machine pistol. 'Parmatia,' he said.

Beyond the windscreen, the world began to move, white stone, pine and juniper, cliff and gorge, gleaming in the light of the blacked-out headlights. The dark puddle on the road behind faded into the blackness of the night.

They headed for Parmatia.

From the top of the ladder in the house by the Acropolis church, Miller could see Mallory at the door. The knocking persisted. Carstairs was up through the hole in the ceiling now. Miller hauled up the ladder, fast. As he pulled its foot through the hole, the door opened, loosing a flood of blue-white light into the squalid ground floor. It picked out straw, rubbish, and Mallory. Mallory with his hands on his hips, glaring at the three soldiers outside, Schmeissers levelled: Mallory shouting in German, walking towards them, out into the light . . .

And that was the last Miller saw of him, because the ladder was up and he was lifting it to the next ceiling, where there was another hole. The floor creaked alarmingly as Spiro headed for the ladder. Miller picked out the joists with a pencil flashlight, shooed Carstairs to the ladder foot, then went after him. Spiro was already climbing, at a speed truly remarkable in one so recently bedridden. Carstairs went after him, more groggily.

At the top, they were in a low attic, whose ceiling was the underside of the roof tiles. 'Leave the ladder,' said Miller, and started to push aside the heavy clay half-cylinders. After five minutes' steady work, his head broke through, and he was spitting worm-eaten beam and ancient bamboo lining into the night air.

In front of him was a low white parapet. Beyond the parapet was the roof of the church, sweeping at one end up to the cupola, and at the other to a belfry, open to the air, with a three-foot parapet running around its edge. The belfry would be accessible from the church, as well as over the roof.

Miller very much liked the look of the belfry.

He took off more tiles, scrambled through the roof, and pulled the other men after him. Then he replaced the tiles, and led them across the parapet to the dark slope of the church roof.

'Shit,' said Spiro. 'I don' likes highness.'

'It's not high,' said Miller.

'Looks high to me,' said Spiro.

'Go,' said Miller.

'No,' said Spiro.

It was quite obvious to Miller that the Greek meant what he said. Hard to blame the guy, really. He had done plenty already, and everyone drew the line somewhere.

Pity it was right here, though.

Something barged Miller aside. It was Carstairs: Carstairs with something held out in front of him, something with a faint sheen under the stars. A very faint sheen: the sheen of the blued-steel blade of a killing knife, nine inches of razor-sharp unpleasantness.

'Ow!' said Spiro.

Carstairs said, 'Listen, greasy boy. You heard what he said.' His arm moved slightly.

'Ow!' said Spiro again.

'We don't really need you any more,' said Carstairs. 'So you give me one good reason to stop me carving out your nasty yellow liver.'

Miller was shocked. He did not, however, intervene.

Spiro became lost in deep thought for about three and a half seconds. Then he started to scuttle up the church roof like an overweight monkey.

Carstairs went after him. Miller followed, moving slow and careful. The roof seemed to be in doubtful condition. There was a nasty springiness to it, a suggestion of sag. Mindful of the fifty-foot drop to a hard stone floor that lay below it, Miller found himself holding his breath.

The belfry parapet loomed invitingly ahead. But they were moving out of the shadow now, and between them and the parapet lay a brilliant wedge of floodlit tiles. Spiro did not like the look of it. His pace was slowing perceptibly. He had chosen a bad place to slow down, because they had moved some distance along the roof, and below the eaves of the church was no longer the crumbling shelter of the priest's house, but the village square. And in the village square, a squad of German soldiers was standing. All it took was for one of them to look up –

'Go!' said Carstairs.

Spiro froze.

Carstairs pulled out his dreadful knife and prodded the Greek's foot. Spiro squeaked, scuttled like lightning up the roof and hauled himself over the parapet. His short legs waved for a moment in the air. Then he vanished. Safe.

Not safe.

In his last frantic scuffle, Spiro had dislodged a tile. It started slowly. It accelerated, rattling down the floodlit section of the roof. Miller stuck out a hand and made a grab for it. For a moment he thought he had it. But Greek roof tiles are heavy affairs, made with plenty of good solid clay, and no human fingertips can restrain one once it has got the bit of gravity between its teeth.

Miller watched that tile loop out into space and fall, tumbling over and over, towards the cobbles of the square where the squad of soldiers stood, only needing to look up.

When Mallory opened the door, light flooded in. There were three soldiers outside, rifles at the ready. Mallory looked them scornfully up and down. 'What the bloody hell is all the noise about?' he said, in a German pregnant with the accents of Heidelberg University, where in his pre-war climbing days he had indeed spent six months.

'Orders to search the house,' said one of the privates, squinting at this nasty-looking *SS Leutnant*, with shadowy hollows on his face and a rifle slung negligently over his shoulder.

'I've already searched it,' said Mallory. One of the soldiers opened his mouth to speak. 'Give me that gun,' said Mallory.

The man handed over his rifle without hesitation. Mallory looked it over with the scorn of an epicure who has found a dead rat in his soup. He pulled the bolt out of the rifle and threw it on to the ground. 'It stinks!' he said. 'Clean it! Now get out of my way!' He marched into the square.

There were a lot of soldiers: a terrible lot of soldiers. Mallory found himself seriously worried. A good search would certainly land them all in trouble. Carstairs he had little confidence in, besides which the man was woozy from his bang on the head. Spiro was a charming personality, but not what you would call a natural athlete. Miller would look after himself. But with that much dead weight round his neck, he was going to need all the help he could get.

Mallory marched briskly across the square, up the street towards the village gates, and turned sharply into Athenai Street where they had made rendezvous. The houses were dark and ruinous. At the end, the cliff face was a pit of blackness in the night. Settling the rifle firmly on his back, Mallory started to climb.

The cliff was steep but pocked with steps and holds where stone had been cut to build the village. Mallory went up until he was looking down on the rooftops illuminated by the blue-white lights mounted on the cliff face. He considered getting above those lights, sixty feet above him now. But he had a feeling that just for the minute, he might be better off below them. He moved along a ledge – a ledge to him, anyway; to anyone else, it was no more than a thread-fine irregularity in the face of the rock – until he came to a broad crack, sunk in black shadow. Into this he fitted himself, and stood invisible.

Below, the roofs of the village shone livid in the floodlights. The streets were stripes of violet-black, except for the square, a handkerchief of naked white under the stars.

In that white rectangle little black shapes moved, precise, mech-anical movements, pairs attaching to other pairs to make bigger blocks, which in turn fragmented . . .

Mallory knew that what he was watching was a search of the town. And what was being searched for was him, Spiro, Carstairs, and Miller –

Something caught his eye. Behind the church was the priest's house, leaning against the bigger building like a small, drunken man holding on to a fat wife. There was movement on the church roof.

Mallory watched the little figures wait by the parapet, saw the first of them – Spiro, it was – move haltingly towards the triangle of light that lay over the tiles. He unslung the Mauser and put it to his shoulder. Spiro swam into the sight's circle; Spiro hesitant, Carstairs at his heel, jabbing. Mallory saw the tiles rock as Spiro pressed on. He saw the tile come free, accelerate, check as Miller got his fingers to it, carry on. The palms of his hands were suddenly damp with sweat. He panned the sight down. A line of German soldiers stood under the eaves of the church, at attention, listening to some officer or other, barking orders. The cross-hairs of the sight settled on the helmet of the soldier closest to the church wall. Mallory squeezed the trigger.

All hell broke loose.

The steel helmet flew off the head and smacked into the church wall. The soldier slammed flat on the cobbles, a dark patch of blood spreading around his ruined head. The report of the rifle rolled like thunder on the flat, hard faces of the buildings. Even before the echoes died, Mallory had his Schmeisser in the firing position and was hosing the square with bullets, the stabbing spear of flame from the gun's muzzle saying here I am, here I am, up here on this cliff.

Down in the square grey bodies rolled and crawled and shouted, taking cover. There was fire coming up from the square now, sporadic bursts, ill-directed, but focused loosely on the crevice in which Mallory was hiding.

But Mallory was no longer there. He had moved away, upwards, in the shadows. Now he was approaching the lights. Below, the village seethed and muttered like a cauldron. Seventy feet above the place he had fired from, he paused and looked down. In the belfry of the church, he glimpsed three heads; visible only from above, those heads.

And what with one thing and another, nobody had noticed anything as trivial as the fall of a tile from a church roof.

Mallory moved on, shoulders and feet, up the crack in the rock. Above him the cliff soared for ever into the wild, cool dark. Below him, the village swarmed like an ants' nest stirred with a stick. Someone was firing tracer, the rounds smacking the rock face and spinning away into the dark until it must have seemed that there were forty men up here, so more men opened fire from the town . . .

Really, thought Mallory, climbing fast and steady, it was a deplorable lapse of discipline. But he had no illusions. Soon the brilliant organization of the German army would reassert itself, and life would become even more difficult and dangerous than it was at the moment.

For him, anyway. The men in the village should be left alone: the Germans would assume that the whole squad was on the cliffs

165

of the Acropolis. All he had to do was keep moving, draw away the pursuit.

Keep moving.

For a moment he hung on the face of the cliff and thought of the precipice above him, crag on crag, a couple of thousand feet to be conquered against gravity. He could taste the old cigarettes in his throat, feel the grit of sleeplessness in his eyes, feel the weary ache of continuous action in his bones. The Benzedrine had worn off. If he took any more, he would be seeing things . . .

Better to see things than to fall off.

Mallory took two of the pills out of the foil and swallowed them. Then, wearily, he began to haul himself up the wall. Forty feet above, he found what he was looking for.

He was on a level with the lights. Bullets still whined and spanged around him, but nobody was aiming. Between the spots of brilliance was only darkness, and it was in that darkness that he existed, anonymous.

He paused, eyeing the face. He could already feel the jump of the Benzedrine at his stomach, his blood beginning to fizz.

Just above his head ran a heavy cable: the cable that brought the power to the floodlights. Mallory pulled the clasp knife from his pocket and wrapped around its handle the rubberized bag in which he kept his shaving kit. He wished he had his commando knife, but the commando knife was gone. He had no idea of the clasp knife's insulating properties, but rubber was supposed to be all right. Go on, the Benzedrine was telling him, it will be fine, you are immortal, if things don't work out you can spread your wings and jump clear over the village and into the cool sea –

Steady.

He reached his right hand up, and positioned the blade on the outside of the thick insulation. Then he began to saw.

The edge of the knife sank into the rubber as if it had been butter. He felt the touch of some kind of armour. Then the blade went through the armour, and shorted out the live and the neutral.

The night suddenly turned blue, as if it had been struck by lightning. Then, just as suddenly, it turned black, as the lights went out. Pitch black: black as the inside of a coal hole.

Mallory left the knife wedged in the wire, and looped his silk rope over the cable. He whipped a new tracer magazine from his ammunition pouch and clapped it into his Schmeisser. He went back along the wire twenty feet, until the rope came taut. Then he fired a burst into the square, and let go of the cable.

The rope took him in a great swinging arc across the cliff face. He felt the scrape of rock at his hands and knees, felt himself rise again towards the cable, reached up a hand, gripped the rubber, and found a hold. In the same movement he fired again, another burst into the square, and swung back the way he had come. From the corner of his eye he could see tracers still spinning and ricocheting down there. He fired another burst, swung back. This time he did not shoot. The enemy would have seen three bursts of tracer virtually simultaneously, from places forty feet apart. There would be at least two men up here, they would assume; possibly more. Two men covering the retreat of a whole squad.

Diversion established, thought Mallory. Now it is time to get away from here. Up; gain height.

He hauled himself up on the cable.

The cable came out of the wall.

All of a sudden he was falling, hanging on to the rubber insulation, trying to remember what the hell happened further down the cliff: a wall to smash into, or merely a long drop . . . He clamped his hands and closed his forearms against the scrape of the rock. He could feel the staples popping up there one by one, the wild rush of the night on his face. It occurred to him that his knife would have fallen out of the wound in the rubber. The circuit would be open again.

Two things happened.

One, a staple held. Mallory found himself hanging there in the night, far above the village, heart pounding, the weight of his two weapons and equipment doing its best to pop his arms from their sockets.

Two, the lights came on. Mallory's over-brightened brain saw quite clearly the cliff as visible from the square: a towering sheet of rock, with a dotted line of brilliant lights, dislodged from their moorings, dangling down its surface, saying: look here, this direction. And on the end, wriggling like a frog on a hook, a small human figure.

For a second, a great silence hung over village and cliff.

* * *

Miller had taken advantage of the darkness to stand in the belfry and assess the situation, secure in the knowledge that nobody could see him. When the lights came on, he had experienced the mild flicker of interest that in Dusty Miller passed for surprise. It had passed through his mind that Mallory, suspended on a bit of wire over about a hundred and twenty heavily-armed Germans, seemed likely to be in some trouble. Miller had already noticed with admiration the streams of tracer that had come pouring from various different spots on the darkened cliff. It had seemed exactly as if a fair-sized body of men was up there. So it would not be amazing if Mallory's colleagues did a little something to cover him.

All this he thought in the time it took to unclip four grenades from his belt, two for each hand, pull the pins, and heave them over the belfry roof and into the square. All eyes in the square had been on the cliff, raising guns for the fusillade that would blow Mallory to kingdom come. The arrival of the grenades in their midst came as something of a shock.

Miller ducked down, saw the flashes light up the night, heard the crash of the explosions, the whine of shrapnel, the screams of the wounded. There was a sputter of gunfire, sporadic and disconnected. It said to Miller that the troops in the square had realized that they were disagreeably exposed where they stood on that brightly-lit rectangle of paving, and had decided to take cover.

But this was of only passing interest to Miller. What got his immediate attention was that the lighting cable, glaring up there on the cliff, now bore only its light fittings.

Mallory was gone.

'Here,' said Clytemnestra.

Wills stamped on the brakes. The lorry halted. Round the corner were the quarry and the landward end of the rail causeway. They were back.

Out in the dark, something moved. Wills cursed gently to himself. There were not supposed to be any sentries until the quarry fence. He flicked on the headlights, feeling a stealthy shift of weight as Andrea, who had been riding on the rear step of the truck, took his departure into the night.

There was a sentry in the lorry's windscreen; a fat sentry with a sullen expression, blinking in the headlight beams that

illuminated the rolls of fat at his belt and the spidery outlines of
the quarry machinery and the shed Miller had burned, vanishing
into the dark behind him. Wills put his elbow on the window and
said, 'Morning.'

The fat sentry frowned. He said, 'Where's Koch?'

Wills' grin stiffened. His German was not up to deep conversation. Presumably, this man was a friend of the driver. The plan
had been to drop Andrea off a mile short of the quarry. But they
had overshot.

'Went flying,' said Wills, trying to hide his atrocious accent by
mumbling.

'Where?'

'Back home,' said Wills.

The sentry frowned again, and switched on his torch. Wills could
feel Clytemnestra rigid in the seat beside him. This is bloody stupid,
he thought. All the way across the island, no worries. Into Clytemnestra's brother's favourite cave for the machine. Grab machine,
drive back towards rendezvous, everything tickety-boo.

And now one fat sentry was going to sugar the whole shooting-
match.

The torch came closer to the driver's side window. 'What the
hell do you think you're doing out here, this time of night?'

'Minding my own business,' said Wills.

'Papers,' said the sentry. Then he said something else – something
with no words, that was the sound of all the air being driven out
of his body for the last time ever – and slumped with a crash against
the lorry door. Behind where he had been standing, a figure that
might have been a bear stooped and cleaned what might have been
a knife on a tuft of dry grass by the roadside. Andrea swung his
pack into the cab. Where he was going, he would need to travel
light. 'Go,' he said. 'Till dawn, at the airfield jetty.' He paused,
slapped the mahogany box on the passenger seat. 'And look after
this thing, yes?'

'With my life,' said Clytemnestra.

Andrea watched the lorry turn in the road and rattle off the way
it had come. He looked across at the Acropolis. There were lights;
too many lights for his liking. Silent as the night itself, he padded
along the road to the quarry gates.

He heard the sound of voices, saw the glow of a cigarette where a couple of sentries were finding courage in conversation. Down the chainlink fence a little, he found a place where the base of the wire was loose. He wormed his way under. The root of the causeway lay just ahead and to the left. Andrea clapped a German steel helmet on his head, straightened up, and began to march steadily along the sleepers towards the Acropolis.

Mallory hung three hundred feet above the village, and wished he could smoke. He had almost forgotten what it was to walk upright on level ground. His bones felt the pull of gravity, and groaned.

As he stood wedged into a crevice, he had the sense that things had gone badly wrong. Below, the village was heaving with German soldiery. Andrea was out there in the night, on an errand that had only the smallest chance of succeeding. Miller, Spiro and Carstairs were treed in the belfry. Benzedrine or not, he was too tired. He needed four hours' sleep. But in four hours it would be getting light. The enemy were waiting for the light, so they could find the scattered elements of the Thunderbolt Force and pick them off one by one. Command and control were what was needed. Command and control. Big words. Words for men who were not so tired that they could hardly move.

Mallory looked down. The church was below him. He needed to regain the belfry: establish rotas, stand watches, organize a way out, make the second rendezvous at dawn. He needed a way down to the church.

There was no way down that did not go straight through five hundred Germans.

In the square below, sentries had been posted. The world had settled. Hot pursuit had cooled. All the Germans had to do was wait. There had been too many operations, too much action, too little sleep. The Thunderbolt Force was fragmented like quicksilver. This looked very like The End –

Above Mallory's head, something made a small noise. To his right, a pale streak had come into being on the dark rock. To his left, another. Ropes.

There was a new noise: a clinking and grinding. Boots.

Mallory knew then that he had been wrong about the waiting. The Germans were on the front foot; someone somewhere had argued his case, and argued it well. They were searching the

Acropolis, pebble by pebble. The *Wehrmacht* garrison would not be combing cliff faces with ropes. This was *Sonderkommando* work. The work of Dieter Wolf, highly professional, utterly deadly.

Mallory unslung his own rope and looked down into the square. There were half-a-dozen men there, no more. The architectural and human debris of Miller's grenades had been cleared away. There were the men descending from above, and the men waiting below. And Mallory in the middle.

From the movements of the ropes on either side, the men were quartering the cliff, poking their noses into every little nook and cranny, methodical at last. It was the least you expected of an élite German unit.

The men down below, possibly over confident, were not in cover. Mallory made his plan.

Reaching out, he grabbed the nearest rope and sawed it off short with a razor blade from his shaving kit. Then he hauled in the other rope. In its middle he tied a marlinespike hitch and placed the knot around a hand grenade. Finally, he took the rope he had cut, coiled it, and belayed it to a little post of rock.

Mallory fitted the flash suppressor to the Mauser, and wished he had a silencer. But silencers cut the muzzle velocity, and their steel-wool baffles only worked for half a dozen shots. He filled the magazine and slotted it silently into the rifle. The scuffling noises from above were louder now. He ran the telescopic sight over the square. Two men in the open. Two behind the buttresses of the church. The gleam of a helmet in the alley.

Mallory made a list in his mind, measuring the necessary movements of the carbine. Then he took a deep breath, sighted on the gleam in the alley, and pulled the trigger.

The gun roared. He moved to the men by the church, one, two; one dead, one winged, but the heavy bullet would do him no good, and the men in the middle of the square were diving for cover as Mallory worked the bolt and pulled the trigger. One of them was down, not moving, the other one a pair of heels vanishing behind the buttress, damn, and the cat was properly among the pigeons now.

Mallory pulled the pin on the hand grenade he had looped into the searcher's rope and let it swing away. He kicked the rope he had cut out into space, grabbed it, and went down as close to free fall as made no difference. There were shots from below, but the bullets went wide. Mallory's boots hit the cliff, and he bounced out, a wide arc, descending. There was a scream from above. One of the searchers had discovered that his rope had shrunk. A body whistled past, bounced once, and crashed into the buildings at the cliff's foot. Mallory was slowing now, crabbing sideways for the roof of a building. The bullets were getting closer. Then there was a heavy explosion overhead, and another body whizzed past, preceded this time by a length of rope. The grenade had done its stuff –

Mallory landed on a roof, let go of the rope and rolled, unhitching his Schmeisser. He was breathing hard, his heart hammering at his ribs. Above him in the lights he saw three men descending, foreshortened. He loosed off a burst at them, saw two of them let go, heard the crash of their bodies coming down. The third stopped in a crease of black shadow. Mallory saw the muzzle flash. Rounds whacked into the roof around him, and grit stung his face. He felt naked on this roasting-pan of a roof. There was no cover. He squeezed off another burst at the cliff face and scuttled to the edge of the roof. Bullets cracked past his head, whipping across the cobbles from the direction of the church. He could feel the breath rasping, the sweat running. Another burst of bullets from on high kicked chips out of the parapet by his head. He took another look at the square, squeezed off a burst, rolled over the parapet and dropped to the cobbles.

It was a long drop, longer than it had appeared. Mallory landed awkwardly, felt his ankle turn as far as his boot would let it, sharp prongs of pain jab up towards his knee. No more climbing, he thought, rolling and firing at the same time, heading for the patch of shadow, ankle hurting like hell and going to hurt worse later, if anything was going to be hurting at all –

He was across the alley and in the shadow. His helmet crashed into stone. A mounting block. He was invisible, in cover. Safe as houses.

For as long as it took someone to unhook a grenade. Say, twenty seconds. There was no way out. Mallory fought the Benzedrine, and the pain, and the weariness, scrabbling for an answer. Miller was up in the tower. Wills was off with Clytemnestra. Andrea was ... well, God knew where Andrea was. The important thing was not to give Miller away. If they found Miller, they found Spiro, and if they found Spiro, Spiro could be expected to tell them everything he knew.

As far as Mallory was concerned, there were no answers.

A great hush fell over the square. Mallory lay ears pricked, waiting for the fizz of the grenade fuse, the rattle of metal on stone that would signal the finish.

But instead, he heard a voice.

'*Herr Kapitän* Mallory,' it said. It was a military voice, with an odd, bubbling hiss in it. How the hell does he know my name? thought Mallory.

'We have recognized you,' said the voice, as if it had heard his thoughts, 'by your skill, at first, it must be said. *Kapitän* Mallory, there are things I should like to know.'

Of course there are, said Mallory to himself. 'Who the hell are you?' he said, aloud. He was surprised he still had a voice, let alone a voice that sounded clear and normal as it bounced from the surface of the buildings.

'*Hauptmann* Dieter Wolf,' said the voice. And to Mallory's astonishment, a man walked out into the light. He wore a high-crowned cap, whose peak hid his eyes. Someone at some time had smashed his jaw, and whoever had mended it had not been a master of his craft, not by a long chalk. The lower mandible was horribly skewed; it looked as if it would not shut properly. Spit bubbled in the corner as he breathed, giving his voice its nasty liquid hiss. It gave him a permanent crooked grin; a crocodile grin. There was a Luger in his hand. No grenades, though.

'Come out here,' said Wolf.

'Quite comfortable where I am,' said Mallory.

Wolf's twisted jaw writhed. 'Let me put it like this,' he said. 'I have men in position who can drop some things into your hole. This would be a pity, I suppose. I have heard a great deal about you.'

Mallory had to acknowledge that Wolf was right, it would be a pity. He hesitated, his mouth suddenly dry: a dryness he had felt before, high on a Southern Alp without a name, foodless at the top of a couloir, the sun coming on to the ice above, freeing salvos of boulders that swept the gulley clean as a whistle. It was the dryness that came when you had run out of ideas, and you had to put judgement on the shelf, and trust to luck in a place where luck was not in plentiful supply.

Mallory pulled himself to his feet. His ankle hurt, now. Everything hurt. It was most unlikely that *Hauptmann* Wolf wanted to talk to him about the weather. More probably, he would want to cut him in half with a Schmeisser. 'Closer,' said Wolf. He had his Luger pointed at Mallory's stomach. Mallory could feel the presence of Miller in the belfry. He schooled himself not to look up.

'So,' said Wolf. 'We are honoured that you have been able to visit, *Herr Kapitän* Mallory. You and your friends, *Kolonel* Andrea of the defeated rabble once known as the Greek army. And of course Corporal Miller, of the Catering Corps.'

'Who?' said Mallory.

The saurian jaw stretched in something approaching a smile. The grin broadened. A thread of drool hung from the corner of the ruined mouth. 'They are both dead,' he said. 'The *Kolonel* was shot. Miller we hanged.'

'Sorry to hear that,' said Mallory. His ankle was killing him. He told himself he did not believe a word of this. But his stomach was hollow with something worse than hunger.

The weariness flowed over him in a heavy wave. Admit it. There were hundreds of them, four Thunderbolts. Wolf was lying about Miller. But Andrea . . .

'And now,' said Wolf, with horrid affability, 'I am going to kill you.' Delicately, he put the Luger back in its holster and secured the flap. Removing his cap, he skimmed it on to the mounting block. Fumbling behind him, he pulled out a nine-inch dagger. Mallory had heard of this dagger. Wolf liked to use it to disembowel people.

'One thing,' said Mallory. 'I'm flattered that you recognized me. How did you do it?'

'I should say that I recognized you from the newspapers before the war,' said Wolf. 'But it would not be true. The fact is that your friend Andrea told me, under torture. Just after he had told me where to find the charges you had placed so amateurishly on the Victory weapons.' It was not just his jaw that had been broken. Without his cap, his whole head looked as if it had been crushed and clumsily reformed. The eyes were cold slits under a whitefuzzed cranium that might have been moulded from dough by a child with a taste for the macabre.

Mallory smiled at him, the bright, enthusiastic smile of someone who has just been given a lovely present. Andrea would not have revealed the time of day under torture. This unpleasant specimen was beyond a shadow of doubt telling lies.

'Now,' said Wolf. 'Come here, Captain Mallory.' He beckoned, with the dagger held out in front of him. As he beckoned, he advanced.

Mallory felt for his own knife, then remembered both of them were gone. He tested his ankle. Not good. He stood his ground, watching the knife.

They were two figures standing on that sheet of floodlit cobbles, feet apart, intent at the hub of their radiating shadows. One with pack on back, unmoving; the other stealthy, feline almost. Both of them focused on the little starburst of light on the point of Wolf's dagger.

Wolf was close enough for Mallory to smell his sweat. It was a sour smell, violent, disgusting. Mallory watched the knife wrist sinking for the first upward thrust. He shifted his weight until it was on his good leg. Wolf's eyes betrayed no feeling. His knife hand came round and up, hooking at Mallory's belly. But Mallory was not there any more. He had arched away like a bullfighter from the horns, grabbing at Wolf's wrist as it came past, to transfer the man's momentum into a twist that would dislocate the elbow.

But as his hands locked on Wolf's wrist, he knew it was not going to work. The SS man's arm was thick as a telegraph pole. It was an arm whose owner had slept well and eaten well. Mallory's fingers were worn with cliff and battle, and his reserves were close to rock bottom. He could not hold on. The arm wrenched away. Wolf brought his left hand round, fast, a closed-fist blow that made Mallory's ears ring. He kept his feet with difficulty. Wolf came in again, hooking with the knife. Mallory aimed a kick at his knee, made contact, but he had kicked with his right foot, the bad foot, and pain shot up his leg and he fell over, feeling something burn his ribs, cool air on his side. Wolf had cut him. Not badly: a surface cut to the ribs.

It would get worse.

He struggled to his feet.

Wolf was waiting for him. His breathing was steady and even. Little bubbles of spit formed and burst in the corner of his wrecked mouth. 'Now,' he said. 'I'll give it to you now.' He came in, knife in front of him like a sword. Mallory knew he was in bad trouble. He had lost sight of the fact he was going to die. There was no time for fear, or thinking ahead. The name of the game was survival, every second a bonus wrenched from the crooked jaws of death.

He got inside the knife, trapped the huge arm under his own arm, butted his steel helmet into that disgusting jaw, heard a tooth or two pop, brought his knee up into the groin, found it blocked by a leg that might as well have been made of wood. The arm was coming round behind him. He tried to cringe away from the knife, but the arms were remorseless, and he was exhausted –

The world went mad.

The square filled with a gigantic noise, the noise of a thousand typewriters, the whine of many hornets' nests kicked to hell, two, maybe more huge explosions. Sensing a minute faltering of Wolf's hold, Mallory smashed his helmet once more into the *SS* man's face. This time the nose went, and the man grunted and reeled, and behind Mallory the knife clattered on the cobbles. But then the arms came on Mallory's neck, tilting his head sideways, and Mallory knew that this time he had had it for sure, and for the first time the fear of death showed itself in his mind, a dark and ugly thing –

But only for a split second.

Because suddenly those terrible arms were off his neck and he was lurching back, free, and a voice was saying, 'Get your weapon.' A familiar voice.

Andrea's voice.

It had, Miller reflected, been a bad five minutes.

They had been sitting in the belfry nice and peaceful. Miller had even managed to get a little shuteye – a very little, seeing that he did not trust Carstairs, and that Spiro was trembling like a frightened rabbit and muttering about bulletses and gunses and getting outses of here. Miller was worrying about Mallory, sure, especially after all that stuff with the lights. But when you knew Mallory as well as Miller, you could tell when he was in real trouble and when he was staging a diversionary action. The stuff with the lights, though it had made Miller's flesh creep, was definitely a diversionary action. When Mallory had vanished from the end of the cable, there had been silence. A silence that Miller had very definitely appreciated. Then had come the shooting, and the voice in the square.

The voice in the square had been different.

It had woken Miller up, a thing he held against it. When he put his eye to the waterspout in the belfry floor, he saw the big man in the breeches and jackboots and high-fronted cap, standing tough and arrogant among the sprawled bodies of the Germans. He saw Mallory hobble out to meet him. Miller's stomach became hollow with apprehension.

It was not just that Mallory looked tired, and the monstrous figure in the jackboots looked fresh as paint.

There were other things to be seen: things invisible to Mallory, but visible to Miller in his eminence. It was what staff would call a fluid situation. Staff could call it what they liked. To Miller, it looked like a mess.

Round the corner from Mallory, out of his line of sight, a machine-gun post had been set up. Miller did not know why, but he had a nasty feeling it could have something to do with reprisals on the civilian workers. He was not actually worried about the civilian workers, because when those rockets went up, the Germans were going to need all the manpower they could get.

What really worried him was something else: a shadow he had seen floating from darkness to darkness in the alley on the far side of the square. A big shadow, impossibly big: a shadow with the shoulders of a bear and the lightness of a butterfly.

He dug Carstairs in the ribs. 'Stand by to give covering fire,' he said.

'You're joking,' said Carstairs, huddling into his corner of the bell tower. 'They'll have us in a second.'

'Listen up, Captain,' said Miller. 'If you don't give covering fire, I'll blow your God damn head off.'

'Who the hell do you think you're talking to?' said Carstairs.

'I'll blow your head off, sir,' said Miller. Then he gave him his orders.

Down below, there was the sound of a dagger clattering on to cobbles. The man in the breeches had Mallory in a headlock and appeared to be breaking his neck.

'Open fire,' said Miller. He stood up, tossed two grenades, sighted the Schmeisser on the three heads inside the Spandau emplacement, and fired two short bursts. Behind him the belfry trap door slammed open, and Carstairs' boots clattered down the ladder. A man stood up in the Spandau emplacement and fell across his gun. The grenades exploded, blowing him out again, accompanied by the two other men. There was movement in other windows as a squad of Germans took cover, Miller waited for the withering fire that would lash Mallory to the ground –

But while he had been disposing of the machine gun, the shadow had detached itself from the alley and moved in half-a-dozen great strides across the cobbles. The shadow was no longer a shadow, but had become Andrea. And Andrea had put a mighty forearm around the neck of the man with the crooked head, and wrenched him away from Mallory, and tucked Mallory in behind him like a hen protecting its chicks, and reversed towards the church door, using the crooked-headed man, *Hauptmann* Wolf in person, as a human shield, though human was not the word anyone who knew Wolf would have used.

Miller found it all very impressive. He heard the church door below burst open, Carstairs open up. Then he flung himself through the trap door in the belfry floor and went down the ladder into the dark, into the middle of a knot of people that consisted of Carstairs and Spiro, Mallory and Andrea, with Wolf instead of sandbags.

Andrea said, 'Get behind me.' The German had a face that Miller did not like. He seemed to be swearing. Andrea's mighty forearm tensed. The squashed-pumpkin skull turned purple under the thistledown hair. 'Now,' he said.

Miller took Carstairs' Schmeisser gently away from him, and gave it to Mallory, just in case. They moved towards the mouth of the alley, crossing the wide floodlit spaces of the square. It felt horribly exposed out here. But none of the SS would shoot for fear of hitting their commanding officer –

A man flicked into view behind the church, wearing field grey, not camouflage, lifting a rifle to his shoulder. Miller put the bead of the Schmeisser's sight on the man's chest and squeezed off a four-round burst. The man crashed back into the shadows.

'Thank you,' said Mallory.

'Don't mensh,' said Miller. But beneath the grin was something they all knew. Wolf's soldiers might not like to shoot their colonel. But the regular *Wehrmacht* garrison would not be bothered one way or the other. With the amount of noise and fuss coming out of the Greek village, it stood to reason that reinforcements would start arriving soon. And that this time, they would do the job properly.

The mouth of the alley closed around them. Ahead, two lines of houses jostled each other on either side of a strip of cobbles. Then the houses on the left-hand side gave way to a blank wall: a wall with steps of ancient stone rising to battlements.

'Up,' said Andrea.

They went up. Behind them, the village was suddenly quiet as the dead under its lights. Mallory peered down the walkway behind the battlements. There was a guard tower, but as far as he could see, no guards.

'Over,' said Andrea.

Mallory unlimbered his pack, tossed the silk climbing rope over the edge. 'Spiro,' he said.

'No,' said Spiro. 'I no go. I stays. High places, bullets, very bads.'

'You go,' said Mallory. 'Rope round your neck, round your waist, all the same to me.'

'But sea down there,' said Spiro. 'Very bad, wets, no swim good.'

'Fields,' said Andrea. 'Not sea. Get in a ditch. Now go.'

He grabbed the fat man's wrists. Mallory tied a bowline round the barrel chest and tipped him, still struggling, between the battlements. He and Miller lowered him into the dark until a sound floated up, more a squeak than a shout. Spiro had arrived.

Still the village lay quiet.

Wolf said, 'You're crazy. Give up now.'

'Carstairs,' said Mallory. 'Go.'

Carstairs took hold of the rope and launched himself over the edge.

'Miller,' said Mallory.

The lights blazed off the cliff. The houses of the village stood bone-white and still. But the world was changing. Outside the orbit of the lights, the sky seemed paler. And from the gates came the sound of nailed jackboots, running.

TEN

Friday 0300-Saturday 0030

As Miller put his foot over the wall, the first grey uniforms came round the corner. He flung himself to the ground, put the Schmeisser to his shoulder, and squeezed the trigger. Two men went down. The others fell back.

'Go,' said Mallory.

Miller would have hesitated, but he knew that when Mallory spoke in that tone of voice you did what he said. He grasped the rope and went down hand over hand. He could hear a voice shouting in German. Andrea's voice. Shouting something about *Hauptmann* Wolf.

Miller's boots hit the ground. 'Where?' he said.

'Here,' said Spiro, in a terrified squeak. 'Thank Gods you come.'

'Now hear this!' Andrea shouted, in German. 'I have with me *Hauptmann* Wolf, a name known to you all. The *Hauptmann* is in great danger. Hold your fire.'

The noise of boots had stopped. The alley below the wall was empty. Silence had fallen. But it was not an empty silence. It was the silence of a village full of Greek labourers holding their breath; the silence of a platoon of *Wehrmacht*, waiting for Andrea to blink. A silence like the silence between the last tick of the timer and the detonation of the bomb.

Then a voice from the alley gave a curt order.

'*Nein!*' yelled Wolf.

But the order had been given by a serving officer of the *Wehrmacht*, and was not to be countermanded by an *SS* man in enemy hands. Half the platoon laid down covering fire. The other half began the advance.

Andrea felt Wolf's body jump in his arms as the first salvo hit. A bullet scorched a track across the skin of his forearm. The body went limp. He dropped it, rolled back, his uniform wet with blood. Mallory was already over the edge. Andrea yanked the pin from a grenade, laid it carefully under the battlement round which the climbing rope hung noosed, grasped the rope and went over the edge.

He slid in silence through the night, rope crooked in his elbow, braking with the sole of one boot on the instep of the other. Against the sky – much paler seen from the thick blackness down here – he saw a head lean over, two heads, heard covering fire from below, finished counting, hoped the ground was close now –

And from above there came the great flat *clang* of the grenade detonating in the angle between wall and stone floor. The rope became immediately slack, the noose cut by the explosion. There were yells from above, yells Andrea scarcely heard because the ground had rushed twenty feet up to meet him and hit him with a bang, and he was rolling, once, twice, away from the wall, and behind him there were two crashes as the bodies blown over the wall hit the ground, but by that time he was on his feet, running away from the dark loom of the wall.

And a voice said, 'Over here.'

Mallory's voice.

Two more steps, and Andrea was in something that from the evil smell of its bottom and the steepness of its sides must be a drainage ditch. Now that his eyes were accustoming themselves to the dark, he saw that his head was on a level with a flat plain, more of the small fields that covered every horizontal square inch of this island.

'Here,' said Mallory again.

Andrea put his head down and began to run. There was tracer overhead. In its lurid flicker he could see reeds, blades of grass, the deep footprints of the rest of the party in the mud ahead. As he ran, his mind went back to a time when he had had a pack, equipment, maps.

Particularly maps.

Andrea was a deadly fighting machine, but fighting ability alone was not enough to make you a colonel. What made you a colonel was tactical sense, the ability to read from a map the features of any given terrain that a force could use to ensure the achieving of an objective.

The objective now was the aerodrome. Between here and the aerodrome, the marsh was at its broadest and stickiest. To the south was the causeway with the road, which would be heavily guarded. To the north, the fields ran up to the beach, and the jetty. According to the briefing, the jetty was heavily guarded too, but less heavily than the road.

It had been obvious for some time that the jetty was the only option.

He caught up with Mallory, who was limping along, bundling the little Greek Spiro along the bottom of the ditch: good man, Spiro, lot of noise of course, but very brave to have got this far. They paused to take stock.

At the base of the Acropolis cliffs, the high walls of the village stood out stark and black. Every now and then a burst of tracer whipped from the battlements into the fields. The shooting seemed to be directed in a northerly direction, towards the causeway. It looked like the spastic twitchings of a military force without a head – twitchings that both Andrea and Mallory knew would not last long. Soon, the superb military organization would reassert itself, and the marshes would be combed, blade of grass by blade of grass, and there would be no escape, for them or the Enigma machine.

'Well, my Keith,' said Andrea. 'I think we must take up yachting.'

So it was that an intelligent owl would have seen a little straggle of men, heavily camouflaged with mud, deploy across the fields of young corn, and start to jog purposefully towards the bay on the northern shore of the Acropolis. They moved in a loose curve, using cover as and when they found it, a clump of oleanders here, a field-shed there. But the focus of their movement was the expanse of hard-packed gravel and mud with the long pier and deep-water jetty, connected to the water gate of the Acropolis by a mile of road.

An hour later, the sky was turning grey, and the island was emerging from the anonymity of the night. Mist hung caught in the olive groves on the slopes of the western massif, and drooled from the notches of invisible hammocks in the high Acropolis. A smear of peach-coloured cloud hung like a banner past the north-eastern capes. Miller was lying in the rough grass by the edge of the road. To the right, the Acropolis loomed in the half-dark. To the left, the shed by the jetty stood dark against the shifting sea. The road connected the two. 'The morning after the ball,' he said.

Mallory blinked his gritty eyes. 'First,' he said, 'the telephone line. Then we move in.'

Miller looked down the road towards the sheds. There were other shapes. Concrete shapes, squat and bulbous. Machine-gun posts, if they were lucky. Eighty-eights, if they were not.

He sighed, rolled over, and cut the telephone line. Then he bustled around, making his preparations.

Up and about the Germans might be. But to Dusty Miller, there was a feeling almost of homecoming. This was the old life, the Long Range Desert Group life, crouching in a ditch in flat land, waiting for the convoy.

Miller had always been a great believer in subtlety. During Prohibition, when others had run booze across from Canada in heavily-armed trucks with supercharged engines, Miller had been a master bootlegger. Having disposed of his principal competitors by persuading them to ram a bargeful of unstable nitroglycerine, he had bought himself a railroad wagon. This railroad wagon he had attached to various trains. It left Thunder Bay loaded with Canadian rye, was shunted into a siding north of Duluth, and unloaded into a private ambulance, whose uniformed driver did the rounds of his discriminating clientele. While others shot each other to bits for the sake of fancifully-labelled cleaning fluids, Dusty's product had been of impeccable quality, and arrived as regularly as the tide. Miller had made a hundred and ten thousand dollars in very short order. Good business was good business, and nothing to do with fast cars and machine guns. It was not his fault that the gold mine he had bought with the profits contained less gold than the average three-year-old child's teeth. Subtlety, thought Miller, dry grass up his nose. Subtlety was everything –

The first truck of the convoy passed. The second was opposite. Miller clicked the switch in his hand. A sun-bright flash appeared under the truck's fuel tank. The truck slewed sideways, blocking the road. Thick smoke billowed from the wreck, composed partly of burning truck and partly of the smoke powder Miller included in his patent traffic reduction bombs. There was very little wind.

The smoke settled in a pyramid over the road, blocking it. Someone somewhere was shooting, but Miller could hear no bullets. By the sound of it, Andrea and Mallory were making space for themselves in the front. Miller went to his allotted place in the rear of the lead truck, shooing Carstairs and Spiro ahead of him. The truck picked up speed. The pall of smoke dwindled behind, covering the still forms sprawled on the road. By the swerve and judder, at least two of the tyres were blown. Spiro's eyes were spinning in his head. Carstairs was stroking his moustache. 'Nice engines, these trucks,' said Miller, looking at his watch. 'Terrible ride, though. Oh, look. They left us a machine gun.'

The truck entered the jetty compound crab-wise, with a tearing roar and a cloud of dust. Faces behind the windows of the harbourmaster's office hut looked pale and nervous. The telephones were dead, and something had happened on the road, there was no way of telling what. Still, it seemed as if the reinforcements had arrived.

A huge man in a *Wehrmacht* helmet climbed down from the truck. The men in the hut relaxed. This guy was the kind of guy you wanted on your side when things looked doubtful. Thank God, they thought, he's one of ours.

'*Morgen*,' said the big man, smiling a huge white smile; Andrea was famous for the size and whiteness of his smile. 'Telephone's down.'

'Tell me about it,' said the under-harbourmaster. 'What the hell's going on up there?'

'Bit of fuss in the camp,' said Andrea. 'SS man found fornicating with a goat. The Greeks didn't like it.'

'Poor bloody goat,' said the harbourmaster, wrinkling his nose.

'We're taking a boat,' said Andrea. 'Checking the aerodrome perimeter.'

'Nice day for it,' said the harbourmaster. 'Coffee later?'

'Maybe,' said Andrea, and loped off. The harbourmaster yawned. It was a lonely life out here on the dusty quay, now that the ships had stopped arriving. All you got was the occasional shipload of stores, and fuel, alcohol and oxygen for the factory, and aviation stuff to be barged across the shallow bay to the airfield landing. Otherwise, the gun crews were getting a tan, and everyone was getting hot, fly-mad and bored. They said there was going to be a

185

rocket firing sometime today. Maybe that was what all the fuss was about –

The big man and his four companions were already on the quay. One of the men seemed to be a civilian. There was something wrong with their boots, but that was none of the harbourmaster's business. They already had the harbour launch started up, and were climbing aboard. Someone cast off the shore lines. The boat puttered off the quay and into the ink-blue bay that lay between the jetty and the aerodrome. It shrank, heading for the aerodrome fuel jetty. Goodness, thought the harbourmaster, yawning, again. They're in a hurry.

That was when the motor cycle and sidecar combination clattered out of the smoke. The man in the sidecar hung limp over his machine gun. The rider climbed off and started banging on the harbourmaster's door, shouting. It took the harbourmaster a good three minutes to get any sense out of him. When he did, he almost wished he had not bothered.

'Awfully sorry,' said Carstairs, 'but how exactly do you propose to get through the fence?'

'I guess we'll think of something,' said Miller. Miller was sitting in the bottom of the boat, the wooden pack open beside him, pushing time pencils into his little buff bricks of plastic explosive. Spiro was looking away, like a child, knowing life was horribly dangerous, but not wanting to admit to himself the full scale of the horror.

'Get us a plane,' said Mallory.

'Of course,' said Carstairs.

'What?' said Spiro, no longer able to deny the evidence of his own ears. 'You steals plane?'

'Steal one. Buy one. Borrow one. Who can tell?' He held out his cigarette case to Spiro. 'Turkish this side, Virginian that.'

'I spits on your Turkish,' said Spiro, mechanically. 'No smoke. Much explodibles here.'

'Oh, for God's sake,' said Carstairs, applying the gold Ronson to a Muratti. 'You can eat that stuff.'

'No!' roared Spiro. 'You want explosion in belly, you eats it! Not Spiro –'

'Quiet,' said Mallory. He was looking back at the shore with his glasses. Men were swarming in the vehicle park by the

186

harbourmaster's shed. There was activity in the 88's gun-pit, too, alongside where they had left the lorry parked. The boat chugged across the quiet blue surface of the bay. They were half-way. Not far enough. 'Left a bit,' he said.

Andrea pushed the tiller with his hip. The boat yawed. In the gun-pit, the muzzle of the 88 flashed. The report came at the same time that the shell kicked water and yellow high explosive smoke in the air eighty feet to the right.

'Right a bit,' said Mallory.

Another bang. This time the shell roared past with a sound like a train, clipped the surface of the bay, ricocheted and blew a hole in the beach. Nobody cheered. They were in a little wooden boat in the middle of a little blue bay, feeling very naked indeed.

'This is it,' said Carstairs. He was pale now. 'The next one. Christ, what are we doing here? Like fish in a barrel –'

'Tchah!' said Spiro. 'Coward! Be a mans!'

The 88 spoke again. This time the shell burst close enough to shower them with chemical-tasting spray. Another shell came, made a smaller splash, skipped, burst on the shore.

'Hah!' said Spiro, who had worked himself into a sort of frenzy. 'Missed again! Bloody square-head fools!'

'Shut up.' Carstairs' composure had cracked. 'We're dead. What the hell possessed me to –'

A huge explosion sounded from beside the harbourmaster's hut. A mighty tree of black smoke grew in the sky.

'Left a bit,' said Mallory.

Carstairs climbed up from the bottom boards, and gaped at the shore. As the smoke cleared it was apparent that the 88 had been blown out of its pit. It now lay on the edge of a vast crater, a mass of twisted metal. As for the lorry, it had vanished clear off the face of the earth.

'What was that?' he said.

Miller gazed at him with blue and innocent eyes. 'I guess,' he said, 'that I must have left a bomb in the truck. Very careless.'

Carstairs swallowed. He did not reply. The boat chugged on. The far shore was coming nearer. Finally, he said, 'Why aren't the machine guns firing?'

Mallory kept his eyes outside the boat. 'It's all that petrol,' he said.

'Petrol?'

Miller pointed a kindly finger at the land ahead. The shore consisted of a strip of white beach with a jetty. Above the jetty was a sun-scorched grass bank. On top of the jetty and the green bank were small, coloured objects. 'Oil drums,' he said. 'Gas cans.' He pointed over the stern, directly behind them.

'There's your guns,' he said. Then he turned, and pointed straight ahead. 'And there's your aerodrome fuel dump. So if they miss us and take a ricochet, up goes the whole caboodle. They have a problem, my man.'

Carstairs thought for a moment of pointing out that it was not only the Germans who would find an aviation fuel dump a problematic place to be in a hail of bullets. Given what he knew of the present company, he kept his mouth shut. It would soon be over.

One way or another.

There were no guard towers along the seaward side of the aerodrome – this far out in the Aegean, the designers of the defences could be forgiven for not expecting shallow-water sea-borne attacks. But as the boat came to within a couple of hundred yards of the shore, a lorry roared down the buff-green strip of vegetation between the security fence and the beach. Andrea gave the tiller to Mallory, sighted down the barrel of the Spandau he had commandeered from the truck, and opened fire. The lorry swerved suddenly and crashed on to the beach. Andrea kept hosing down the little figures that crawled out of the back. Soon none of them was moving. Just to make sure, he loosed a burst at the drums on the jetty. They felt the blast of the flat, oily explosions, smelt the sweetish reek of the black smoke that rolled off the burning drums. Then they were ashore, low, crawling to the fence. There was no time for delicacy. Mallory opened the decompression valve on the boat's engine, unscrewed the lever, and put it in his pocket. Miller shoved a brick of plastic explosive against the bottom of the wire and snapped the time pencil. 'Down!' he yelled.

Thirty seconds later, a roar and a fountain of sand announced that the fence was now metal rain. Odd shots were coming in from the wreckage of the lorry. The Thunderbolt squad used the explosion crater as cover, hauling themselves and the Spandau up the sparse, burned slope of the berm. On the other side, fenced in by a mound of earth, was a half-acre field of oil drums, and a bowser.

'Well,' said Miller. 'They're not going to do a whole lot of shooting in here, I guess.'

Spiro could not speak.

Mallory had sized up the situation. Now he took control. 'They won't do anything to endanger their fuel dump,' he said. 'We'll hold it here. Carstairs, how about you?'

'Transport,' said Carstairs. He was looking white about the lips and pinched about the nose. He took out his cigarette case. 'Turkish this side, Vir –'

'Not here,' said Mallory, mildly. 'Now you get over there with Miller' – he pointed to the dumpy fuel bowser parked by the entrance – 'and he'll hot-wire it for you, and you and I will go and steal an aeroplane, and then we will come back and get everyone.'

'Piece of cake,' said Carstairs.

Five minutes later Carstairs came back in the bowser and Mallory climbed in. They rolled out of the fuel dump and across the aerodrome. Andrea gave quiet orders to Miller, who trotted over to the far end of the dump. When he returned, there were two people with him: Clytemnestra and Wills.

'Good morning,' said Andrea, with old-world courtesy.

'Morning,' said Wills. Clytemnestra was holding his hand.

'You found your way.'

'Been here most of the night,' said Wills. They walked back to an above-ground firefighting pond. Beside it, lying casually in the dirt, was a polished mahogany box with a webbing handle.

'Yais,' said Spiro. 'Yais, this is the damn bloody machine that will make us all killed. I spit on him' – he spat – 'and curse him to hell.'

'Sure,' said Miller.

'Better take cover,' said Andrea, shoving rounds into the magazine of the Mauser. 'Here.' He handed the rifle to Wills, and said to Clytemnestra, 'Do you want one?'

'What do you think?' Her eyes flashed dark fire.

Andrea shrugged. 'Cover me,' he said, and gave his orders.

Miller and Clytemnestra went to the top of the grassy earthwork protecting the fuel. The surface of the aerodrome stretched away under the sun, a yellow-dun billiard table shot with shining patches of wind-flattened grass. And on that billiard table, small figures were advancing.

Andrea had been busy. He had rolled two fifty-gallon drums of aviation fuel to the top of the bank, siting them six feet apart. Between the drums, he set up the Spandau. Miller kept working, rolling the barrels up the slope, placing them along the crest of the earthwork.

'Bloody hell,' said Wills, whitening somewhat beneath the peeling mahogany of his face. 'It's an Aunt Sally.'

'What does that mean?' Clytemnestra was scowling down the sights of her rifle. The nearest soldier was four hundred yards away.

'If the Germans shoot at us,' said Wills in a dazed voice, 'they stand a good chance of hitting one of those drums. If they hit one of those drums, they stand a good chance of knocking it down and setting it on fire, and rolling it down into a lot of other drums, and blowing up their principal fuel dump. Their supply ship has been sunk. This is precious stuff. They won't want to lose it.'

'So?' said Clytemnestra, shrugging her broad shoulders. 'They won't shoot. This is good, no?'

'Of course,' said Wills, weakly. 'It's just not . . . normal, that's all.'

'Nothing is very normal,' said Clytemnestra. A German soldier was walking on top of her rifle's foresight. Her finger tightened on the trigger. Even as she squeezed, Andrea's Spandau started to chug heavily. Out there on the bare brown plain tiny figures began to drop and roll.

Wills sighted and squeezed, worked the bolt, sighted and squeezed again, and felt the barrel grow hot in his left hand. There were a lot of them: a terrible lot of them. They were not shooting back, though. Thus far, the gasoline drums were a success. But there were too many. They would be able to capture the position by sheer weight of numbers. Unless . . .

Wills knew with a sort of gloomy certainty that Andrea would have other plans, featuring the destruction of the fuel dump and everyone in it.

The machine gun jammed. The enemy trotted on over the shimmering grass. Any minute now, thought Wills.

Then from behind the line of attackers and to the left, he heard the cough and roar of an aero engine starting; first one, then another, throttling up, then back into a steady clatter. And from the direction of the huts there taxied a twin-engined Heinkel.

The aircraft stuck its nose on to the yellow-dun grass and swung towards the advancing Germans. A heavy, road-drill clatter added itself to the roar of the engines.

'My God,' said Wills. 'He's machine-gunning them.' And even as he spoke, the front line of the advance began to collapse. The Germans faltered and stopped. The Heinkel swung back towards the fuel dump and taxied, fast. It came to a halt by the dump entrance. Andrea said, 'Go. I'll come.' He had cleared the Spandau jam. There was still movement out there; squads were re-forming on the grass, and NCOs' yells drifted down the breeze. As they ran for the entrance, they heard Andrea's Spandau begin to chug again.

The Heinkel's door opened. Mallory looked out. Beyond him, Carstairs sat at the controls, smiling an odd smile; a smug smile, cat-gets-the-cream.

'All aboard,' said Miller, swinging the mahogany Enigma case in his hand. Mallory jumped down, and went to fetch Andrea. Miller heaved the case up and into the plane. Carstairs reached down and grabbed it. Miller was starting to help Clytemnestra on to the step when Carstairs said, 'I don't think so.' There was a Schmeisser in his hand. The muzzle trembled slightly. It was pointing straight between Miller's eyes.

'What?' said Miller.

'Bit of a load, six people plus pilot,' said Carstairs. 'Not a good idea.'

'What the hell are you talking about?'

'We don't want to take any chances with the machine, do we?' said Carstairs. 'I mean, who can you trust, nowadays?'

'You bastard,' said Wills. 'You absolute bloody –'

Miller stopped him. He said, 'What are you going to do with that thing?'

'Take it to the Allies,' said Carstairs. 'Trouble is, I haven't decided which ones. Everyone wants it. The Yanks have got dollars, the Russians have got gold, and even the poor old Brits have got a couple of bob stowed away in a sock, I shouldn't wonder. And they don't like each other much. I'm going to have a little auction, that's all. Now stand back.'

Miller stood back, pulling Wills and Clytemnestra back with him. His face was completely blank. 'Goodbye,' he said.

The door slammed. The engines throttled up. The Heinkel began to roll. Wills raised his Schmeisser. Miller knocked it down with his hand.

'You can't let him get away,' said Wills. 'He's a bloody thief. A traitor. You –'

'Hush,' said Miller, and Wills observed now that Andrea had come down from his post. 'The Germans think we're all on that plane.'

The Heinkel reached the end of the runway and pivoted on one wheel. The engines crescendoed as the throttles went through the gates. It began to roll. It rolled faster and faster, shrinking with distance, the tail lifting, the wheels rising on their suspension until there was daylight under them and the undercarriage came up. A hand came out of the pilot's window and waved. Then the aircraft turned over the buildings and headed out to sea, chased by the impotent black puffs of a couple of anti-aircraft shells.

'Hell,' said Wills. 'Oh, bloody hell.'

The Heinkel rose steeply into the deep Mediterranean blue. Soon it was no more than a dot, headed north-west, for Italy. Spiro was watching it as if it were a ghost. All his work, said his slack jaw and fishskin jowls; all his massive bravery, his tolerance of Captain Helmholz, his feigning of coma, his sliding around on ropes in the dark; all in vain.

Wills was not so tongue-tied. He was pale and shaking with rage. 'Sir,' he said to Mallory. 'I must protest. I must jolly well tell you that I shall be submitting a report to my superiors about this shameful, pathetic –'

He stopped. The black dot hung high in the blue vault of heaven. And then, shockingly, it changed. There was a brilliant white flash, and a puff of smoke, and comet-tails of falling debris. And later, several seconds later, the small *bap* of an explosion.

'It blew up,' said Wills. 'It just bloody well blew up.'

'Goodness me,' said Miller, mildly. 'So it did.'

'But he had the machine,' said Wills.

'Yeah, well,' said Miller. 'I knew there was something.' He was leaning on the concrete lip of the firefighting pond. He pulled a string that led into the murky deeps. On the end of the string was a chunky oilcloth parcel. 'This here is the Enigma machine,' he said. 'Captain Carstairs only had the case. I guess someone must have put something else in it.'

Wills gaped at him, then at the Enigma machine; the key to the deliberations of German High Command, a window into the enemy's most secret responses to the Allied second front, due to open any day now.

'There is a game you play with three cups and a pea,' said Mallory. 'Corporal Miller is the world champion. Now let us find somewhere to lie up for the day.'

Spiro's face was a miserable bag of sweating lard. 'Lie up?' he said. 'You crazy. They searches everywhere, finds us, catches us. We deads, matey boy.'

'Speak for yourself,' said Miller. 'Personally I am alive. And I have an idea that people in the great wide world are going to think we were on that plane.'

Spiro's face suddenly shone with hope and anticipation. 'My hell!' he cried. 'By the Godsalmighty you are one hunnert per cents!'

Andrea came down from the bank. 'They're coming,' he said.

'Time to leave,' said Miller, looking at his watch. Like ghosts, they flitted over the earthwork and were gone.

Feldwebel Braun approached the fuel dump wall with his usual briskness, his squad well scattered over the ground, as per the tactical manual when advancing in the face of enemy fire. Except that there was now no enemy fire. The defenders of the dump had gone quiet – not surprisingly, since they had all flown away in that Heinkel. There had been a lot of disorganization and general unpleasantness these last few days. Braun looked forward to a more normal life in which regulations would be observed and there would be the minimum of fighting.

Crouching slightly – from habit rather than the expectation of enemy fire – he led his squad to the earthwork and into the fuel dump in a succession of short, textbook rushes.

But the dump was empty. He wandered into the stacked oil drums. There were signs of occupation: spent cartridge cases, a foil wrapper from a bar of chocolate. But they were safely out of the way; out of the sky, too, he thought, chuckling heavily. All that remained were the oil drums, like the stumps of a forest turned to steel.

There was a fungus on one of the stumps. Braun walked closer, to examine it. An odd brown growth, with a pencil-sized object sticking out of it, a pencil with a black stripe on the shaft.

Braun opened his mouth to shout. He never made it.

A black time pencil means a ten-minute delay at twenty-five degrees centigrade. It was a warm spring morning, so the corrosive action of the liquid in the pencil's barrel was accelerated. As Braun ran towards the oil drum, the fuel dump blew up in his face.

They were sitting in a deep creek in a clump of reeds when the explosion came. The dry stems hissed and shook, and a blast of heat passed overhead, a waft of air hot enough to fill their nostrils with the smell of scorched grass. Then the smoke rolled up, and blotted out the sun.

Mallory put his head on his pack, and squinted up at the lip of the creek. Andrea was up there, standing sentry. When you are dead already, thought Mallory, you don't have to die . . .

At which point he fell asleep.

The sun was going down as the four *SS* men and two civilians wound out of the marshes and started along the fence of the aerodrome where it ran by the sea. The wire was bent, the angle-iron posts melted. The launch was where they had left it. Over on the Acropolis, all was quiet.

Reverently, Mallory laid the Enigma machine on the bottom boards of the boat, lifted the engine cover, and screwed the decompression lever back into place. He wound the starting handle, dropped the decompressor. The engine caught with a big, heavy chug.

'Nice night for a test firing,' said Miller. The sky was a vault of blue velvet pricked with stars. He looked at his watch again. 'They must have found the primary charges,' he said. 'They should have gone eight hours ago, easy.'

'Cast off,' said Mallory.

'*Wer da?*' said a voice from the shore. And suddenly there were figures there: dozens of figures, light gleaming on steel helmets and guns, and Mallory felt a great lurch of the heart, because the

Thunderbolt squad were tired and sore and their identification would not stand up to scrutiny, and they had the most secret machine in the world in a sack on the boat's deck.

'Out,' said the voice in the dark.

'What the hell are you talking about?' said Mallory.

The voice said, 'Show us your documents.'

'Go to hell,' said Mallory. 'Refer to *Hauptmann* Wolf.'

'*Hauptmann* Wolf is dead, thank God. Out,' said the shadowy figure.

The not so shadowy figure.

The whole island was suddenly lit by a gigantic white flash. It illuminated with a pale and deadly light the twisted fence. It flung the shadows of the platoon on the shore up the scorched black berm of the fuel dump, and brought the glare of noonday to the black sheet of the water and the sugar-white houses of the Acropolis.

After the flash came a blast wave that raised a four-foot ridge of water and knocked most of the soldiers on the beach off their feet. The boat lurched high, then down again, bounced off the coping of the jetty. The people on the boat had been facing away from the explosion. The men on the shore had been looking into it. Their vision was a series of red blobs, shifting and wavering. 'Must help!' shouted Mallory, ears ringing. 'Quick!'

The boat's engine hammered. Water churned under her counter. She moved away from the jetty, towards the Apocalypse.

The mountain was burning. From tunnels and shafts and galleries there spewed gouts of flame and sparks. And from the top of the mountain, presumably the launching area next to which the fuel tanks had stood, there rose huge and twisting tongues of fire that burned and detached themselves and rose into the smoke that climbed and spread like a roof over land and sea.

'Most impressive, Corporal Miller,' said Mallory.

'I was born on the Fourth of July,' said Miller.

Under the roof of smoke the launch, with Wills at the helm, chugged across the dark water towards the jetty on the opposite shore. Some three cables short of the jetty, anyone watching would have seen the boat turn hard-a-port, run parallel with the eastern shore of the bay, continue its course past the headland and out to sea.

But there was nobody to watch small boats going about their business. All eyes were on the mountain of Antikynthos, erupting for the second time.

The boat's engine became a fading heartbeat, and vanished into the inky shadows offshore.

Two hours later they were at the rendezvous, on the long, glassy corrugations of the sea. Andrea found a bottle of brandy in his pack. They passed it round. There was a fishing line in a locker. Miller dangled it over the side, smoking and dozing. Mallory lay against the engine box with his eyes closed. Spiro sat and shivered, his eyes jerking left and right, his face a jaundiced yellow in the light of the lantern on the stubby mast. And in the shadows, close together, Wills and Clytemnestra sat holding hands. Into Wills' mind had come the certainty that the currents of war that had thrust him and Clytemnestra together would soon start running in new directions. He should have been relieved that the long ordeal was over. Instead, sore, battered and burned though he was, he felt something approaching sadness.

Miller was singing 'Your Feet's Too Big' and hauling in his line, when there was a commotion in the water nearby. A long, dark shape rose against the sky. A voice floated across the water. 'Any of you chaps called Mallory?'

'Yes,' said Mallory.

'Come on, then. Tea's brewing.' Pause. 'Nasty smell of smoke,' said the voice.

Mallory's eyes went back across the water to the hot orange glow that had once been the V4 plant.

There was a clang of boots on a steel pressure hull, the slam of a hatch, the whine of ballast-pumps filling tanks. Then there was silence; silence except for a sound that might have been the fading pant of a single-cylinder diesel, and the great, stirring rumour of the sea.

EPILOGUE

The sun was shining brilliantly on an emerald-green lawn, laid out for croquet. At the end of the lawn stood a small figure in an impeccable tropical uniform: Captain Jensen, a captain no longer, his sleeves and cap incandescent with bullion in the bright noonday. With him were Andrea, Mallory, Miller, and Wills; Wills looking faintly shifty in the presence of so much scrambled egg, the rest gaunt and hollow-eyed, and apprehensive, as if they were waiting for something.

The debriefing was over. The Enigma machine was already in a Hurricane *en route* for Tangmere, with a large and well-armed escort.

'Well,' said Jensen. 'That's that, then.'

Mallory said nothing. It would not have been politic to mention Admiral Dixon. Carstairs' role had already been explained. But Mallory was not feeling politic. Carstairs had been first a liability, then a danger, and finally a traitor. Carstairs had been Admiral Dixon's idea.

So Mallory said, 'We'd expected to find Admiral Dixon here.'

Jensen grinned, his alarming tiger's grin. 'I bet you had,' he said, and Mallory, as so often when he was with Jensen, knew that he had been outplayed and outmanoeuvred by a master. 'By the way,' said Jensen. 'It isn't Admiral Dixon any more. Captain Dixon, RN, Retired.' He looked down at the bullion on his arm. A broad stripe had joined the narrower gold hoops. 'Only room for so many admirals in the Service,' he said.

They looked at him: Andrea, hulking against the sun, Miller with his hands in his pockets, apparently half-asleep, and Mallory, the flesh bitten away from his face by hunger and exhaustion. That was Jensen for you. They had thought they had been playing one game on Kynthos, and they had played it well. But they had been pieces in another game, the game of intrigue and back-stabbing that Jensen had been playing against Dixon –

'Just one of those things,' said Jensen. He nodded at Wills. 'He doesn't mind, even if you do.'

But Wills was not listening. His mind was back on the submarine, standing in the conning tower, feeling the last pressure of Clytemnestra's hand on his, watching her steer the boat into the smoke-reeking night, heading for Parmatia. The turbulent currents of war had washed them apart, sure enough. In the smoother flow of peace, though, he would be back . . .

Jensen was saying something. 'Well,' he said, briskly. 'All's well that ends well, eh?'

'Yessir,' said Mallory.

'And I am very glad to see you. Very glad. Particularly glad today, as it happens . . .'

'Oh, no,' said Miller, under his breath. 'No, please.' Andrea was staring at Jensen, horrified. Mallory opened his mouth to speak, but Jensen put up his hand.

'. . . because I have a job for you,' he said. 'Just a tiny little job, really. And I thought, since the three of you are here anyway . . .'

Mallory sighed. 'We would be fascinated to hear about it,' he said. 'But we will need brandy.'

'Large amounts of brandy,' said Andrea.

'Five star,' said Miller. 'Roll out the barrel.'

'Of course,' said Jensen. 'And then we will begin.'

HMS Ulysses
Alistair MacLean

'A brilliant, overwhelming piece of descriptive writing'
Observer

This is one of the great war novels of our century and one of the finest achievements of Alistair MacLean's best-selling career. It is the story of Convoy FR77 to Murmansk – a voyage that pushes men to the limits of human endurance, crippled by enemy atack and the bitter cold of the Arctic.

'A story of exceptional courage which grips the imagination'
Daily Telegraph

'It deserves an honourable place among twentieth-century war books'
Daily Mail

'*HMS Ulysses* is in the same class as *The Cruel Sea*'
Evening Standard

ISBN 0 00 613512 9

Storm Force from Navarone

Sam Llewellyn

The action-filled sequel to Alistair MacLean's *Force 10 from Navarone*

Alistair MacLean's gritty heroes from Navarone are not dead, and definitely not forgotten. Mallory, Miller and Andrea, the surviving commandoes of *Force 10 from Navarone* are sent on operation Storm Force – a perilous mission through the Pyrenees to disable the greatest threat to the success of the D-Day landings – the 'Werwolf' U-boats.

The Storm Force have less than six days to locate the submarines and destroy them. With communications in-secure, the Force must operate outside normal channels, cut off from any back-up. Their Basque guides declare it mission impossible.

But of course they have never worked with Mallory.

Full of action, intrigue and betrayal, *Storm Force from Navarone* is a truly worthy modern successor to the original novels.

Now available in hardback

ISBN 0 00 225296 1